KINGS OF SEDUCTION

THE PLEASURE ROOM

TPR

3

M.o. Absinthe

Sign up on www.moabsinthe.com to my newsletter to get a FREE extra-steamy bonus scene featuring Bea and her kings

TRIGGER WARNINGS

This book is written and intended for mature audiences 18+. This book is considered Reverse Harem, meaning our main female character has a relationship of sexual nature with multiple male characters. Scenes in this book contain sexually explicit acts, and graphic language which some readers may find offensive. Our male main characters are morally gray in nature and our female main character is a little too innocent for their world but is snarky and manages to hold her own.

This book is not recommended for the faint of heart. This is not a perfect love story, it is dark and twisted. It pushes conventional boundaries and your imagination.

If any of the following are triggering to you, this book may not be for you, please turn back now. Your mental health matters.

TRIGGER WARNINGS

Abuse

Alphaholes

Attempted Rape

Attempted Somnophilia

Blackmail

Beggary

Bullying

Blood

Child Neglect

Degradation

Drugging

Dub Con (Dubious Consent)

Exhibitionism

Extremely explicit sexual content

Grief

Humiliation

Knife Play

Manipulatin

Mental abuse

Mental traumas

Murder

Psychological Abuse

PTSD

Reverse HaremVarious kinks

Trauma Violence

Slavery

Voyeurism

Villain MMCs

And the list goes on and on

Table of Content

For all you book babes who need to hide the book you're reading under the pillow whenever someone comes into the room,

I've got you!

THERE IS NO LOVE WHERE DARKNESS GROWS,
BUT YOU COULD LEARN TO LOVE THE DARKNESS

CHAPTER 1

B^{ea}

Bea

A breath of air!

A breath of air, as if I had just surfaced from the depths of the ocean. The first breath of life after having been plunged into total darkness. Light was finding its way between my eyelids, slowly forcing them to open and acknowledge reality.

I was alive.

"Bea?" The faded letters floated somewhere in the background, a blur mixing with the mystifying clouds in my mind.

I didn't need to see the face or hear the voice to know who it belonged to. That scent. The mesmerizing scent that invaded all of my senses, bringing alive the memories of his lips, passionately moving against mine.

"Cole," I breathed out, without realizing at first that

speaking would come with such effort. Something was wrong—completely wrong. My body was responding to every single one of my moves with pain as if something was punishing me even for lifting a finger.

The room slowly began to appear before my eyes. A place I'd never been before, though I knew exactly where I was—a hospital. The blue and white walls along with the beeping sound of the machines gave it away even before I could rotate my head and take a better look—not that I could actually move my head.

I was in pain—severe pain, echoing through every inch of my body so loudly that I couldn't even tell what exactly was hurting. If that wasn't enough reason for me to worry, Cole's warm hand gently caressing my cheek was sending me into full panic mode. He was never *that* kind. So, either he had some sick fantasies with me on a hospital bed, or I was dying.

"Hold on, Bea, I'm going to get the doctor." He rushed to calm me while storming out of the room.

My eyes kept closing as if hit by the strongest fatigue. It was taking extraordinary effort to try and keep them open, over and over again, until I noticed the door crack open, and Cole returning with the doctor.

I tried to speak, but this time just a long sigh managed to come out. I was losing my will to keep myself awake.

The image that flashed before my eyes as my head fell to the side caused panic within me—needles with tubes were sticking out of my veins while my hand looked as if it was part of a corpse.

I was as white as the bedsheet I lay on. It felt like I was

waiting for death, and that's exactly why I couldn't be there any longer. I couldn't remain bound to that hospital bed. I tried getting up. "I don't want to be in a hospital." That's all I could say, and all I could remember. The next second, everything turned black, and I drifted back into the darkness that had surrounded me.

I don't know exactly when I woke up, but the same cologne was floating in the room. Cole was there with me, and his warm hand was resting on the side of my face again. I tried opening my eyes. Thankfully, the task seemed a little easier this time around, but it still took me a few minutes to come to my senses. I wasn't in the hospital anymore. Of that I was certain. The dark Victorian wallpaper and new gothic furniture led me to believe I was in Ferris's mansion.

"Take it easy." Cole was trying to stop me from moving too much—not that I was able to move in the first place. Everything seemed to still be hurting, just not as badly as last time, which made me wonder how long I had slept.

"Water," I mumbled. My throat felt like razor blades were gliding through it, tearing at every inch of flesh along the way.

"Nurse," Cole hurried to call out for medical assistance, creating a déjà vu sensation in my mind. Last time, I didn't get to take a good look at him, but the image of the man sitting right next to me was far from similar to the one of the Cole I used to know. Dark circles had appeared under his eyes while his usually styled-to-perfection raven hair looked more like the messy bed hair he used to get in the morning.

"You look like shit." I may not have been able to speak much, but I couldn't hold back from making that observation.

"Are you sweet-talking me, Mouse?" He ran a hand through

his hair, arranging a few loose strands, trying to fix his image. "You should look in a mirror. You're not looking that great yourself," his tone amused rather than upset that I had offended his good looks.

I couldn't say the same for Ferris, who stormed into the room. "Watch your fucking mouth, Cole."

I found it strange for Ferris to roar at Cole, unless—unless there was something seriously wrong with me. Glancing down at my body, I realized I looked exactly how I felt—shipwrecked.

I didn't get a chance to butt into their *discussion* because the nurse entered the room.

"She wants water," Cole immediately instructed, keeping his position next to my bed.

I wanted much more than water. I wanted to know what happened to me since my mind was momentarily refusing to take me back to when my anguish began.

At least I got my first request fulfilled. "Just a few tiny sips." The nurse brought a straw to my lips.

"I'll hold that." Cole was playing the perfect gentleman, taking the bottle out of her hands, and making sure I was properly hydrated.

My throat seemed to be doing a little better. At least well enough that I could speak. "What happened? I can't remember."

No response. Just a 'Shhh' from Ferris, who glanced toward the nurse. She wasn't supposed to hear the answer to that question, and that was blurring things even more for me.

Brax... The glass wall—no, that wasn't it.

Ferris... The balcony? Did I fall? I most certainly would be sitting in a grave by now, so that couldn't be it either.

Then what?

Did I make it to... The governor! The blow that sent me to the floor... but it was all so dark from there on, except...

"Sebastian!" I called out as bits and pieces were beginning to make sense. I tried to get up, though with no real success.

Cole caught me by the arms before I had a chance to move, using his body weight to keep me on the bed. "Your brother is okay. The transplant was a success. He's already back from the hospital."

"Back? How long have I been out for?" I looked at Cole's tired face, and it was almost unrecognizable. He had lost some weight too. "Has it been years?" My voice trembled, preparing for some sci-fi revelation.

"You watch too many movies. Chill, it's only been a couple of weeks." Cole was putting some sense back into me, as a ten-year-later scenario was already playing in the back of my head.

A couple of weeks were far more acceptable. I could live with missing out on that.

Still, why couldn't I remember anything?

I couldn't ask the guys since the nurse was still checking my vitals. At least the tubes from my arms were gone, though not too long ago since the pain and the bruises from having them was still pretty evident on my skin.

But there was something I could ask for, "I want to get up." I felt so painfully numb; the way you feel when you sit in a place for too long, and for me, it seemed like I'd been sitting there forever.

"Not yet. You still need rest. You just woke up," the nurse scolded me as if I was a child.

Just wait until she leaves. And that's exactly what I did, nodding along to everything she said, just so I could try a never-do-that-at-home trick the instant she was out the door.

"What the fuck do you think you're doing?" Cole barked, seeing me trying to get out of bed.

Of course, Ferris followed the next second, rushing from his spot to stop me. "Get back in there."

"Cut the politeness. It's not like any of you really give a shit anyway," I cut them off without too much consideration. Imagine waking up on the wrong side of the bed after two weeks asleep.

"What's that supposed to mean?" Cole was playing victim just as I was trying to get up. He knew exactly what I meant. He and the other two kings used me for their own satisfaction, even if, despite the rest, he was the only one who didn't lie to me.

Ferris didn't say a word. He knew exactly where things stood—he was now the enemy. An enemy I was still bound to because of a deal. The same deal that was also binding him to me.

"You know well enough what it means." My answer to

Cole came with a delay. Strangely enough, it didn't seem to affect his newfound attitude. His arms still opened to support my weight, helping me get up while Ferris was doing the same. Though there was a difference. If Cole's touch seemed strikingly warm, Ferris's was deathly cold. Our last face-to-face encounter caused a change in the perception my mind had of his touch.

Even if I had any intention of hiding it, my body jolted toward Cole, instantly rejecting any interaction with the King of Darkness himself.

Luckily, Ferris got the message quickly enough, and before I could offer an explanation, he took a step backward, letting Cole be the one to help me walk to the mirror—not that I believed I needed any kind of help.

"I'm fine by myself." I was letting Cole know he was free to go.

I guess I didn't think things through since the instant he heard the words, he really let go of me, causing my knees to buckle as I was heading for the floor. "Are you, now?" he asked as he snatched me back up before I could harm myself further. "Are you sure you want to do this?"

"Yes... I need to," I whispered in a much humbler tone, realizing that this wasn't the best time for any mutiny.

"Okay. Just don't bite my head off when we get there." He was acting nice again without a single comment about my behavior. It had to be bad, and I was about to find out exactly how bad as I approached the mirror.

A face I didn't recognize anymore was staring back at me. Bruised eyes, bruised lips... bruised everything since I was looking like a yellowish green balloon ready to pop at any second.

I couldn't control my silent whine as I was trying to accept the reflection, mostly horrified that I couldn't tell exactly what was broken anymore and what was not.

"It's okay, Bea. Everything's going to be okay. You'll heal." Cole's arms came wrapping around me, helping me to still stay upright.

"It's not okay," I said, feeling panic settle in. I was never one to care much about beauty, but I now had the face and body of a monster.

The air was getting sucked out of my lungs, and all the strength in my feet was melting into the ground.

... and it was dark again.

Like a loop repeating itself, I was waking up once more in the same room, with Cole still by my side, only this time, uncomfortably dozing off in an armchair.

"Don't you ever go home?" It was probably the stupidest thing I could say, but I had no idea how to react to him watching over me. It was something so far out of his normal selfish behavior that it raised more than a few questions swirling my mind.

"I have a new fetish for sleeping on a chair," he mumbled as his cobalt blue eyes were opening.

"Could have offered you a spot on my king-size bed, but now that I know why you sit over there, I wouldn't want to interfere with your fantasies." At least I kept my sense of humor. For some reason, I didn't feel like lashing out at him—not this time.

"Is this an invitation to get in bed with you? Because you do know that most of my fantasies do include *you*."

"I thought you didn't need an invitation. It's your prerogative." I was becoming a poisonous bitch.

"A prerogative that I gave up." He seemed serious about that.

So what was he doing in the same room with me if he didn't want me to keep my end of the deal anymore?

"Still, that doesn't explain why you chose the chair," I pointed out since the bed I lay on was huge, and Cole was never the shy type.

"I didn't want to hurt you in my sleep or something like that. Though now that you're awake, I can change that." He leaned over me just to find a spot to rest his head somewhere above my shoulder, next to my neckline. "You scared the fuck outta me there for a second." His words were warm, filled with real concern, while his arm slid over to bring the side of my body closer to him.

His gesture physically hurt me, but I didn't say a word since his closeness was doing me much more good than the anguish it was causing me. He was honest this time. It wasn't a trick to sneak a hand down my panties or who knows what thorough check of my other curves. It wasn't a game. I guess he stopped playing games the moment we left Emerald City.

I have no logical explanation why after all he had done, my arm wrapped around his neck, holding him in place. I just needed to feel him close.

Still, the moment couldn't last long since there was another thought that didn't let me be at peace. "Cole, can you take me to my apartment? I want to see my family?" I definitely needed his help since the last time I was on my own feet things didn't end up too well.

"They're not there anymore. It was easier to move them here so we could keep an eye on Sebastian and Natalia. Don't even know which one of them needed more supervision." He laughed as I recognized my sister in his words. The apple didn't fall far from the tree in her case. "They don't know what happened to you. We weren't sure what to tell them, so we just said you had to go on a study trip with the University. Your sister didn't really believe us, but Ferris kept her busy with his black card."

"Little gold digger," I laughed, although laughing wasn't such a great idea since everything seemed to be still hurting as I moved. Still, I did need to know something else, "What happened to me?" I could only remember bits and pieces of what had happened that day. My memories seemed to be stuck on the part where I was going into the governor's house.

"The governor caught onto our plan. He... fuck..." He paused. I could tell whatever he said next was difficult for him to say. "He beat you before we could intervene."

Suddenly, the governor's fist coming straight to my face was the shocking image my mind reproduced while my eyes instantly closed, trying to block out the rest. "What—what do you mean, *intervene*?"

The plan!

What happened to our plan?

Cole raised his head a little, breaking the embrace, but remained leaning over me. "Brax freaked out, and went all Rambo on the governor's ass."

"Nooo. Everything we tried to do is lost." A state of desperation engulfed me, suspecting that everything I'd fought for was in vain.

"Not exactly... but I want to have this conversation with both Ferris and Brax present. They'll explain exactly what happened. Besides, I was with Seb at that time, so you're better off with them telling you."

I never imagined Cole doing something without personal gain involved, so the whole situation was still a little shocking to me. "Thank you for that, you know... for keeping an eye on my brother," I murmured.

"I had a lot of free time on my hands." He rolled his eyes all away to the back of his head like not even he was buying into that bullshit.

My hand stretched across the sheets to reach his. "Cole... I..." I was making a mistake that needed immediate fixing. "I need some make-up so I can go see Seb and Nat."

"They don't produce enough makeup in the entire world to fix your face. What you need is a fucking miracle." He seemed thoroughly amused, but his smile suddenly faded as Brax entered the room.

"I see you're feeling better," my mobster spoke, keeping a fair distance. The limp in his leg was almost gone, but his dark green eyes seemed as tired as Cole's.

I wanted to hate Brax. I really did, but the malfunctioning part of my brain kept staring, completely mesmerized by the way his black jacket clung to him. He looked exactly as deadly beautiful as he truly was—a perfectly chiseled demon with the goal of enslaving me—body and soul.

I hope he wasn't expecting an answer because he should've known better than that; I wasn't going to give him one. At the same time, I knew he wasn't one to give up that easily. "Did the nurse give you something for the pain?" He took a step closer to me, trying to get a better look.

"Do you even care? Or are you just asking random questions?" My tongue was sharper than ever, fueled by all the previous intentions he had of breaking me.

This time, it was he who didn't answer. It didn't mean that it would get me to keep my mouth shut. "I'm not the pretty face you dream of, Brax. I am sure you can find a replacement for me—at least until I recover."

He wanted a toy, and that's exactly what I was—his toy that got severely damaged, and now had to spend some time in the repair shop.

My tone didn't seem to agree with him. But I wasn't, in any case, going to watch out for his *feelings*. He didn't have any, to begin with. "Get out, please," I hissed a request that made perfect sense. I couldn't *serve* him at the moment, because of my wounds, and it wasn't the right time to talk about any kind of plan—at least not before I could get myself together, and function properly.

Things were simple; neither of us could take any action

regarding the deal at that time. And since the *deal* was the only thing keeping us together, he could just as well find a better use for his time.

It seemed I didn't need to expand on my statement, because in the next moment, he was heading toward the door. "I'm going to find Ferris."

"What the hell was that about?" Cole decided to ask, probably confused about the lack of an actual reaction from Brax. I'm sure he'd killed people for a lot less than that.

"I can't give him what he wants right now, so he has no reason to be here," I explained what should have been simple math in my book.

"You think you have us all figured out?" I seemed to be amusing Cole again.

"They're primal instincts. There's not that much that needs figuring out."

"Oh really? So primal instincts made him *camp out* in the hospital lobby for two weeks until we brought you home?" Cole asked, arching an eyebrow as if I needed a new reality check.

I wasn't expecting things to pan out like that, but it didn't mean Brax managed to redeem himself in any way. He was just looking after his property the same way people protect a piece of real estate.

"Maybe he felt he was losing his investment. How should I know? Brax always has an ulterior motive. You of all people should know that by now." I was still denying any sign that Brax could ever act like a human being and show sympathy without having something to gain in return.

"Look, I'm not defending him, because Brax is... Brax. Besides, he can defend himself if needed. But he doesn't always have an ulterior motive. I'm living proof of that."

Cole had a point since Brax seems to be his protector, but I, for one, wasn't going to fall down that rabbit hole again. "Well, I'm living proof of exactly the opposite. So, spare me the theatrics."

"When did you become so bitchy?" Cole seemed surprised by the new *me*.

"It comes with the crown, Cole." I smiled bitterly, reminding him that he was the one who pushed me down this road.

Be careful what you wish for, Cole.

"So what about my family?" I continued pressing. "When can I see them?"

"You should probably wait at least a day, until you can walk on your own. The doctor said no shocks or stressful situations for Seb. And I think seeing you crawling or having me as your human crutch would be stressful enough."

"Okay." I nodded, although, for some reason, my eyes filled with tears. I guess the situation was making me more emotional than usual.

Cole reacted to my fragile state of mind by leaning over to bury his face in my hair and resting his head on my shoulder. "It's going to be okay, Mouse." He whispered against my neck while peppering kisses along it as his body made room next to mine on the bed.

His gesture—far from sexual, much more connected to an attempt to offer comfort as the warmth he was emanating against my body was creating a feeling of safety.

And that's exactly what I needed. To feel safe.

I lost track of time, bathing in his scent. He felt different. Good different. So good that I snuggled into his chest, putting my arm over his body, getting him as close to me as humanly possible.

Too bad I forgot about my fragile condition. The innocent movement triggered excruciating pain somewhere below my breasts that yanked a cry out of me.

"Slow down. I know you can't resist me, but you still have a few broken ribs." He raised his body to arrange himself closer to me, though this time with his arms wrapping around me.

The fear still vivid inside of me was making me want him there. Or maybe it was *something else* too. But I wasn't ready to admit that. I just wanted him to... "Stay," I breathed as I was beginning to dread the moment he would let go. "I won't tell anyone, if you don't."

"Tell them what?" he asked, his hand gently threading through thick locks of my hair.

"That you have a decent bone in your body." I nestled my head against his own.

"The fuck if I want a single living person to know I've cuddled." He let out a charming chuckle, getting his lips to melt on the top of my head until my eyes closed.

I was still exhausted from fighting to stay alive, and sleep came over me again, a natural part of the healing. But this time, I managed to hover somewhere between reality and dreams. Maybe it was just fate, keeping me like that to hear his words. "You know, Mouse. You fucked me up really good. Not going to willingly admit it to your face, though." Cole let out a secret confession that I didn't think I was really supposed to hear. Or perhaps, unconsciously, he wanted me to know the struggle tormenting his soul.

Knowing my kings, it could very well be a trap. Only time would tell.

His words seemed to have brought me an unexpected peace, helping me find my sleep, knowing that one way or another, things had changed. And most importantly, I had changed.

I wish I could say I'd slept like a baby, but my dreams carried me to a dark place. A place where hope was gone, and all I could ever feel was excruciating pain, expanding to every cell in my body. A fist kept slamming into my face, knocking me to the ground, followed by so many kicks to my stomach that I just lost count. And that voice. That anger-filled voice echoed through my skull like someone had implanted a loudspeaker in my head. *Who do you work for?* The question repeated itself between all the blows to my face, along with the rest of my body.

I was ice cold. Like a corpse cold, feeling the life draining out of me. But my will was still there, fighting with all of my strength to get away. I was screaming and kicking back through the darkness in a futile attempt to protect myself. Until vicious arms grabbed me, holding me so still that I could barely breathe.

"Shh... It's okay... It's okay."

I recognized the voice calling me back to reality, chasing away my monsters. It belonged to a man who fought monsters of his own. A man I didn't want next to me anymore.

"Ferris?" I stuttered, strands of his light brown hair falling over his sculpted face, perfectly framing his dark night eyes.

I was still trembling, but the image of him standing right next to me managed to make my heart stop for an instant. I couldn't allow myself to have any reaction, yet my body seemed to be ignoring my conscience, letting the effect he had over me visibly make me tremble.

Except, this time, I wasn't going to let him win. I wasn't going to rest in the arms that were trying to bring me brief comfort. I knew damn well where that comfort would lead. So instead of responding to his embrace, I peeled myself away from it, putting distance between us.

He instantly noticed. Ferris was no fool and recognized my gesture for exactly what it was. I wasn't only detaching from his embrace. I was detaching myself from him, from everything that he meant.

"I'm fine," I muttered, trying to rearrange myself on the bed.

He seemed temporarily lost for words. Barely a moment passed before those cold eyes peered straight at me.

"I heard you screaming. You had a nightmare." I picked up the worried tone of his voice. He knew the definition of nightmares all too well.

"It's pretty difficult not to, after..." I could only remember bits and pieces of the events, but I was sure it was better that the memory was coming in flashes rather than all at once. I didn't think I could handle everything at once.

"I know the feeling." He let out a deep sigh, reminding me of his own bad dreams. "Do you feel better now? Do you want me to stay here with you?"

I thought I already had a guardian. "What happened to Cole?"

"He had to run to the University."

My head fell back to the pillow. I didn't want Ferris here, and he knew that. But we still had a deal, and there was nothing I could do about it—yet.

And it seemed he sensed I was miles away from the girl he used to know. "Do you want to be alone?"

"Yes," I said without raising my eyes to look at him.

I couldn't have him here, waiting for me to get well just so he could break me once again. That time would come. I was sure of that, until the moment when there would be nothing stopping him from fully destroying me.

Like a shadow, he followed my request, slipping out of the room before I could even raise my eyes and look at him. I may have hurt him, but he also hurt me.

I tried staying in bed after Ferris left. I really did, but my feet were itching to get out and stand for even just a second.

With slow careful steps, I made my way back to the mirror.

I was a trainwreck, inside and out.

A few cuts were starting to heal, and the swelling around my eyes had gone down a little, but the pain was still there— just as sharp as when the blows first landed.

I was going back to my bed when I heard the door open again. Initially, I thought that it was Ferris or that Cole had returned, instead a whole different person was entering my room. "Why are you here, Brax?" My tone was crisper than ever before, and even if I'd wanted to mask it somehow, I wouldn't have succeeded. The bitterness he left after our last private encounter was still too fresh in my mind.

"I came to see you," he said, trying to seem relaxed, but I could clearly notice that my tone was bothering him.

"Well, I can't function right now. So you can leave." I had nothing that I could have given him that day.

"You think that's what I came for?"

"I *know* that's what you came for," I snapped back as a new idea formed in the corner of my mind. "Or perhaps you would enjoy having me like this. Maybe my suffering turns you on."

Tugging at the strap that was keeping my nightgown together, I let the material fall to the ground. I was completely naked in front of him. It was far from being a pretty sight, and his eyes confirmed it, forcing his head to bow to the ground. At least my bruises got a king to bow in front of me.

"Put that back on," he groaned, picking my hospital

nightgown from the floor.

"Why, Brax? Do you want to fuck me with my clothes on this time?"

"You're lucky I know this is the trauma speaking and not you." He made an angry move with his hand, menacingly bringing his index finger right in front of me.

Strangely, his hand looked as bad as my body, healing bruises mottled with their purple, green and yellow coloring; his knuckles all swollen and cracked. But I didn't have time to get the story behind that, especially since my blood was beginning to boil in his presence.

"Let me help you back on the bed." He was playing Mr. Nice Guy this time around—too nice, if you ask me.

"Listen. Nursing me isn't a part of the deal. So, either you get me to spread my legs, or you leave. There isn't any *in-between* when it comes to us." I guess my words were clear enough because the next moment, he stormed out of the room. I was getting good at chasing my kings away, even if the knives I was sending their way were returning to me, like boomerangs, no matter how hard I was trying to stop them.

My gaze fell upon the mirror that was reflecting back to me the image of my naked body. Every inch of me seemed to carry the bruises and marks of my *plan*. I was shattered to pieces, but the truth was, I'd been broken long before I ended up in that house. My kings made sure of that.

I was weak, and I paid the price; all the events conjoined saw to that. But everything has a limit, and once the line is crossed, you can never return to what it was. My last drop of innocence was gone, and a dangerous plan was taking shape in my mind.

A new road lay ahead. I didn't want revenge for what my kings did. It was just a part of a deal that I agreed to, no matter how fucked up that was. I wanted something that would change the course we'd initially set.

I wanted them to seek *redemption*.

CHAPTER 2

"**M**ouse... Mouse!" Cole's voice managed to break through to me just in time to notice him pulling a sheet from over the bed and wrapping it around my body. "Mouse, are you okay?" he asked with genuine concern as he lifted me in his arms and placed me back between the pillows.

"Y... Yes. I can get back into bed myself, thank you," I grumbled in an annoyed tone. My kings may not have realized it, but I was much stronger than they believed.

"You were standing completely naked in the middle of the room. I called you about five times, and you didn't even move a muscle. I think it's safe to say you *couldn't* get into bed yourself," Cole snarled back at me while his gestures didn't match his tone. His hands kept arranging the bedsheet over me, making sure I was comfortable the way he laid me.

"Cole..."

"What?" He sounded more concerned than angry.

"I want to know what happened... and what's happening right now."

"Right now, I'm trying to keep your stubborn ass in bed." He was trying to avoid the subject. In the past, though, he never let me avoid *any kind of subject.*

And I wasn't going to cut him any slack just because he decided to play the good guy for twenty minutes. "You know what I mean. What's happening outside? In the city."

"We'll all meet in a few days, and we'll talk about it then."

His reply chasing away the last of my patience, "Don't you understand? I can't wait a couple of days. You'll have me committed for a breakdown by then. I need to know now."

"As I said, *now* isn't the right time." He kept rearranging the sheets to cover me, while I had no intention of remaining in bed.

I tried standing up again, but it was impossible to overcome Cole's body weight. "What do you think you're doing, Mouse?" He warned me to keep my ass in bed.

"I need answers." Just because he didn't agree with me moving, didn't mean I had to stay grounded to the mattress.

"Maybe I didn't make myself clear enough. You'll stay in bed even if I need to tie you to it." The low credence of authority echoed through the walls, causing an unexpected chill to travel to the depths of me.

But that didn't mean I would stop. It was just time for a

change of tactics. "Cole, please," I sobbed, burying my head in one of the pillows.

"Listen, I'll talk to Brax and Ferris about it. But I can't leave this room knowing you'll be running around here naked."

I reached for his hand. "I won't, I promise."

"I don't quite believe you. But the nurse will be here at any minute to check up on you, so at least I'll know you won't be alone."

"Thank you." I squeezed his hand in gratitude, only for him to withdraw it the very next second. I guess affection wasn't what he'd bargained for.

"You can thank me by not giving me any more trouble." I could feel the exhaustion hidden in his words. If only he knew how many times I've felt the same exhaustion. And especially how many times he was the one that helped cause it.

Maybe it wasn't the right time for a discussion, but I felt that the wait was only prolonging my agony. "I won't. Just help me out with this. It's killing me."

"I will be the one who kills you if I don't find you in the exact same position when I return," he warned me again.

"I'll behave," I murmured, sinking deeper beneath the sheets just to convince him to go.

"It gives me a fucking hard-on when you talk like that," he muttered, hearing my words of obedience, and the next second stormed out the door.

I didn't have much time from the moment he left to

when the nurse replaced his presence, checking up on me, and making sure I took all my medicine. At least it kept me busy until Cole returned with a response. "Brax cursed every single bone in my body, but both he and Ferris finally agreed that it's probably best for your peace of mind that we meet; the sooner, the better. I brought you something to wear. I've heard bedsheets won't cut it at the fashion week this year." He gestured toward Alfred, who was just bringing in a hanger with a clothes cover on it.

"I hope it's not a cocktail dress. Not sure if my nurse would approve of that." I giggled, trying to raise onto my elbows.

"Hey, I heard that. And *she* wouldn't approve of any cocktails either," the nurse scolded me from somewhere in the lobby.

"See, your party days are over. And it's not a cocktail dress... more like a bag than a dress, if you ask me, but at least it's loose enough not to give you any discomfort," Cole said, opening the zipper to reveal a loose pink dress, perfect for what I needed at that moment. "Brax will be back later tonight. He has some business meetings first. To be honest, I'm surprised he's even coming back at all."

"Why? Because of the way I treated him?" I asked.

"What do you think?" I could detect Cole's sarcasm.

"I think he deserved it. Besides, I can't help it if the truth bothers him." I shrugged, playing the innocent when I was far from being that.

"You know what? I'm done with this subject. You two can work it out on your own. You've asked me to talk to him, and I did. It's your business if he stays and tells you what happened, or you piss him off the second he walks through the door. Just keep me out of it." Cole was losing his patience, and I could feel it wouldn't be long before he'd be the one who would walk out the door.

"I'm hungry." I quickly changed the subject with the first thing that popped into my head—food. My stomach was feeling pretty neglected, especially since I couldn't remember putting something in my mouth since... since the day I entered the governor's house.

"Alfred was on his way to the kitchen to bring you lunch when I was coming over here." Cole stopped to look at the door. "There he is now."

I looked up to notice Alfred walking in, holding a tray of... of... "What the hell is that? It looks like horse crap," I uttered.

"I'll send your compliments to the chef." Alfred bowed, barely holding back from laughing his ass off. "It's broccoli and chicken pudding. The doctor said your first meals should be crushed vegetables and light meat."

Cole took out his phone. "I'm filming you when you eat that."

"Can I have my IV back? Seriously, I think I preferred the needles over this *pudding*." There was something wrong with that food. No meal should look like that.

"You won't get better if you don't eat." Alfred was playing mom on me.

And I just decided to let him know I noticed. "That's how you speak to children."

"Maybe it's because you're acting like one. Now eat before I send the chef in to present *his finest creation*." Alfred put the breakfast tray on the bed in front of me. "It does look like crap," he whispered to Cole on his way out as they both made fun of my misery.

At least it didn't taste as bad as it looked... Okay. Who was I lying to? We're talking baby food best-case scenario. Let's just say I barely finished my first meal in days as Cole was kind enough to describe every possible junk food he'd ever eaten, from crispy chicken strips to Turkish delicacies.

"You're pure evil," I grumbled, handing him the tray so I'd have space to get out of bed.

"I promise to take you to the best pizza place in town as soon as you recover." He helped me dispose of my dishes, then returned next to my bed.

"That's the best you can do, pizza?" I asked as images of cheesecakes and burgers were spinning in the back of my mind.

"Someone's picky." He arched an eyebrow.

"No... I didn't mean that's all you can manage when it comes to a fancy meal... More like when it comes to calories." I laughed, amused that he thought I would ever choose a luxury restaurant over any kind of street food. "I want a burger and fries... *and* a banana split. Extra-large."

"Banana split. Really? I'm not sure about the split, but I already have the banana." He laughed at his own joke. Narcissist.

"Since you're acting like a monkey, I guess it's a win-win situation. You can eat it yourself."

"Ouch. You grew fangs, Mouse. Not sure if that pisses me off or turns me on." A satisfied grin surfaced on the corner of his lips. No need to decide which one of the options he was leaning toward. "Burgers and bananas. Sounds like a perfect plan to me."

"Just drop it and help me get dressed." I tried moving my feet a little, but it was pretty obvious that I couldn't do it on my own—at least not yet.

"I've already seen you naked once today. So, why not?"

"Can you just be a decent human being for a second?" I was already doubting my judgment for asking him the question in the first place.

"I'm not sure. Never tried it before." Again, with his jokes...

"Well, you should start now." I tried to lift myself higher on the pillows, but the instant I made an effort to rearrange myself, a sharp pain shot from my ribs to my spine. "Arghhh." I couldn't help but let out an enraged sound since my body was barely mine to control. And I didn't mean it in the mesmerizing way in which my kings majestically claimed me as their own. No, I meant it in that helpless, anguishing way in which the pain was much more than I'd bargained for, and I had to fight for each breath of air.

"You asked for my help, and the next second you went on to fuck things up all on your own. Just don't move. That green shit you just ate didn't magically glue your ribs back together." He jolted from his place to snatch the dress and place it on the bed.

Not a single word on my part this time. I just followed him with my gaze as he returned to gently pull the sheets down from my body.

An instant knot formed in the pit of my stomach, letting the old me surface in the awkwardness of the moment. Sure, I was also sitting naked in front of him less than an hour ago, but that was just a crazy impulse. This time around, it felt as if I was raising a storm on a sea that had just become still.

Maybe it wouldn't have felt so tormentingly real if it wasn't for his cobalt blue eyes roaming over every goosebump of my exposed skin. Yet, they were doing just that, feeding off each involuntary shiver, his teeth clenching, seeing the greenish-yellow bruises that were still covering my body.

"Can you raise your arms?" he asked while arranging the dress so he could put it over my head.

Could I? I tried lifting them, but they only rose about ten inches above the sheet. "That's about it," I murmured, trying to hide my slight state of panic.

"That's okay, Mouse." Cole suddenly turned serious on me. Without letting me wait too long, he glided the dress over my head, then brought my shoulders to rest on his taut chest. "It's going to be okay," he whispered again while wrapping his arms around me. "Not sure if I'm going to be okay though. You've already got me breaking my own rules." He pulled a pair of new panties out of one of his pockets. "Who would have ever thought I'd be helping you put them on instead of taking them off?"

"I guess there's a first time for *everything*," I said, lifting my head enough to meet his deep, reflective gaze.

Why did it feel like it was the right time for that *everything*?

My lips twitched with the urge to touch his, but I knew I couldn't give in. I couldn't let myself fall into a trap. I was the hunter this time, and no matter how appetizing the thought of kissing him might have been, I had to resist it. I never would've thought it could be so hard, especially as he drove his hands over my feet, to slip that tiny piece of material to where it belonged? His fingertips lustfully brushed over my thighs, gliding up the curves of my hips, as he carefully adjusted the edges of the material.

My throat went dry as a coil of tormented need tightened in my core. As if he knew that, his thumb ran over the center of the fabric, straightening it to perfection and forcing an uncontrollable gasp to escape my lips.

"You know, I'm terrible when it comes to figuring out how to arrange these things. I think it would normally take me an hour to get it right," Cole said with hidden under-meaning rolling off his tongue. "But you have that fractured rib, and the doctor said don't move too much for another minimum of two weeks. So, I guess I'll have to leave them as they are." He ran his hand over the material again while I was praying he couldn't feel the pool of desire he'd just stroked to life.

But as usual, luck wasn't on my side, and his lips moved to tell a truth I didn't want to hear. "I bet you're wet by now."

So much for my keeping things undercover.

At least he didn't get a chance to go on as Ferris stepped into the room. "Brax's plans changed. He has a meeting with an Annelid leader later this evening, so he came earlier."

"I'll get right up." I tried to maintain some façade of dignity when the best I could do was to crawl out of the room.

Fortunately, Cole saw right through what I was trying to do. "Yeah, right up," he grumbled, sneaking one arm beneath my knees and one around the small of my back. "Put your arms around my neck so the move won't be too sudden when I lift you."

It felt oddly surreal that someone set to break me was now helping me at such an intimate level. But I wasn't going to question his new attitude, especially not at a time like this. I just let myself be swept away into his arms, at least for the ride to the living room.

"Is here okay?" he asked, helping me take a seat on a divan sofa. .

"Yes, thank you." I gently parted from his embrace under Brax's hard gaze while Cole secured his own spot next to me. It wasn't jealousy—far from it, more like a wave of anger that I was rejecting him, and still allowing Cole to get impossibly close to my body and my soul. Something changed during our trip to Emerald City, and it was becoming more and more obvious that nothing would ever be the same when it came to him and me. Now all I could do was wait and let time decide if, in the end, that was a good or a bad thing.

"I don't have much time to waste." Of course, the one with the attitude had to be Brax. He was *wasting* his time on me, and I was beginning to think he was right from his point of view. I had nothing to offer in those moments, so it was only fair that he wouldn't want to offer anything in return.

Determined to relieve him of any duties I may have placed

on his shoulders, I decided to broach the subject. "Then tell me what happened that day. I remember bits and pieces, but I can't seem to figure out the bigger picture."

To my surprise, it was Ferris who decided to elucidate the mystery for me, and not Brax, the one I had initially asked. "Do you remember the previous day?"

"Yes. I remember. I also remember going into the Pleasure Room to take the letter, then arriving at the governor's mansion... and then..." Sudden fatigue almost melted my whole body into a helpless puddle as flashes of images that weren't adding up ran through my mind. A glass, a red dress, the earpieces, a bathroom, all spinning in crazed circles, aiming to extract the very last drop of air out of my lungs.

Everything almost turned black when Ferris's arms shook me back to reality. "Bea, get back here." I could hear him roar as he was trying to get my attention.

"What... Why is this happening?" I was confused, trying to understand where the reaction was coming from and, most importantly, why I couldn't remember anything.

"It's called post-traumatic stress. Different people react in different ways to it, and it seems your body is blocking memories of the events that triggered the stress." Ferris definitely knew what he was talking about, especially with his past always being there to haunt him. "I'll carry on telling you what happened." He pulled a chair in front of me. "But I need you to tell me when to stop. Got that?" He needed to assure himself I was well enough to continue listening to what they had to say.

"Got it." I nodded, bracing myself to keep back the nightmares from surfacing.

"Okay. I'll start from when you went into the house. You tried seducing the governor into taking you to different areas of the mansion so you could search for any leads where he might keep any sex footage of him and whomever... surprisingly that worked."

"Surprisingly?" I snarled, with a certain irritation in my voice. Was he underestimating my intelligence?

"Be careful, Ferris. I don't see such a bright future for you if you keep pissing her off." Cole decided to intervene, making fun of my outburst. If only he knew what I had planned for them.

"Oh, I know she's much more powerful than she lets on to any of us." My king of darkness cast a genuine smile, shadowed by a tint of silent agony. He, of all people, understood best, and he, of all people, should have known better than to continually test me. "Resuming what I was saying—you managed to get him to ditch his guards, and when the time was right, slipped a little something into his drink to get him to pass out.

"Meanwhile, I got a call from my people down at the hospital. They had found a kidney donor for your brother. We needed to act at that moment or wait for who knows how long for another opportunity. We had to act fast. So, Cole decided to go be with Sebastian at the hospital to ensure everything was going smoothly.

"I think Cole left around the time you returned to the governor's safe. Unfortunately, there was nothing that we could use in it, so the next stop was his office." Ferris took a short break to check up on me. "Are you okay? Can I go on?"

I nodded again in confirmation, though I couldn't say I was

truly okay. Anxiety was building in the center of my chest, slowly transposing me there again as prey to the avalanche of fists.

"Okay... Shit, here comes the hard part. Seconds before you managed to download all the data from his computer, the governor came into the room with half a dozen of his men. He..."

"Hit me... I remember now... so many times and so forcefully. The pain... I couldn't get up, and he kept kicking me in the stomach..." I could barely breathe and found myself needing to bury my head against the backrest in a feeble attempt to hold back my tears.

"It's okay... it's okay. It's over," Cole's voice was trying to soothe me as he pulled me to the safety of his chest.

"Did... did he—" I could barely ask.

"Sexually abuse you? No. He only managed to rip your top off, but Brax arrived just in time." Cole was the one who answered me.

"What happened?" I asked. I already knew Brax had come to get me out, but I couldn't understand exactly how.

Ferris decided to continue. "Brax freaked out when he heard through the mic that the governor had come into the room."

"I did not fucking freak out. And you, of all people, should not be judging me for freaking out. Or do I have to remind you what happened to the governor?" Brax was... *freaking out* again, his biggest flaw exposed in front of us—he was human.

"Both of you cut it out. Do you want us to be here until morning?" It was Cole who was losing patience this time.

And Ferris, the one who got the message, "Okay, so Brax called all his men, and busted into the mansion."

"But how?" I asked. "Even the guards had guards there."

I could see Brax huff in annoyance. He wasn't going to answer, so it was Ferris's job to clear things up, "He took the men who were with him in the van, and walked straight through the front gate."

"It wasn't straight through the fucking main gate." Brax somehow felt he needed to recount things as they happened. "There was some shooting, and I had to act quickly before his guards got a chance to regroup. I had four men against two dozen, and we managed to break through the first floor before any backup arrived."

That's probably how he got the bruises and cuts on his knuckles. But I wasn't going to ask. Curiosity would only force me to acknowledge what he did for me, and going into a war zone with suicide mission-level danger wasn't part of the deal he bargained for.

"I blew those motherfuckers' brains out of this world. Literally." Brax was going further with the story.

"Literally?" I couldn't hide my surprise at the enthusiasm he was displaying.

"I had to because a certain *someone* lost it and made spaghetti out of the governor." Brax shifted his gaze toward the person sitting on his left.

"Ferris?" I asked with a bitter aftertaste of what Ferris *losing it* really meant.

Brax took it upon himself to clear up any confusion. "So, here I fucking am, trying to replace twenty-something guards with my own, wiping the house clean in less than an hour, making sure you got to the hospital okay, and keeping that piece of shit of governor alive. Then Ferris walks in, spends ten minutes in the room with that dickhead, and all that's left of the governor is chopped meat."

"I said I was fucking sorry for not sticking to the plan. I... I just lost it when Cole sent me a picture of Bea in the hospital." Ferris jumped to his own defense since no one else would.

"I almost fucking popped a vessel trying to contain myself from putting a bullet between his eyes," Brax barked, as he still seemed pretty upset about not being the one who had ended the governor.

"What about the body?" I couldn't hold back *that* question.

Apparently, it was Brax who held the answer once more. "I made it look like an accident. Ferris found some pictures of him playing with fire, some kind of pyro kink. So, after planting a few drugs in his bedroom, I caused an explosion so large that he would only be recognized by his dental records."

"What about the guards? Wouldn't people know the guards are different?" I added.

"No one ever pays attention to the guards. I just replaced them with my men. They were only there when the police arrived; then they scattered around the city since their *employer* was ashes."

"What about the plan?" I felt exhausted since nothing was going according to what we initially discussed.

Ferris pulled his chair closer to the sofa. "You know I met with the governor a few hours before you went in to see him."

"Yes, we decided it didn't really matter since my going in was the new plan."

"Yeah... well, it mattered because he had some supporters amongst the Elite. Like the mayor. He was one of the biggest contributors to his campaign. Luckily, I leaked a few photos to the press showing both the governor and the mayor attending a... let's just say an unconventional party."

"So who is running the city now?" Things still weren't adding up in my mind.

"My dad." The answer came from Cole, his eyes rolling at how things had panned out. "He's been temporarily *chosen* due to a little support from Ferris. But it won't be long before the gambling debts will blow up in his face. That's where Ferris steps in and takes the keys to the city into his own hands."

"The keys are only returning home. Isn't that right?" I asked Ferris, aware of his royal origins.

"I'd prefer it if they would find a new home. I don't really want to do this." His answer didn't come off as a hundred percent true. Maybe not recently, but I was sure there must have been a point in his life when he had dreamed of this position of leadership.

"So, next thing on the list—early elections. For both the governor and the mayor." Cole intervened once more.

"This isn't exactly what we planned, but I think we can work with it." I let out my thoughts. We may have solved two problems in one go; I just didn't like thinking about the price we all paid for the result. "We just need to find ourselves a mayor now."

"Not exactly," Brax growled, lighting himself a cigarette.

"Not exactly?" He had me totally confused once again. Why can't these guys just say what they have to say? It's like they're purposely getting on my nerves, especially making me play dumb and ask a million questions.

"Erick, my right-hand man, will take that seat. We'll back him as a representative of the Pit. The Elite can't do shit about it with everything going on in the city. It'll get things to calm down for a little while," Brax finally continued. "We need absolute control, and this will be the best solution."

"For the city or for you?" The question involuntarily slipped.

I might have stepped on Brax's nerves. "Don't play innocent with me. This was the deal. *We* take the city. Besides, the problem is far from being solved. We may have the Elite under control for now, but we still need to deal with the Annelids. The riots are still brewing to happen. We need changes, and we need them now."

Every single piece of information put together was adding up to only one result—we made it. We'd actually pulled it off.

Sure, Cole was right. I'm just replacing one psychopath with another—or actually two, in this case. But they were my psychopaths. And gaining total control over them had just

47

become the next step in my plan.

CHAPTER 3

B rax soon left, and Ferris retreated to his room, leaving the burden of carrying me back on Cole's shoulders. Not that I would let either of the other two touch me anyway.

"Come on, let's get your ass up the stairs again." Cole chuckled seductively, reaching to grab me.

"When you put it like that, I'm considering just sleeping here on the couch." I was running my mouth, though my arms wrapped around his neck so he could carry me back.

Of course we couldn't go without another comment from Mr. Smarty-pants. "Grab on tight, Mouse. I know you want to feel those muscles."

"Arrogant jerk."

"Stubborn prude," he cackled.

"Prude?" I was surprised by the term he used. "I'm pretty sure I'm far from being a prude."

Cole scoffed while carrying me. "Yeah, right."

"What's *yeah right* supposed to mean?"

"Say cock," he said, a smile tugging at the corners of his lips.

"Excuse me!"

"See, that's exactly what it's supposed to mean." Cole let out a loud laugh, clearly making fun of me.

"Just because I'm civilized doesn't make me a prude."

Did it?

Cole was backing me into a corner. If I kept quiet, it would mean that he was right, but if I was to keep talking, he would maneuver things into getting me where he wanted. I had a feeling that I was going to lose either way.

"It's not because you're civilized. It's because you're fucking Miss Goodie Two Shoes. I bet you never say ass or tits, not even in your mind."

Was he right?

Now that I got to thinking about it, I didn't really use the words he mentioned. I find it difficult to speak them out loud, but that didn't make me a prude. "I just don't think talking like that does me any favors."

"Since you're such a lady..."

"I never said I'm a lady. I just don't find the need to use those words."

"Okay, so if I was to take you back to your room, get rid of the panties I just put on, then carefully attend to every single need of that tight pussy of yours until you cum all over my cock... maybe then you could find a use for the words."

I blinked, utterly dumbstruck. The vivid image he painted was suddenly crystal clear in my mind, like a hologram projecting behind my eyes. My body, as if responding to his words, tingled with a surge of heat.

"I was just proving a point, don't get excited over something that won't happen." The devilish smirk on his face confirmed he was enjoying this way too much while my own body betrayed me, reacting to his words as if they held power over me. "You're just afraid of the idea of sex, even though you like it much more than you let yourself believe."

Jesus, it was like he was peeking directly at what was going on in the deepest, darkest corners of my mind.

"So, now, Ms. Prude, let me tuck you in before I feel forced to come up with extra examples of how much of a prude you really are."

Couldn't quite argue with that, so before he got a chance to continue, I let him arrange me on the bed and pulled the covers over myself. "Goodnight, Cole."

"Nighty night, Mouse." At least that lightened the mood, leaving me with a full night of rest to help me regain my strength.

I know I said I would wait, but the tormenting feeling of not seeing my brother since his surgery made me stand up, trying to walk across the room first thing in the morning.

Success was on my side. I managed to reach the door, and then walk back to the bed. I wasn't going to push my luck. Besides, it was enough that I could enter Seb's room without him getting suspicious.

"Can you please bring my makeup today?" I didn't even give Cole a chance to say hello as he walked into the room.

"It's nice to see you too," he snarled, arching an eyebrow, then throwing some notebooks on a chair that was in the room.

"What's that?" I asked, gazing at the notebooks he brought.

"Your courses." He was clearly pissed off. His tone made me aware of that.

I was surprised he'd even made the effort to get them for me. "My university courses?"

"No, your chef school courses." He said with a roll of his eyes as he handed me the notebooks. "Of course, your university courses. I had some students write down the course work for the classes you've missed."

"Thank you... I don't know what to say."

"Nothing. I may be forced to kill you if you bring it up." Cole didn't need words of praise, maybe just a little gratitude. But he already knew he had that. "I should go grab your makeup bag since you're so determined to go see your family."

And he did just that, bringing me my makeup essentials along with a mirror.

"I'm going to check on Ferris for a few minutes." He

practically stormed out of the room so that he wouldn't need to learn the basics of applying concealer or foundation equally.

It took me longer than expected, but with a little effort, I managed to cover all the bruises and signs of what happened.

It seemed Cole returned just in time for a shock as he came to discover a brand new *me*. "Fuck! Are you like one of those *'take her to the pool on your first date'*, girls?" Cole asked.

"Well, you first saw me in the pouring rain." I could barely hold back a smile.

"That's not when I first saw you. It was on your first day when you were walking into the university." His eyes gleamed with mischief, conscious that he was giving me a peek into his world.

That didn't mean I couldn't play dumb for the sake of it. Getting that confession out of Cole felt pretty good, so why not try and go for another one? "You probably didn't even know that I existed back then."

"Oh, I knew, Mouse. Now, let's go. I have some business later, so let's get this part over with." He didn't let me walk to Sebastian's room, just took me in his arms, and carried me all the way to the door; despite my protesting that I could make it myself. If I were to be honest, that was probably best since I wasn't sure if I was ready to walk and stand for that long. But I wasn't going to tell him that. I just played grumpy and turned the doorknob.

"Sebastian!" I exclaimed, rushing to get to his bedside.

"Sis! When did you get home?" His happiness could barely be contained.

I hated that I needed to lie to him, but desperate times call for desperate measures. "Just now. I... I was on a study trip with limited phone access. I just found out about the surgery."

"Bullshit," my sister was the one calling me out as she was just entering the room.

"What did I say about that language?" Cole, of all people, was the one who decided to educate her. Not that it was bothering me in any way. He was one hundred percent right in his actions. I just found it a little strange that he even noticed she was cussing.

"Sorry." Nat rolled her eyes, still trying to defy him. I could tell that she was doing it out of embarrassment, being unsure exactly how to act. "I still don't believe you, though."

"Natalia!" Cole barked, motioning for her to follow him into the hallway.

"What's she talking about?" My sister's mutiny seemed to have piqued Seb's interest, although I couldn't let him in on what had really happened.

"She's just upset with me being absent on the day of your transplant. But I really didn't know. I would have done anything to be there with you if it had been possible."

"I know. You could make it up by taking me to the auto show. It's in a couple of weeks." He smiled devilishly as I was becoming certain he'd had this idea in mind for a while now.

"If you're well enough, we'll go." I couldn't really deny him anything he wanted, especially after what he'd been through.

This promise was followed by many more since my brother had the talent of manipulating me into making all his childhood dreams come true. By the time I left the room, I owed him a trip to the auto show, a PlayStation, a long... long list of robots, some toy cars, and apparently a dinosaur. At that point, I was just surprised that he didn't actually ask for a living one.

And if that wasn't enough, I stepped out into the hallway to a very angry Natalia. "Where were you? And don't tell me 'a study trip' because I don't buy it."

I couldn't lie to her. She would see right through me. But I couldn't tell her the whole truth either, so I improvised... *a little.* "Okay, I was involved in a car accident."

"Oh My God! Are you okay? I knew there was something wrong with that trip excuse." Nat seemed to be genuinely worried. At least she bought it. I felt it was far more complicated trying to explain how I seduced the governor than claiming a car accident.

"I'm a lot better now. I still need some time to fully recover, but I'm slowly getting there."

"You should have told me. I could have handled it." Nat put on a grumpy face, although telling her was never an option.

"I didn't want you to see me like that, especially with Sebastian having his surgery. That was enough stress for you two to handle. Now, drop it, and tell me how you're doing in school," I cut her off, steering the conversation to something that had been on my mind for a while now.

"Good..." she murmured, letting her sight fall to the floor.

But the doubt in Cole's voice didn't convince me that what Nat was saying was the truth. "Nat..."

"Okay... I'm a little behind," she grumbled, keeping her glare to the ground. "But I'll catch up soon."

"She changed two home tutors in three days." Cole was getting me up to speed.

"Maybe because I don't need a home tutor—or you and Ferris constantly on my back about it. I said I'll handle things, and I will." Nat's attitude shining through.

An attitude that was apparently also my fault. "I wonder where she gets that from," Cole muttered, preparing to leave the room. "I can't handle the two of you at once. Nat, just so you know, you're not getting your phone back until you show me an A." Cole waved his hand, holding what was apparently my sister's new phone.

"How did you get that?" She almost burst into tears, witnessing the *cruel injustice* Cole was subjecting her to.

"I was the one who gave it to you, and I'm the one who is taking it back." I could hear him calling out as he was walking down the stairs.

I wasn't sure if Cole's trick would work, but it was better than nothing, and by the look on Nat's face, she was going straight to her study so she could get her social networking back. Even our chit-chat was cut short by her impatience to get back to homework. Imagine that.

I guess Cole really knew what he was doing by giving her a phone, just so he could use it to blackmail her into learning.

I knew he was good at blackmailing and manipulating people. But who would've thought he'd be so good at parenting?

***

I found myself settling into our strange new normal. Three weeks of barely getting out of bed, just moving from one sofa to another. Nothing important happened. Brax came in a few days ago to announce that his man had won the mayoral elections, not that it was a surprise. Ferris was up next for the governor's position while the Pit residents were standing still, waiting for the outcomes.

Besides those meetings, I only interacted with my family and Cole, but his visits became less frequent with each passing day. I wasn't going to shed my cold attitude, and he was quickly growing tired of not holding the lead. Plus, from what he told me, Ferris and Brax were slowly getting pissed off with him. I guess it was one thing sharing, but quite another picking favorites. And since I was only speaking to him from the onset, he seemed to be by far my *dearest* king. Though the main problem was, none of them was *dear* to me in any way—not anymore.

It was finally time to return to the University, but first, I had something to do—something I should have done a long time ago.

"Let's go," I called out to Jenna, who seemed to be only one step away from fainting.

"Are you sure about this?" Her feet were trembling in her

57

new stiletto shoes as she was asking.

"Positive. Now, let's go." I rushed her.

As always, the ride to the ECU was much shorter than I wanted. No amount of time could prepare me to face the wolves, though things were about to change. "Through here, Jenna." I was leading her straight through the front door.

"Three years, I managed to survive here just so that you could get me killed in my final one." That was all I'd been hearing from her the whole morning. I couldn't blame her. But I couldn't let her live in fear anymore either.

"Stop being a drama queen; I can handle this." I walked forward, unwilling to give up my plan no matter how much Jenna would whine about it.

Cole wasn't there yet, and that was just perfect for what I had in mind, especially with the jackals already circling.

"What's she doing here?" Kellie, one of the Elite's main representatives, stepped in to ask, sickening me once again with the spiteful attitude so specific to all of them. In this world, common sense decreases proportionally to your wealth.

"She's here with me," I grumbled, visibly irritated by the defiant tone of her question. It was time to learn who their Queen B really was.

"You know the rules," Kellie continued, trying to force me to back down. Jenna wasn't part of the Elite. She didn't belong in their world, even though I made every effort that she would be dressed according to their *standards* so she wouldn't stand out amongst them. It was the same egotistical attitude that had sparked the rebellion.

"Well, rules change, so you can either stay here with us or go to the other end of the hallway and remain there. It's your choice." I was finally stepping up to my role, and they'd better listen.

Despite my bravado, Kellie didn't seem to react at all. She just stood there dumfounded, staring at me as if she was having trouble processing my words.

But my knight in shiny armor—a leather jacket—was here to save the day. "Didn't you hear her?" Cole's voice came from somewhere behind me, making sure that my message got through to her.

I wasn't positive whether he agreed with me, although publicly disagreeing would do him no favors. So that helped *me* be the manipulator this time around.

Kellie soon vanished somewhere into the crowd, but I was certain she was still eavesdropping on us.

"What the fuck do you think you're doing?" Cole barked menacingly between his teeth.

"Just making a decision, as my role permits me. She's my friend, and I'm sick of hanging around these marionettes."

"I think I should go." Jenna tried to excuse herself, though I wasn't going to let her give up so easily. This was about trying to change the rules, and backing out of my second challenge wouldn't have been a good start.

"No, you shouldn't." It was Cole who answered, agreeing with me, to my staggering surprise.

"Stay. But you, Mouse, you're coming with me."

"What? Why?" I crossed my arms defiantly, refusing to give in to his command. He did say the deal was off, so he had nothing on me now.

"Mouse, I guarantee that you *don't* want to see me pissed off. And right now, you're only *one word* away from doing just that."

I didn't say anything back, just locked my eyes on the blue of his own.

I wasn't saying any *word*, was I?

That managed to infuriate him to his limit.

He had a message.

One that was only meant for my ears to hear.

Cole tilted his head, sneaking his chiseled lips between the curtain of my hair. "I promise that if you don't do as I say, I'm going to remodel your friend Darryl's face. And I'm going to let everyone know whose fault it was."

I didn't doubt that he would go through with his threat. Maybe if he had chosen any other random person, I would have tried to call his bluff, even if I knew it wasn't the case. But I couldn't risk it, especially sensing the annoyed arrogance in his voice.

Cole didn't wait for an answer this time. He just walked away, heading toward a secondary hallway, convinced that I was going to follow.

He didn't leave me much choice but to do just that.

It was pretty difficult to get a moment of intimacy, especially with everyone around us focused on our every move, but Cole was an expert when it came to controlling the crowd. It didn't take more than a sharp gaze from the *king* before all pairs of eyes were pointed randomly across the space, just pretending to dismiss our presence.

They weren't really ignoring us, but mentally, it helped me way more than having them stare at us would.

He finally stopped in front of a classroom—the same chem lab he used before to meet with me. It was empty. Not a single soul around. Just him and me, all alone.

The door closed behind us, and the instant the echo of the snicking sound scattered in the air, Cole's roar replaced it. "What the fuck do you think you're doing?" he barked, his frustration palpable.

"I was just playing my part as *queen*. I thought I was allowed to make decisions on my own."

"Not decisions that change the way things work around here," his tone carried a note of warning.

"So let me get this straight. When you wanted a piece of my pussy, it was okay to bring me into your world, but now that I'm here, I don't have the power to bring a friend?" That was me *not* being a prude any longer.

Angered flashed through his eyes. "Things were different with you."

"Different how? You broke the same rules you're now

giving me attitude about." I was just stating the obvious.

"Different... because everyone knew I owned you," he snarled, letting out a truth that stung me.

"Oh, so I was only the king's toy." I was trying to get him where I wanted.

But things were never easy with Cole. "I officially made you my fucking girlfriend, so don't give me attitude about it."

"Right... because you liked the way I trembled in front of you." I took a step closer to him as I was speaking, defying the air of superiority he projected. I was far from trembling in front of him or being *owned* by him now. "So tell me, Cole, how do you like me more, to tremble like a slave?" I let my lips slightly shiver as I was closing in the distance to his ravenous mouth. "Or to rule beside you?" I ran my hand over his, intertwining our fingers, then slowly guided his thumb to press against my bottom lip. "Slave or *queen*?" My tongue ran across the tip of his finger, luring it inside my mouth to play with it like the most delicious toy I'd ever found.

I was slowly reopening the door he had slammed shut a month ago. Maybe I was crazy, but I was also addicted to him. And if I initially had my doubts, the days spent without his presence had managed to erase them.

I mentally kicked myself for being so weak a thousand times before. But the lustful flicker in his eyes, as I kept sucking and nibbling on his thumb, was encouraging the thought that my plan was going to work. Because the real question was *king or slave?* And I was just assuring myself that we would stick to the former.

Cole raised a brow, but it wasn't out of dissatisfaction. More like disbelief. "What do you think you're doing, Mouse?" he asked, his voice low and teasing.

"Ask me to stop, and I will," I murmured, guiding my body against his own as I continued teasing his finger.

"I wouldn't exactly ask you to stop. Maybe just change the body part you're playing with." He smiled, probably hoping that he would get me running to unzip his pants.

"You know as well as I do that isn't going to happen. This time, I want things done like they're supposed to." I stopped to look back at him, allowing him to retrieve his thumb. I was waiting for what he had to say. Did he want some fun in the locker room, or was he being serious about making the girlfriend phase a real part of his life?

For a moment, he seemed confused, almost shocked by what I had just said. He may have suspected me of many things, but the guts to step up the food chain alongside him was never among any of those.

"We can play games if that is what you're also into, but don't think for a single second that I'll let *you* play a game with me. Got that?" The way he said it—it wasn't a threat meant to protect his ego. It was a threat meant to protect his heart.

"Yes... I got it. Now, excuse me, I have to get to class." I just left him there, storming out the door. For the first time, he couldn't hold me in a place as a result of our deal, and it felt fucking awesome to regain that kind of freedom. Besides, I needed to leave the room as the pheromones floating in the air were seconds away from clouding my judgment. He had that undeniable sex appeal. Every word that left his lips sent a coil of molten desire to everything located around my mid-waist, bringing that place to a boiling point only with the intonation of his voice. Like mixing honey, poetry, and lust into a potion carefully brewed to melt the panties of all living breathing females.

I was shaking when I finally got to my seat in class but carefully masked it so that no one would ever notice the true effect he held over me.

No other challenges arose the rest of the day—not even Cole, who seemed to have evaporated into thin air. Not that it was actually bothering me. It just left me more space to do whatever I wanted, including having Kellie bring lunch for Jenna and me. Imagine the embarrassment of an Elite serving two Annelids.

Maybe I really was a bad bitch after all.

The time spent ruling over my new *kingdom* turned out to be way more tiring than I'd expected, especially because it was the first day since the visit to the governor that I was leaving the house.

It would have been nice to say I crawled into bed and stayed there until morning. But Seb was just emerging from bed rest himself, and both he and my sister needed a few hours of family time.

I was still disappointed with Ferris, so I found it only fair that I shouldn't show him any kind of attention. Fortunately for him, he wasn't one to insist, especially given his own experience was so close to mine.

When I finally did crawl into my room, I was running on emergency batteries, though what was waiting for me there had suddenly brought me back to life. "Cole?" I uttered, finding him sitting on an armchair with a glass of whiskey as his companion. "What are you doing here?" I asked, a hint of surprise and annoyance in my voice.

"I was waiting for you."

"And you couldn't find the light switch? You scared the hell out of me." I wasn't kidding; my heart was literally threatening to escape my chest at the encounter.

"I just wanted to be alone with my thoughts."

"Did your parents kick you out, or what?" If he had *something* to say to me, I thought it only fair to make the task impossible. It's not like he ever listened to anything I had to say, at least not when he was taking full advantage of the *payment* resulting from our deal.

"They didn't. My mother is actually expecting you for dinner soon. But that's not why I'm here," he said, taking a sip of whiskey.

I feigned detachment. "Why are you here, then?" In reality, curiosity was gnawing at me.

I guess the answer was more complicated than I had initially suspected since he felt the need to down the full contents of the glass in one sip before expressing the most unexpected desire. "I want to spend the night."

I instantly lost all track of thoughts, and my mind went blank. "Cole... I—"

He cut me off, "I didn't say I want to have sex with you. I said I want to spend the night."

What did that even mean for us?

"Come here." He stood from his chair, gazing at me with an inviting charm.

Maybe the way he said it was in the same signature way, trying to impose himself. But this time, it hit differently. It felt like I was heading to safety.

There wasn't much thought put into my actions. My feet just carried me next to his muscular frame, immediately letting me be captive against his chest. I was skipping all the steps I wanted to follow in my plan for them to ask for redemption, but it felt so good—too good to resist. I just buried my head against his shirt and let my eyes close, taking in everything that he represented—power, seduction, but most importantly, warmth. A warmth that was only for me to relish.

"I don't want you to fall asleep standing. Let's get you into bed." He slowly peeled me off him, pointing to the red flannel pajamas that were waiting for me on the bed.

"I haven't seen them since Emerald City. What on Earth made you choose those?" I giggled, just imagining him going through my drawers.

"It helps me with the *no sex* part," he snarled while helping me remove my jacket so I could get ready for bed.

"I'm taking these to the bathroom with me." I snatched the pajamas and went in for a shower, only to return disguised as a new version of Santa Claus.

Cole seemed to have made himself comfortable in the meantime, already waiting for me between the sheets after having disposed of his clothes. They were all neatly stacked on a chair; no sign of his boxers though, so he at least must've kept those on.

Almost to confirm my thoughts, he lifted the blanket to invite me into my own bed. Though the invitation was much more devious than I would've ever thought. That ink on his chest perfectly fit the display of sinful lines and shapes, melting the last drop of resistance with every breath he took, calling me, luring me to get lost in that charming delirium.

And that voice... that demanding voice, "Come, Mouse," summoning me to join and obey every single thought that could flow through his devious mind.

Without realizing it, I was sinking between the sheets, molding to every rocky curve of his torso.

If only things were that easy.

But they never are.

Drawing me closer, his lips sought that spot on my neckline he loved so much while his hand ventured between my thighs.

If I had a single drop of sanity left, I would have asked him what he was doing. Or maybe I would have even leapt out of bed. But I couldn't bring myself to risk him stopping. I craved his touch, breathlessly waiting for him to go on... to do something, *anything* to temper the ache building just by thinking about what pleasures he could instill in my body.

Though, he didn't continue. He just remained there as a silent torture of what it could be like if he took things further, turning the wheel again, and creating a dangerous addiction for each sensation he could create.

And since it seemed I was an emotional masochist, my eyes only closed after half an hour of uselessly hoping that he would come up with some devious plan to seduce me. Because at that point, even, *"Hi,"* would have me all wrapped around his little finger.

How fucked up was I to crave something that I spent so much time running away from?

Maybe I had brain damage, but all I could think about was *him and me transforming the sheets into a silk ocean in which he would... ahhh...* Just hopeless dreams at that point, especially since he decided to plant a goodnight kiss on my lips.

His eyes finally closed to sleep, not before he murmured a truth that changed everything, "I need this as much as you do, Mouse."

This wasn't about sex; it transcended any physical need.

It was *the next level.*

CHAPTER 4

"**H**ow long have you been awake?" Cole asked, holding me close, refusing to let me slip even an inch from that chest tattoo that I managed to drool over—literally.

I couldn't really answer that question, not without totally embarrassing myself and admitting to only having dozed off a couple of times throughout the entire night.

I was deadbeat tired, and that was far from my plan. But I had a feeling that my time to rest was approaching an end.

I needed something else.

I needed that earth-shattering adrenaline rush that stormed through my senses.

I needed him to bring *me* back to life.

Not that I was ever going to admit any of that. "I woke up a few minutes ago."

"When did I ever lie to you?" He let the sentence drift into the air, underlining a fundamental truth—he never had.

Even if in the past he said it himself, I never put much value into the thought until now. I even found it difficult to admit the truth. "You never did," I murmured, my gaze still averted.

"Then why do you feel the need to lie to me? You're safe with me, at least when it comes to someone judging you. I perfectly understand that you can't keep yourself from drooling on me."

"Cole." I pulled back, finally meeting his gaze.

"Don't make things hard on yourself. I could feel you throughout the night. You were having trouble sleeping. And so was I." He wasn't kidding when he said he wouldn't lie to me, and since it was confession time, the hard part was just about to begin. "And you know why I kept waking up?"

I was dying to hear the answer. This time around, it was impossible to seem indifferent or hide my curiosity. "No, why?"

"Well, except for the blue balls that you gave me by fidgeting against me the whole night, I had another reason. One that will either send you running away or kiss me."

I was intrigued. "Now you really have my curiosity."

"I want to take you out on a date. No deals or obligations. Just us—Bea and *King* Cole."

"You forgot to add the *modest* King Cole." I knew he was making fun of me, but he was the one who decided to go there in the first place.

"I have zero reasons to be modest, and you know enough of

them not to differ." He smirked like the devil he was, sneaking a hand on the small of my back and letting it slip on my ass. "So, what do you say? Are you going to break my heart or let me surprise you?"

I pouted my lips, trying to visualize a moment in which he would act normal. "I can't really imagine you out on a date."

"I can't imagine it myself either, but there's a first time for everything."

"What do you mean *first*?" I was a bit taken aback, thinking that he probably knew all the restaurants in town along with every possible pick-up line.

"*A first* as in I never fucking needed a date. Things just happened without the effort." He shrugged, a reminder of how easily women would fall for him.

"Oh, so you're putting in the effort so you can get me in bed with you? When I'm already in bed with you." *Confused much?*

"That's not what I was trying to say, and you know it. I want to try this with you. And if things end up in bed, it would be like a bonus."

"Arrogant jerk."

"Call me whatever. You know you can't resist me." And the truth was I couldn't—especially with the motive behind his invitation still a mystery. I mean, why would he give up the payment he got out of the deal just to go through all that trouble to get to the same result—sex?

Was he serious about wanting the experience, the dating, and whatever comes of it?

He had to be.

It was the only thing that could make sense. Though there was an aspect that wasn't too clear to me. "If you want to do this... see where things go, then what about Ferris and Brax?"

"What about them?" he asked as if *them* still being in the equation was normal.

"I still have deals with them that imply..." I trailed off, just couldn't really say it out loud.

"Having sex with them. I know. I told you that you were a prude; you can't even say the words out loud."

Maybe I was a prude because I couldn't bring myself to say anything else *out loud.*

"I told you how I see Ferris and Brax. They're like a part of me. I'm not against an open thing."

"*Thing* as in relationship?" I needed to clear that part up.

"Yeah, whatever you say." It seemed, the word didn't really fit into his vocabulary.

"Apparently, you're the prude when it comes to emotions and interacting." I was pointing the finger the wrong way, because so was I.

"I'm not a prude; I just don't like labels," he muttered, annoyance creeping into his voice as I pushed him.

But I wasn't backing down. "Maybe you don't like labels when it comes to you, because you label all the rest: Annelids, nerds, the Herd, your girlfriend—who you don't have a relationship with..."

"I'm king there. I can do and say whatever I want."

"Exactly my point." I shot him a *knowing* look.

Despite being unable to label what we were going for, Cole did seem to have a solid grasp of how relationships work—at least the parts he was directly interested in. "Is this our first real fight? Because I'm sure I want the make-up sex."

"Get out of my bed." I giggled, playfully pushing him deeper into the sheets, yet still lazing around next to him for a couple of extra moments.

"You have to be at the university in twenty minutes." He stretched his hands and feet, finally getting out of bed to get dressed.

"Me? What about you?" I asked, sensing from his tone that he was likely skipping classes again.

"I'm going to the Governor's Office to see what my dad is up to, then help Ferris prepare for an interview."

"Is he ready for what's coming next?" I asked, uncertain about what Ferris had been up to lately. We had those brief meetings, but since I didn't want him around, I hadn't rushed to ask him what was really going on with him. Plus, my recovery time was drawing to a close, and I was certain that the nights spent in his room were approaching faster than I'd imagined. In a way, I even wanted to go. For too many nights, I clung to my sheets not to follow the sounds of his misery. His nightmares had returned; I could sometimes hear his anguished screams. I couldn't shake the feeling that my plan had sent him spiraling back into his past. Still, I couldn't do anything to support him. I just kept telling myself *maybe tomorrow,* hoping that *tomorrow* I'd find the strength to confront his demons once again.

But tomorrow never came.

Cole echoed my concerns regarding Ferris's current mental condition. "I'm not sure if he's ready, but we'll be there to make sure he's up for it. We'll back him up."

For such a jerk with everyone else, Cole was totally different when it came to Ferris and Brax. It was like he was keeping all the compassion and support he should have had for the rest of the world only for his two besties. "I'm going to leave before I'll be late. I'll come pick you up at seven."

"Wait, you want to go out on a date today?" I was slightly shocked, feeling like I needed more time to prepare myself for this—at least a century or so.

"When else? Just wear something short, so I can reach second base." He cackled, pulling up his black jeans, preparing to leave the room.

"Who knew you're also a comedian?" I muttered, turning my back on him and pulling the quilt over my head.

"Okay, then let's settle that now." Cole lifted the cover just enough to sneak a hand beneath the sheets and pinch my ass. "Objective accomplished." He planted a small peck on the top of my head, even if I was still hiding between the pillows. "Now I really have to go. I need to swing by my house to change, and I'm already late because of you."

Of course, his tardiness was on me too. "Am I to be held accountable for all possible evil in the world?" I asked, rolling my eyes.

"Just for all the bad things in my life." This time he was leaving, but not without finishing his thought. "And for the good ones."

Obviously, he didn't stick around to clarify what he meant by that, but it drew a pretty clear line as to where we were heading.

The day at school was pretty normal. The Elite seemed to have learned quickly enough not to underestimate or contradict me. I could say I was some sort of a female version of Cole, only it wasn't the Herd that should fear me—it was the Elite.

Despite the bossy attitude, I was feeling pretty goofy. Like I couldn't control my clumsy nature, letting my thoughts rule most of my actions.

I was a little excited about the date. Okay, extremely excited, although I was pretty convinced that I didn't have a plausible reason to be so. It was just Cole. I'd spent time with him before in every possible way.

And I do mean *every possible way*!

Maybe it was because of the promise of something different, that was making me even more nervous than usual.

Against my better judgment, I spent a little extra time in the mirror, fixing my makeup to perfection. It wasn't much different when choosing the outfit either. I managed to speed-try half of the clothes in my dressing room. Same for the lingerie. Choosing between some grannie panties and a few sexy straps of silk seemed impossible. My mind urged me to go with the parachutes while my body instincts were screaming for the almost invisible material. And since the black over-the-knee skirt I chose didn't go well with the retro knickers, I ended up with some mini string thong and a garter belt that I just stumbled and fell into... Besides, I needed something to keep my leggings in place—it was freezing outside.

I blame it all on fashion.

My king arrived at 7 p.m. sharp. I could hear him parking the car outside. That didn't mean I couldn't pretend I didn't know he was there. It was just a womanly thing, not wanting to seem overly excited, especially since I knew Cole's ego would feed on any sign of weakness. Though Alfred interfered with my plans, announcing Cole's arrival even before he got out of the car. "Mr. Clayborne has arrived."

"How did you know it's for me?" I asked, not realizing that the whole house was up to date with my schedule.

"Mr. Ayers hasn't returned yet, so unless he's into third-age British butlers, I'm fairly convinced it is you he is looking for."

"You have a point," I chuckled. "I'd better get going. Just keep an eye on my sister and Sebastian, please."

"I'll order pizza and cheesecake, and they'll babysit themselves." Alfred was trying out his British humor on me.

But I must admit, he did make me laugh.

"Oh, I wasn't joking, just adopting the new babysitting style around here lately," he continued, exposing the kings' secrets.

"Ferris?" I asked, curious to know who was spoiling my siblings.

Alfred shrugged. "All of them."

Just great. It was me against the world now.

"Don't worry, I, for one, was kidding about the pizza. It's nuggets night.'" He smiled, disappearing down the hall.

Even Alfred was making fun of me.

What was I doing wrong?

Still, it felt kind of nice seeing him loosen up a bit. I guess having a full house of *infants* must've helped him with that. And I wasn't referring only to my siblings.

It was time to leave, and since Alfred already thwarted any attempt to mess with Cole's schedule, I had no choice but to head straight to the car.

"Hop in," he spoke from the driver's seat, gesturing to the front right door that he had already opened.

I could notice him analyzing me from head to toe the moment I climbed in, but I couldn't tell if he was pleased or unimpressed.

I, for one, was definitely impressed with him. The black leather jacket that made me want to melt under its scent, the ripped black jeans, and the t-shirt that perfectly molded against his gym-worked body; all those combined could be the new tux replacement in my book because he looked fan-fucking-tastic.

I just wasn't sure if I was dressed okay, or at least okay for where we were going. "I didn't know what to wear." I tried excusing myself.

"What you're wearing is perfect. You look pretty hot, Mouse."

"Yeah, Alfred just pulled me out of the oven." At least Alfred's humor seemed to have been contagious.

"And funny. If I didn't know better, I'd say you were trying to seduce me." He pressed the car's start button but took an extra second before we pulled off to give me one last glance.

"So, where are we going?" I asked, curiosity not letting me keep my mouth shut.

He was already driving away from Ferris's mansion. "Where I promised to take you."

"Pizza or burgers?" I asked since I wasn't exactly sure which one of those two he had chosen.

"You said burgers. Don't tell me I cleared out a whole restaurant for nothing." He seemed dead serious.

Although I *knew better* than to believe him. "You didn't."

"No, I didn't. I just wanted to see what you would say. I don't want to hide you. I'm not the type to be afraid of competition." He seemed to be in an extremely good mood. So good that I could barely recognize the Cole I had first met at ECU in the man sitting next to me.

We kept riding downhill until we almost reached the line

between the Hills and the Pit—pretty close to where The Pleasure Room was located.

Our destination was a location I'd never seen before. It was similar to a diner, and judging by the cars parked outside, most of the customers must've come from the university.

"I didn't even know this place existed," I murmured, letting Cole escort me out of the car and into the restaurant.

"Call it an Elite fast-food restaurant. It's different from the usual Michelin-starred restaurants, but that doesn't mean the junk food isn't exceptional." He seemed pretty excited about the place.

"I hope I'm not getting caviar burgers." I was expecting anything when it came to the Hills residents.

Cole smiled. "Nah, they took those off the menu a while ago."

"You're kidding, right?"

"Not exactly, but it wasn't a burger. It was some appetizer. And I think they could still make it if you wanna give it a try."

"No, thanks." Caviar was a little out of my league, especially since the fish species that produced it were extremely sensitive to pollution and nearly extinct.

"Okay, burgers and fries it is." His palm ran along the small of my back, showing me to a booth right in the center of the diner.

The inside of the diner had a retro vibe—red leather booths, neon signs, and a jukebox in the corner. It was surprisingly charming, though clearly catering to a high-end crowd. Despite the casual feel, there was an air of exclusivity that made it clear this wasn't your average burger joint.

Every single pair of eyes was locked in on us as if some celebrities had just walked in. I should've gotten used to the attention by now, but it still made me feel uncomfortable doing everything under such close supervision.

"You couldn't get a table in a corner?" I couldn't keep my mouth shut about this one.

"Picky much?" Cole raised his eyebrows, hinting I was probably acting like the Elite. "As I said earlier, I don't want to hide you. I want to show you off. Besides, I was under the impression you didn't care about what everyone thought."

"Yeah, but I can't exactly stuff my face while they're looking."

"Oh, so that's what it's all about? You're afraid you'll get your fingers dirty, and they'll notice? You can do whatever the fuck you want; just act by this rule, and everything will be just fine. I promise." He had a point. That's how he lived his life. Just do whatever the fuck he wants, and the world will fall at his feet. I guess that's why we rushed to order half of what was on the menu, literally stuffing our faces with everything that I had missed over the past few weeks—at least, I had an excuse for doing it.

"Better now?" Cole asked as I pushed away a banana split that had no chance of finding room in my stomach.

I gazed at him, defeated by the earlier food challenge. "I think you tried to kill me."

"Let's go, drama queen. I know a cozy place where you can recover from my murder attempt." That sounded heavenly.

It wasn't long before we were back at his car, heading back toward the Hills.

"Is that place you were talking about my bed?" I suspected him of a devious master plan but never of what followed on that night.

"No, we're actually here." He took a right and pulled into a drive-in cinema, where at least two dozen cars were already lined up to watch the movie that was about to start. "Have you ever been to one of these before?"

"No, we didn't have a car." I didn't go on since starting to talk about my family was bringing up old memories, and the night wasn't about that. It was about making new ones. "I didn't know they were open in winter."

"Just as long as it doesn't rain or snow too much. I checked the weather, and we should be good."

I was becoming amused by how much trouble he had put into this date. "If I didn't know better, I would say you're trying to impress me."

And my observation made Cole go into defensive mode. "I've never struggled to impress a girl, and I won't start with you."

"Okay." I barely kept myself from laughing.

"Okay, what?" he groaned, growing agitated that I was on to him.

"Okay, don't impress me," I turned to look at Cole, making it clear that he wasn't doing a really good job at covering up his intention.

"Never mind. I already know you're impressed by me."

"And how's that?" I asked, barely managing to keep my smile hidden.

"You've seen me naked." He casually shrugged like his perfectly sculpted body covered in mesmerizing tattoos and the alluring shape of his manhood could never fail to impress me... Okay, maybe I was just a *little* impressed, but he still had a long way to go before I'd fall head over heels.

And it seemed that the road to my heart was paved with Belgian truffles. "I got these on the way." He took a box of deluxe chocolates from the backseat, and placed it on my lap. Another part of the *I'm not trying to impress you* project.

The movie was pretty cute. We watched a comedy, a nice change compared to the apocalyptic movie that was running at the party or with the sports channel that was always on when Cole came to visit me.

The comedy seemed to bring him into a whole different mood, and his arms glided around my waist, bringing my head to rest on his shoulder. As weird as this might sound, he came across as normal, at least in those moments. And even weirder, we probably were as close as it got to a regular couple. Only we would always be miles away from that. Not necessarily in a bad way, but certainly in a different one.

"Are you tired?" His question came as soon as the movie ended, just like he had been waiting for a while to ask it.

"Not really. Why? What do you have in mind?" He piqued my curiosity about what was going through that handsome head of his.

"You'll see." He sounded mysterious and didn't say another word as we drove off, heading toward the top of the Hills.

I reckon we were a few streets away from Ferris's mansion when Cole veered off the main road, taking a few turns until we ended up on a hilltop. The same cliff that I could see from Ferris's balcony, though it didn't look so menacing from this height. Yet it still looked deadly—amazingly beautiful, and altogether lethal.

Dark purple hues danced in never-ending fuchsia shades of toxic mists at our feet as the promise of some wandering stars was gently twinkling high above us.

"So, what do you think?" he asked, although I wasn't sure what I should really think. The view was amazing, but it was not his style to be skywatching.

My curiosity could not be contained. "Why have you brought me here?"

His eyes gazed deviously at me, as if he was expecting a reward for choosing this place. "I wanted a change. And I imagined you would appreciate this place. I'm under the impression that you didn't have these kinds of getaways back in high school."

He'd either laugh his ass off if he knew what high school was like for me, or maybe he'd just feel sorry for me. Who knows? "I didn't exactly have too many dates back in high school. I was more focused on the *school* part than the guys.

Plus, as I told you, people in the Pit don't usually have cars, especially not in high school."

"Then you're lucky you met me." The king of modesty was taking full credit for any kind of joy I may have had in this lifetime.

I pressed my palms together, thanking heaven I met him. "I feel blessed."

All jokes aside, what he did was pretty amazing.

"You should feel blessed." He let out a laugh. "I never saw myself before as the type who would ever come here. Most girls in college only want dick. They skip this part. But now that I'm here, I kinda like it. Things seem different from up here."

"Different how?" I barely opened my mouth to ask, my breath hitching.

"Different as in this." He leaned his body over mine, gliding his hand against my jawline and bringing my lips closer to his in incredibly slow motion. It was like he wasn't doing it fast enough, and my mouth had been suffering from loneliness for a lifetime.

He was laying the foundation for something new, stopping time to savor each swirl of my tongue the same way all my senses were gradually blooming back to life.

With visible effort on his side, he tried not to rush things, although I could feel his internal fight reaching a heightening level with each composed kiss.

Surprisingly, he finally managed to find himself a sensual rhythm where his lips danced with mine while one of his hands was tangled in my hair, playing with a few rebellious curls. That should've been perfect. It should have been enough. The only problem was that *I* was the one who couldn't keep herself composed anymore. Cole was turning into everything I wanted him to be. And that was awakening a vicious craving to feel him much closer than he decided to let me in those moments.

I kissed him back, fiercer, but without breaking the spell. Just nipping his bottom lip, calling forth the demons within him to come out and play. I wanted him in every way possible, but I didn't want to be the one to ask. And my plan seemed to be unfolding perfectly. With each purr, his hands were clenching harder on my waist, bringing me closer to his body to take advantage of every last inch of physical space.

He was becoming restless, and although I knew he was trying to fight it, his urges were overpowering any rational thoughts. "We need to slow down, Mouse, before I can't go back." Cole said with the exhaustion of a man who had reached the end of the line.

"Is that what you want?" I asked, pausing to meet his gaze.

He let out the loudest sigh I had ever heard. "You know what I want. You're fucking beautiful, and if it were up to me, you'd be on top of me in the driver's seat. But I'm trying to behave, and you're complicating things."

Didn't he know that complicated was my new life motto? "Cole, what if I let you in on a dark secret?"

His eyes sparkled with curiosity. "Do tell."

"I don't want you to behave."

85

CHAPTER 5

I couldn't tell how long it took us to get back to Cole's mansion, but it felt like we got there in no time. Despite my nagging, streetlights were invented for anyone else except us, and he couldn't care less, especially since he seemed to be craving a moment of privacy for too long.

In our crazed entanglement of limbs, we almost fell over a statue in the main lobby. Fortunately, his agility didn't let it crash on the ground and wake up the whole house. Not that we hadn't already woken them up with Cole fumbling the keys at the front door for what felt like an hour as his hands were far too busy gluing themselves to my ass to open the door.

"Why didn't we go back to Ferris's mansion?" I was a little surprised that he didn't want to return to the estate, especially since he's been living there for the past month.

"There are too many people in that house. I didn't want to risk running into someone, and them interfering with our evening. Besides, my room is soundproof. I used to play the guitar." The image he was painting made me laugh. I'd seen a guitar in his room, but I could never picture him actually using it.

"I want to hear you play it," I whispered as he lifted me and carried me to his bedroom.

"*And* I want to hear you scream. Guess which one of us is going to get their wish tonight." He crashed his lips to mine before I got a chance to speak another word. Not that I had much to say anyway since he was probably foreseeing things correctly.

In the past, every time Cole would kiss me, it felt devious. It wasn't just passion—it was as if he was always planning each step, what he was going to do to me next. I loved that tricky sparkle in his eyes, but now... now it was beautiful madness and uncontrolled spontaneity. He wasn't trying to guide the events, just letting everything flow with the beats of our hearts.

Previously, I would've felt that tremble settling in, questioning myself what I was doing and why. *This time* things were so much different. Lust and desire flared between us with heat, Cole didn't need me to melt into the ground but hold on to him, embracing what was coming next.

We only stopped in front of his room, where instead of breaking the door open, he set me back on my feet. His forehead fell to rest on mine under my confused gaze as a deep groan escaped his throat. "Fuck it, Bea. I promised myself I wouldn't do this today. For both our sakes, please be a good girl and tell me to calm down. I swear I'll listen," he groaned, voice tight with restraint. He was letting the burden of the decision fall on my shoulders, and that was making me want him even more.

He'd changed in the last month. Whether intentionally or not, he'd been proving that to me every day since our return from Emerald City.

If I had stuck to my plan, I would have tormented him a little longer. But in reality, I was only tormenting myself as every cell within me was yearning to feel him vibrating against my skin.

My mouth couldn't open to say the words that would get him to stop; instead, it searched for his own, letting my silent answer propel us into his bedroom.

I couldn't see a thing in the dark, but I could hear objects clattering all around us. That was until I found myself up on his dresser as the trip to the bed was apparently too far a journey.

In a race to recover whatever time was wasted with his hesitation, Cole rushed to run his hands on the contour of my panty line. Pushing them aside, he allowed the cold air in the room to crash upon my heated core, at the rate he was going he would be driving into me in the next few moments.

"Slow down," I whimpered, unwilling to end the evening so quickly, especially since that night was so special to us—a new beginning.

"You had your chance to back down. Now, you just have to enjoy the ride," he growled as I felt his belt buckle coming undone, freeing his hard cock.

I couldn't deny the frustration building at how fast things were escalating. I had envisioned this night differently, with a lot of teasing and foreplay. I was supposed to make him wait, torture him with every touch. But somehow, the tables had turned, and I was the one indirectly being teased. Not that it mattered anymore. The instant he pushed himself inside me, all my thoughts had become focused only on the sensual movement that made me tense both in agony and ecstasy.

With raw strength, he pulled me onto him—so close that I could no longer tell where one of us ended and the other began. The moves seemed hypnotic, bringing his mouth to devour mine in a way that was stealing the last breath of oxygen out of my lungs. The sensation of being out of air only heightened the tantalizing tornado that was brewing on my inner walls. He felt raw and primal, destined to shatter me into the most sublime pieces of ecstasy to the point he made me feel embarrassed of my fragile construction. The dresser I was on began skidding across the room, but the sound seemed silent compared to our ragged breaths. I just prayed he meant it when he said his room was soundproof, although I doubted that what we were doing could have been concealed by any insulation. His fingers dug into my thighs with bruising force it almost brought me to tears—yet I wanted more. I wanted him to make me his, because this time, it wasn't just my body that belonged to him. It was my soul as well.

I could feel the familiar tingles of my building release gathering like angry black clouds of storm upon me. I didn't even know if I was kissing him anymore or just moaning through the rough thrusts. One thing was clear, the strong hands that were clenched on my thighs were guiding me in one direction only—ecstasy.

I tried to prolong the moment, searching his cobalt eyes with my gaze only to find a few loose strands of raven hair tumbling over his face, highlighting all the masculine assets he mastered so well. His jaw tightened, noticing the beautiful rapture in my gaze as my attempt to force some self-control failed me dramatically. I was focusing on him just so that I could slow down the overwhelming sensations that were piling up inside me, and without realizing it, that was the main contributor to the uncontrollable pulsing between my thighs.

He was right about me screaming his name, although my screams drowned themselves down his throat like honey melting on his tongue. It wasn't long before a long groan filled the room while some violent flickers of orgasmic pleasure were reignited to race deep between my thighs.

My body was satisfied, but my conscience didn't let me off the hook. I felt disappointed with myself for letting him rush things along. I was supposed to make him suffer, yet somehow I ended up ravaged by pleasure. And since I still had all my clothes on, I was beginning to wonder if I should stay or go.

Chances were that Cole already knew what I was thinking, especially since his lips pressed back on mine. "You think I've rushed things?" he asked, voicing what was already on the tip of my tongue. But what was done was done. No sense in going back.

"Well, I still have my clothes on." I couldn't keep that one to myself, even though I was as guilty as he was for skipping foreplay. Besides, my legs were shaking. Who am I kidding? My insides were shaking as well, and we nearly broke the damn dresser. Not to mention that my ass was literally hurting from being on that piece of wood for so long. It was just that I hoped *I* would play hard to get for a little longer.

"The keyword is *still*. You see, I haven't exactly been with anyone since I started everything with you, so I was a little eager." Cole was making the strangest confession. We weren't even together, let alone was he forced to make a vow of celibacy. To be honest, I was expecting he'd have tried to catch up with someone from his fanbase after all the sexless days I put him through.

"Eager?" I asked, trying to get him to say more.

"Okay, my balls were on the verge of exploding. Happy now?"

"Not really; it wasn't my intention." I giggled, although that was exactly my intention.

"Intention or not, be prepared for a very long *night*," he snarled like the devil he was, helping me off the comforter.

"I thought..." I didn't really know what to say. I thought *that* was *the night*.

"You obviously thought wrong." He didn't let me go on, and I could only feel a wave of relief wash over me. I would've probably been terrible at speaking my thoughts anyway. "Now get out."

"Excuse me?" I stuttered.

What happened to the *girlfriend* part?

He couldn't possibly throw me out right after sex.

Could he?

Who was I kidding? It was Cole we were talking about. The guy could throw me out of a moving train if he ever got tired of me.

Still, that didn't manage to leave me less disappointed, no matter how hard I kept telling myself I should have seen it coming.

"What are you doing? I thought I told you to leave?" He was

dead serious about it. No doubt in my mind.

I could no longer hide a disgruntled expression as my heart began furiously pumping inside my chest.

Though no sound was wasted on him.

"Mouse? Are you okay?" he asked, his brows frowning in concern.

No answer from my side.

"You didn't... Did you?" His eyes narrowed with the most intense thoughts while his hand moved to support his chin as a result of such an extraordinary crashing of neurons.

It only took one second before his hysterical laughter filled the room. "Leave, then walk back into the room. That's what I meant. I want to start this part of the night all over again." His explanation made sense, but my cheeks that had reddened with anger were now flushing with embarrassment. I was one step away from throwing a tantrum when in reality, I didn't really understand what was going on.

"Are you serious about it?" I finally regained my voice.

"Yes. Just let me fix my clothes first." He seemed so determined to do this right, it was downright amusing.

I wasn't sure how getting his cock back in his pants was going to change the dynamic of the evening, but I said I would give it a try.

Adjusting my outfit, I stepped outside into the hallway.

I gave him a few moments before I decided to knock, but

my knuckles didn't get to touch the door before a woman's voice made me jump from my shoes. "Good evening, Bea." Cole's mum was crossing the hallway, probably on her way to the kitchen.

"Good... evening." I was so dumbfounded that I could barely repeat her own words, let alone say anything else.

"You kids have a lovely evening," she completed with a certain tone—that *I know what you two've been up to* tone.

I didn't even know if I was knocking out of panic or eagerness, but the very next second, I was banging at Cole's door to get in.

"I've been expecting you," Cole's voice was greeting me, filled with amused pathos.

This time I could actually see inside the room. The light was on, and to my surprise, the mess we made in the darkness was magically gone.

"Well, I had time for an encounter while I was away. Your mum just greeted me in the hallway," I said, my voice still shaking as if I'd seen a ghost.

"Don't bother with her. She's probably just messing with you. She knows my room is off-limits. But don't stand there. Come in." He was acting much weirder than a minute before when I chose to play along with his game.

The whole scenario seemed ridiculous. We just had sex a few moments ago. I had the scarlet indentations on my thighs to prove that.

"My room was a mess. That's why I kept you waiting before

inviting you in." He was keeping up his game, and it was starting to amuse me. At least he was making me loosen up.

"I've seen your room messy before."

"That was a part of our old relationship," he said, a smile tugging at his lips.

"Enlighten me. The old relationship that ended when we returned from Emerald City or the one that ended a few minutes ago when I walked out the door?" In my *expert* opinion, Cole sucked at *new beginnings*, but I couldn't help but appreciate the effort he was putting into making things work. Funny how now the arrogant king of ECU was trying to impress me, even if he would never deliberately admit it.

"I could return to old habits any time." He let the corners of his lips raise into a grin this time. "But I prefer trying out new ones." He took a step closer. "Don't move."

To my surprise, his *new habit* was miles away from anything he'd ever done before. The tip of his tongue traced over my lips with just a small peck, then descended to other needy areas of my body.

He hauled my shirt over my head, careful so that the small crystal decorations wouldn't get tangled in my hair, then tossed it on a wooden chair.

"Oh, you came prepared." He let his fingers trail the straps of my bra that were running across my breasts.

Damn, my cover was blown. I knew I should've gone for the granny underwear.

"This was the first thing I found in my dressing room." Like he was ever going to believe my excuse.

"I'm sure it was." He pushed the cups of my bra down, freeing the full weight of my breasts. A throaty groan sealed the encounter of his tongue and my aching nipples, getting them to pebble on contact.

I watched him savor each movement, rolling that damn tongue piercing over the softness of my skin with soul-wrecking desire. Each time he stopped to look at me, he seemed to be someone new—an improved version of whoever I wanted him to be, bringing our chemistry to reach astonishing proportions.

No inch of my skin was left untouched by his mouth, and no inch without the goosebumps born from the answering rush of desire rising within me.

I wanted to whisper to him that he was doing all the right things, at the most flawless pace, so he could engrave the moment somehow in his mind and put it on repeat anytime. But I knew the beast lurking beneath his good-guy facade. Any validation of the powers he had over me would only feed it, reviving his limitless ego that stood between any acknowledgment of real feelings.

The delicious exploration of my breasts sent a coil of heat building low in my belly, weakening my knees as if an invisible weight was forcing me to the ground. As if I wasn't devastated enough, my skirt slipping to the floor was letting me know that his vicious torment was far from being over.

The weight of his palms molded to my ass as he pulled me closer to him, just to drag my panties down with his teeth. If I ever had a moment to think about it, I would imagine the gesture as cringe-worthy. But it wasn't. It was sexual, erotic, leaving my pussy pulsing with the thought of what he might actually do to me.

I just had sex ten minutes ago. The memory wouldn't leave my mind as I was unable to understand how it was that I felt even more eager than before. The storm that set out to ravage me was back again, and so was that sublime delight of having his full attention on my body.

I tried to hold back my cravings. I didn't want to break into ecstasy in less than five minutes for the second time tonight, especially since he seemed to be so focused on thoroughly exploring each moment we shared.

With no panties in sight, the warmth of his tongue slipped between my folds, getting that piece of metal that resided inside his mouth to run over my clit.

I jolted from the uncontained thrill, clenching my fingers between dark strands of his hair "B... Be..."

"Bed?" he stopped to ask, savoring the sparkles of his incoming victory.

I nodded, trying to control my breathing.

Maybe he recognized I was surely about to faint this time around, or maybe he wanted a position from where he could explore my weaknesses better. Whatever his reasons, he guided me toward the edge of the bed, gently laying me down on the mattress.

He didn't join me, just remained kneeling next to the bed frame, continuing what he had begun, cradling me against him while draping my leg over his shoulder. Now he had full access to every part of me, and the intrusion of his tongue within me was making me clench a fist full of sheets for support.

I had no idea what stunt he was trying to pull, but the need bubbling below my waist was leaving me with no option but to surrender to his game.

As I remembered, after the six minutes I lasted in front of this tantalizing assault in his tub, I felt that someone should have given me a medal. Tonight, I'd be lucky if I could last even two minutes under the spell of his tongue.

The new intrusion of my senses was doing something to me, *with* me, turning me not only into an addict for this man, but also a piece of a grand puzzle where he held one of the main leads.

As if I wasn't falling apart fast enough, he drove his mouth to completely ravage my clit as he slid two fingers inside.

My heartbeats quickened with every curve and nibble that were fueling my body to pulse with longing. I could barely withstand his presence on my skin. Until I couldn't resist it at all. With the shuddering of every molecule inside me, I arched into the mattress, ripped by a mind-blowing orgasm. It felt so intense that I dug my feet into the bed and tried to lift my body weight higher to escape the irresistible torture.

"Going somewhere?" Cole asked, keeping me on the spot to roam the length of my core with his mouth a few more times, only to assure himself that my body had given up on obeying me. I could see the satisfaction in his eyes as I could barely choke back a moan, let alone make any kind of movement.

I could feel him pushing me higher on the bed until my head rested on the pillows. The next moment, he was advancing on top of me, balancing his weight on his elbows, and caging me under his weight.

Strangely, it felt as if I was in bed with him for the first time that night. It wasn't only the heat of the moment; there was something much more complex, something primal, radiating from within him. Like he was luring me to be his. Like he desperately needed me to be his in every way possible.

His mouth parted slightly as he flexed his hips forward to ease his length into me.

I was barely coming down from the high, and he was threatening to send me to a new one. His tongue moved to invade my mouth as my nails dug deep into his back muscles. I could feel myself heading into overdrive again, much sooner than I'd expected. With long molten strokes, he drove himself inside of me, with each thrust, surging deeper than before. He wasn't in a rush this time. On the contrary, we were floating somewhere above all timelines, gliding between the sheets with fluid moves.

One of his hands was locked on the back of my head while the other molded over one of my breasts to hold me in position. Pressing me completely under his weight, I could feel the heat spiking between my thighs, higher and higher, threatening to set me on liquid fire.

"My King," I murmured, slipping an acknowledgment of his supreme powers. Only this time, the king would treat me like a queen and not a slave.

"I can't fucking get enough of you," he snarled back, biting my lips, and sneaking a hand beneath the small of my back to drive me completely against him.

My eyes flew wide open as his hot, hard length was buried completely within me, happy to extract the very last of my moans.

It all became too intense. Sky-heightening. Irresistible.

I could feel his jaw clenching from how hard he was grinding his teeth together with faded attempts not to break the rhythm, and jump straight to that crazed pace that would blast us both into rippling pleasure. It wasn't time yet; he still needed me to feel every single gesture he had to offer—the warmth of his body, and the warmth of his soul when it came to me.

In the light of this acknowledgement, I kissed him more fiercely, tugging my body toward him to withstand his thrusts, letting the impact of our union amplify the effect he had on me.

I was drawing air from his lungs clinging to him like he was the only thing keeping me afloat, purring with every single thrust of his hips until that tightening sensation snuck up on me. I didn't stand a chance. The tingles inside turned into a detonation of my senses, leaving me no time to brace for what was to come. My core was spasming so strongly that with each new thrust, something else was exploding within, stronger and faster until I couldn't do anything more but cry out in pure ecstasy.

I could barely recall what happened. The moves were shocking places I didn't even know existed, as his arousal seemed to be even thicker than before. If I was to be honest, I was preparing to make a run for it—at least up on the pillows —when a burst of satisfied laughter filled the room, and the warm sign of his elation coated my still pulsing channel.

"Why are you laughing?" I asked with a dying breath.

"I think you just went to war with my dick," he said between groans, trying to come down from the high. "It felt like you were about to murder me down there."

"You had to say something." I wasn't angry this time, just amused that he was admitting *defeat*.

He rushed to catch my nipple between his teeth. "Get used to it." Oh, I was going to get used to it for sure, especially since I had two others just like him.

My hand glided to tangle in his hair, holding him there, dragging out the last moments of our first real night together. That happened for about three to four hours... we had fallen asleep.

I woke up in the middle of the night, my lips resting on the wings tattoo that spread from his shoulders to his neck. His pulse was merging with mine into a silent melody. He felt so peaceful, and so did I—even though peace was so far away from me.

"Shh," I heard him whisper into my ear. It was almost morning, and I could still feel my hand trembling from the nightmare that had even woke Cole. The fists, the fear, the beatings—the same nightmare on repeat almost every night. He was probably getting used to it by now. It wasn't the first time he heard my cries, and it likely wouldn't be the last. But it was the first time he found a quick remedy to my anguishing memories. His lips magnetized toward mine, drying my tears with promises of something no man ever offered me before.

Love.

He didn't need to say it. Feeling it made so much more sense.

And I did. I felt it with every thumb that ran across my cheeks, and every fragile kiss that pressed against my lips.

He was falling in love with me.

I had won my first battle, and the king of ECU had won a piece of my heart.

CHAPTER 6

It was morning—again. Late morning if I was to look at the time, but it was Saturday, so no classes for us.

"Sorry for ruining your sleep." I wrapped my arms around Cole's neck, casting a sorrowful smile.

"You mean last night when you kept me prisoner between the sheets or this morning?"

"*I* kept you prisoner?" I teased, trying to get away from the cage of his arms.

But that only got the corner of his lips to curve into a smile. "What exactly are you trying to do?"

"Get out of bed," I murmured, not so convinced of my own words.

It didn't seem to convince Cole either. "I can see that, but why?"

"Do you really want to laze around here all day long?" I chuckled, the thought sounding more tempting by the second.

"Lazing wasn't exactly what I had in mind." He snuck an arm to the curve of my back, moving his mouth toward mine.

"I... have... to... go... back... to... the... mansion," I breathed between kisses that were just about to ignite last night's torching fire.

He frowned, clearly not thrilled with the idea. "Now?"

"I promised Seb and Nat I'd spend the day with them. We won't have too much time to be together now that I'm back at ECU and they're in school... Plus my deals." I lowered my voice as a silent reminder that I'd have to face the real world soon enough.

Cole didn't seem too bothered about the other *tasks* I might have to perform. "I'm free for the day."

"Are you saying you want to spend time with us?" I couldn't deny that I was surprised he was willing to get involved at this level, but the thought of him actually spending quality time around my family was raising a strange emotion.

"Don't worry. No decent thoughts here." He flashed a mischievous smile. "I was thinking more like all of us playing cards or something like that, and when I win, I would get to give you your dares a little later in the bedroom."

"*If* you win," I raised a finger as a warning.

Not that he seemed the least bit fazed by my threat. "Oh, I would certainly win, Mouse. I always do."

"I wouldn't say always." I tried dodging him and sneaking out of bed.

"Always." He grunted, tightening his grip on my waist and pulling the sheet on top of us.

He was craving a round three, and from the way his lips teased my nipples, I had no chance of escaping the will of his body.

Except, Cole's mom knocked on the bedroom door. "The brunch starts in about ten minutes. The guests have begun showing up. I hope you're getting dressed."

That earned a quick growl out of him as he felt the need to abandon his mission. "Shit! I totally forgot about that," Cole whispered, just so only I could hear him.

"I hope you didn't forget." Apparently, Mrs. Clayborne was a psychic.

"No... I was just getting dressed." Cole's voice was muffled from somewhere between the sheets.

And I had to make fun of his misery. "From where I'm standing, it looked to me like you were getting undressed."

"I completely forgot about this. My mom is friends with all the rich hags around here. Everyone who is anyone in Echo City is going to be at this brunch. I need to charm my way to get them to choose Ferris as governor."

Half of the Echo City Elite drooling over him didn't really sit well with my temper. No matter the age. "Hmm. What does charm your way mean?"

"Whatever it may take," Cole answered so casually that I almost believed him.

"Are you for real?" I was already out of bed, getting dressed to leave.

That certainly stirred a smile on Cole's lips. "I was only joking. But now that I see how worked up you are about it, I might just put it into practice. I like seeing you boil. It turns me on."

I wasn't thrilled with his humor, well at least when it implied someone else getting their hand on him. "Then maybe you can arrange to have the hags also fix your *manly problems*?"

"A—I'm only going to this brunch because you got me involved in all this *saving the city* thing. B—I only want you to fix my *manly problems.* And C—you're the biggest prude I've ever known. Who says *manly problems* anymore?"

"Educated people," I muttered, trying to end the conversation.

"This isn't about education. It's about exploring your sexuality." He jolted from bed, tossing the sheets that covered him away. "This is a dick, not my *manly thing.*"

"Jesus, Cole." I covered my eyes, trying not to look at him naked for too long.

It only made things worse since the devil decided to come my way, pulling my hands away from my face. "I'm going to have so much fun over this."

I tried ignoring him without any real chance of success. "Can you put some clothes on?"

Quite the opposite, his lips sneaked through my rebellious

curls to whisper in my ear, "When you think of it, what do you even call it in your mind? How much of a prude are you?"

Judging by what he said, a hundred percent prude.

"I don't think of your..." Worst excuse ever.

"My..." He was expecting me to fill in the blanks eventually.

Shit, maybe I didn't turn into as much of a badass as I thought.

Obviously, I wasn't about to keep that conversation going.

And also obviously, he didn't leave things that way.

"Dick." Cole laughed the word out, heading to his dressing room to find something to wear. "No offense, Mouse, but there's not a chance in hell you're not thinking about *it*."

"Maybe if you would stop walking around naked, I wouldn't think about *it*."

"Problem fixed," he said a moment later, zipping up a pair of black dress pants, then moving upwards to button up a white dress shirt.

Yeah, like that would fix anything.

I just blankly stared at the way the white piece of material divinely wrapped around the defined shapes of his muscles, letting a few black strands of ink peek from under his collar. My thoughts suddenly began scrambling with lightning speed to the point where I was beginning to question if he looked better with his clothes off or on.

His Elite genes were glinting through the elegant outfit, radiating melting energy that seemed to be having a devastating effect between my hips. He was hypnotizingly attractive, a wolf dressed in sheep's clothing, ready to impress any female audience. He was going in for the kill, and if that wouldn't get them to support Ferris, I don't know what would.

"You could join me. My mother has to have something you could wear." Cole eyed my leather skirt, which was miles away from anything someone could wear to an Elite brunch. They were all too goodie-two-shoes for that—more the society-clubs stuck-up vibe than my modern dress-to-kill style.

"No, thanks. I'll pass on this one. Besides, I wouldn't want to deflect the attention coming your way. Plus, seeing you flirting with an eighty-year-old would definitely ruin my day."

"Fifty is my limit. I prefer MILFS to mummies." He probably considered himself to be funny.

I had to strike back. "Then I should probably go flirt with a sugar daddy myself."

But I never expect it to backfire so fast. "I thought Ferris was your sugar daddy." His tone sharper than I liked.

"And I thought my deal with Ferris didn't bother you. I have my reasons for doing this, and you know it."

"It doesn't bother me. I guess I'm just stressed because I have to spend my day acting nice."

"And that's such an awful thing for you to do." I rolled my eyes to the back of my head. Cole had many qualities, but being nice definitely wasn't one of them.

"Pretty fucked up on my end," he muttered, smoothing the last strand of his jet-black hair into place. "Speaking of Ferris, I think you should go easier with him. He's not going through a good time."

Great, Cole was clearly choosing sides when it came to his friends and me. "And you think I am?"

"You seemed to be having a pretty good time last night," he said, arrogance dripping from his voice.

"You can't fix everything with your magic dick."

"So you finally admit it's magic, and made your first step into not being a prude. Win-win for me." He was starting to get on my nerves. I guess the time spent with Cole always had to have a limit so that I wouldn't feel the need to strangle him to death.

"I have to go see Nat and Sebastian. Have fun seducing the oldies." I kissed him goodbye, then walked straight out the door before he would get a chance to get into who knows what subject.

"I'll try to swing by after I'm done here." He made sure to let me know we were still on for the rest of the day, although his new fans didn't seem to agree. The brunch extended into lunch, and lunch into dinner since nothing could stand in the way of good gossip and rich people showing off their latest purchases.

Despite my power of self-conviction, I felt a little off because Cole couldn't join us for the day. I kind of got used to having him around, and no matter how much I tried to avoid the feeling, his presence was missed.

I caught up on some family time and even got to bed early. My siblings had an earlier curfew than my usual bedtime. That made me roll between the sheets two hours ahead of my normal schedule.

Not that I could ever get enough sleep.

I planned a surprise visit to Brax's office the next day, and I was starting to believe I would need all the energy I could get.

I think it was well past midnight when an excruciating sound echoed through every brick of the mansion, waking me up with my own cry out of panic.

I wished it was just another of the nights when I could ignore it, but I knew that time eventually had to come to an end. I could no longer remain in bed and listen to Ferris's nightmares push him to the edge of madness.

Yes, a part of me hated him, but there was also a part that felt responsible for sending him deeper into the hell he'd created for himself.

Without even realizing it, my feet were already carrying me through the dimly lit corridors, closer and closer to the darkness that seemed to be calling my name. Once again, I was defying every single step of the plan I had regarding him. But when it came to Ferris, I always had to expect the unpredictable.

The lump in my throat was almost preventing me from breathing as I found myself in front of the door I dreaded opening the most. The place still preserved the shattered remnants of a beautiful dream that had plummeted straight off the edge of the world.

He was still asleep when I got there. Well, as much as his nightmares allowed him to be, tossing between the sheets as tormenting thick black clouds of madness were hovering over his world.

I wish I could say I rushed to save him from his monsters, but each step toward his bed was a strong reminder of how fundamentally broken I was when I first stepped into this place. My feet could barely advance as the realization of how close I was to following him down the same path kicked in. I was becoming the temptress, driven by obscure demons to do whatever it took for the success of my plan.

Maybe I was even more devious than him since the source of his breakout was caused by blurred moments of madness, while mine was deliberate, a strategy to rule the game. But I needed to do it, if not for me, then maybe for him. This seemed to be the only chance for a fractured normality.

Cold beads of sweat clung to the messy strands of his light brown hair, multiplying with every twitch of his face.

I had to put an end to all of the madness.

Slipping next to him, I took a seat on the bed. The movement didn't seem to have any kind of impact on my king, but my arms wrapping over his torso did. His eyes shot wide open, staring at me as if I wasn't really there. He was looking straight through me, or more like it, glancing directly into the heart of all his nightmares.

Before I got any chance to react, he pulled out his knife from beneath the mattress, resting it on my thigh so firmly that its tip broke skin.

The gesture instantly snapped him back to reality, forcing his eyes to stare into mine with horror. Though that wasn't enough, it was just a momentary consciousness while I needed him to remain with me for the long run.

Driven by madness—or maybe desperation–I placed my hand over his, pressing the blade deeper into my flesh. The pain spread so deeply into my senses that it felt like it was awakening something unknown within me. It was an instinct of self-preservation and, at the same time, the most twisted form of arousal; inflicted by the anguish reverberating through every cell in my body.

It traced back to what happened in the governor's house, with the fear and pain I endured that day. It took me to the point that I had to accept the suffering just so that I wouldn't completely cease to function. I guess that stayed with me— the acceptance of pain until I managed to trick myself that it was pleasure. A fucked-up repercussion of our road to victory. A path that brought me closer to Ferris's insanity than I ever imagined.

The blood quickly rolled out onto his fingers, getting them to completely open, letting the knife plunge straight to the floor. The impact had a certain sound attached to it. The noise made by the blade scraping against the wood was awakening all primal senses, forcing a surge of basic instincts to rush through our veins.

In essence, we'd become so much alike, and that was all I ever needed to get my plan to work. Join him in his madness, to either bring him back or be lost there with him forever. Only time could tell as the first step in this journey had already been taken.

Unlike anyone else, his first instinct wasn't to get up and help me, but to stare at the red blood that was coating my thigh along with his fingers. No denying that he was in a slight shock, but it was something else besides that—a dark glint lurking in his eyes, waiting for the liquid to blanket my skin completely.

It wasn't about words this time; they seemed useless now, overshadowed by the connection of our bodies. Though almost silent sounds were escaping him as the realization of what happened was gradually sinking in. He was still caught somewhere between his nightmares and earthshaking reality, and the few grunts that evaded his lips had to be shushed. My finger rushed to keep them shut as the red trace of my blood came as a seal that brought his ultimate silence.

I leaned in to kiss the path I just marked, feeling his pulse racing beneath my lips with incredible speed. It was slow at first, catching him off guard, allowing the sensual fusion of our souls to stir forgotten memories. And even if it was a show I put on display solely for him, I couldn't avoid the effects it was also having on me.

It felt both heartwarming and excruciatingly painful, and I wasn't talking about a physical level. I hovered somewhere between building him up or breaking him down, and no matter the result, I was the one who would wear the scars.

For Ferris, it was seduction in its purest form, and that was putting him exactly where I wanted. If, in the past, he was obsessed with me needing him, this time he would be the one that needed me. I was going to make sure of it.

I slid my tongue against his, shifting my leg over his waist, straddling him between my thighs.

Probably realizing I wasn't wasting time on patching my wound up, his hand slipped to cover the cut as I was arching to feel the shape of his arousal. He was as caught up in the moment as I was, and with every roll of my hips, his dark coal eyes grew hungrier and his lips intensified their strength.

We couldn't be kept separated any longer.

With his hands firmly clasped on my thighs, sending a sharp rush of pain to storm through me, I pushed his boxers aside along with my panties, slowly lowering myself to take him.

It was like stopping time for a second, and despite the detached attitude I was aiming for, my mind got caught up in exactly what I was doing. We were together again, bound in an ephemeral moment that took me swiftly back to the foolish girl who'd first entered his room a few months ago.

Funny, how I still felt I belonged to that place, and implicitly with him. Yet in a cruel twist of fate, I didn't quite feel complete without the other two kings in my life.

Unable to let my mind trail off that way, I shook my head, focusing on the present. Pleasure coursed through me in warm waves, foreseeing delirious moments of ecstasy.

I was taking what I needed from him, the same way they all had taken what they wanted from me. He was the tool of my desire, except, completely opposite than in my case, he was happy to be used. I could see that in the satisfied smirk tingling the corners of his lips as each one of my moves was completed by the strength of his palms that were guiding my body.

All I could feel was us, locked in the purest moment of

intimacy as my hips instinctively sought that pleasure that would soon be ripping through me.

I looked down on him, gazing at the deep pools of his eyes, trying to live through the pain, and let the full effect of his intrusion create the enchanted spell that each time pulls me back into his universe.

Part of me wished for him to be free, but all I was succeeding in was freeing his monsters, inviting them to join me and dance in the lights of the orange flames coming from the fireplace.

I felt him give in, living just for the thrill, moving from underneath me with a pace designed to drive us both into the waves of ecstasy.

The sound of our breaths filled the room, quickening in sync with the rhythm of our heartbeats. I wanted him in ways words couldn't describe, and from the deep groans escaping his lips, the feeling was mutual. He was slipping between shock, rapturing pleasure, and devilish joy as his palms clenched once again on my thighs. It was clear that he couldn't contain himself any longer, and the truth was, I couldn't either.

With every cell tensed to its max, I almost fell on top of him, shaken by the maelstrom that was blowing us into micro pieces of sinful satisfaction.

Our lips weren't touching for kissing anymore, but to moan our pleasure down each other's throats, letting the sound of our ecstasy shake the wooden bedposts. I found myself in a place between delirium and a hazy sense of normality, uselessly clinging to the illusion that I had any chance of defeating him at his own game.

I still had to play it cool. For that, I didn't need him to hold me. I just needed him to believe he owned me to the point he couldn't go on without this feeling. And that had all chances of success. I could see it in his eyes, in the hunger that could no longer be contained with just a few minutes of ecstasy.

"I should find something to fix this." He stroked off the drops of blood that were rolling down my leg and to the sheets.

"Your maid is going to think this is a murder scene." Bad joke on my part, but the thrill of the moment didn't let him get mad over it.

"Stay here. I'll be right back." He placed me between the pillows, on his side of the bed, rushing to bring a wet cloth to clean me up.

He felt responsible for my injury, mostly because he really *was responsible* for it. Before I could tell what was going on, he was already cleaning the blood and patching me up, placing an extra-large band-aid over the cut. Funny how he didn't say a word regarding what had happened, just chose to play the silence card until his mind could process the events.

The pain had mostly faded, just small jolts reminding me of the blade as his hand smoothed once more over the bandage to fix it. His palm didn't leave, just remained there, circling the former trace of my red liquid. He had just warmed up, swept up again in a whirlwind of new sensations.

He felt alive again.

Locking his gaze on mine for silent confirmation, his hand slid inside my nightgown. Lust and murky thoughts were boiling into the depths of his onyx eyes, reigniting the same passion that had burned between us just minutes before. He was determined to try for another repeat, and who was I to let the night end?

CHAPTER 7

No words were spent to determine what had happened between us. There was no use for any. Everything could be considered as another part of the deal.

Ferris's lips didn't leave my skin until dawn, trying to catch up with all the lost nights spent in separate beds. Things were just following their usual course for him, while I had to make sure my plan was still on its original track.

I tried displaying a certain tenderness, pretending to fall straight into his spell for one last time, though each attempt of faking a loving touch was backfiring on me in ways I never thought possible.

I let my fingers trail the sculpted path of his jawline over and over again, bringing his own hand to trace my lips in response. I wished I could say it was just a touch, but it was made of ropes tying me back to every deranged bone in his body. I felt like I was teetering on the edge, trying to cling to fleeting moments of clarity.

How could a man so perfect be so irreparably broken?

But maybe being broken was what made him so astonishingly sublime. A prince of darkness, forged in misery and pain, wrapped in the trappings of wealth. My hero in so many ways, an antihero in so many others.

One may think this was the moment for a happy ending, but we were so far away from reaching that. He still hadn't gained anything from this experience, and this path would only lead to where the old one took us.

I think it was well into the afternoon when I first decided to speak. "Can I ask you something?" I hesitated, unsure of what answer I really expected.

"Sure. Anything," his eagerness to answer me made him promise more than he had to give.

"I don't think you meant that *anything*." I let out a chuckle. "And it isn't that serious either. I was just wondering what will happen to the apartment where we were staying now that I'm better."

He took a moment before answering my question with one of his own. "Are you asking if you'll be moving back there?"

"Something like that," I said, avoiding his eyes.

"Would you like to go back?" His question put me in a position of some difficulty.

I couldn't deny that the thought crossed my mind several times, but I couldn't really make up my mind. Part of me was hoping he had a plan for when it came to where I would live. That he'd make the decision for me. "I'm not sure what I want. I was just thinking about your privacy." I knew he wasn't fond of company, and having me here meant also having Nat and Seb around too.

"I initially brought you here because it was easier to keep an eye on everyone. Now I have gotten used to a fuller house. It still doesn't keep the nightmares away. But I hoped *you* would at some point."

"Ferris..." It felt unfair to be putting all that faith in me, especially since I had so many insecurities of my own. I couldn't also be responsible for his dreams and nightmares, even if I was beginning to think he was considering me to be his last hope of salvation.

"Sorry, I'm probably being a little extra with what I said. I don't want my troubles to be on your shoulders." He realized the burden he was placing on me.

"Never mind. I was just worried we were bothering you. Nat can be a little pushy at times." I let out a chuckle, trying to diffuse the severity of the discussion.

"Nothing that a shopping session can't fix," he said with a smirk.

"Yeah, about that... I appreciate what you're doing for her, but I don't want her getting used to a life she won't be able to afford." Mostly, I didn't want her to think money comes for free. There's always a price to be paid, even if she's not who's paying it—at the moment.

Yet, I'd seemed to have offended Ferris. "What do you mean *she won't be able to afford it*? Am I going bankrupt and I somehow missed it?"

"Our deal won't last forever. There are a million things that could happen. I just want her to know what life is really like, to never forget where she came from."

A dark sorrow set upon his face. "You're right. It probably won't last forever." No other explanation or words. Just him putting his arm around me to pull me to his chest while I braced myself to go straight for his bleeding heart.

"Why so serious?" I cast out a laugh, rushing to cover his lips in a hundred foolish kisses.
Drama needed to turn into something else this time, and I needed him to be pulled into the fantasy I was creating, not let him drift away.

"I still have a few minutes before I leave." My voice was drenched with passion, changing the rhythm with which my tongue was trailing his lips to open.

"Minutes?" His tone sharpened, causing my defensiveness to creep in.

"It's a manner of speaking." I made my hand disappear beneath the sheets, guiding it straight to that erect part of him.

All drama was spared for the moment, making room for way better feelings.

"Definitely not minutes." He murmured, sealing his words with a kiss.

"Show off."

"You know they're not just words." He wasted no time *proving* his point, making room between my thighs to add another rope to the chokehold he had me under.

Half an hour later, and just barely getting back from the high, I finally managed to slip out of his room. Had to do it the second I got the chance since remaining there would only lead to another entanglement of limbs and sheets. Besides, I had somewhere else to be. It felt like I'd set a wheel in motion, and I couldn't allow myself a moment to pause. Maybe it had something to do with the fact that I was too afraid I'd get cold feet if I stopped.

I followed my daily routine, trying to spend a little time with Nat and Seb. That's where I took my strength from, although they also seemed to be draining the last drop of energy I had left.

I think I stared at all the exquisite dresses hanging in my dressing room for an hour. I just couldn't decide what to wear—until a black piece of material was calling me from the corner. It was a trip down memory lane, and that was exactly what I was going for. The same black dress I had bought for Brax, charged with the passion of the moments spent together.

I was betting on that passion to ignite a certain fire within him, without me actually having to say the words out loud. It wouldn't work like that with a man like him. I had to be extra careful and play my cards right because I had a single shot at this.

I headed straight to his office. I subconsciously hoped he'd be there, not at the club with the glass wall. I still found it hard to picture him spending time in another female's company, but I knew that if he was in the office with the glass room, I had every chance of not finding him alone.

It was my lucky night since the bodyguard at the club's front door nodded, confirming Brax was in his office. The man didn't seem pleased with my unannounced arrival, especially since I wasn't on any guest list. But I still managed to convince him to sneak me in.

I wasn't exactly out of the woods yet, and the scenario of what an unexpected visit to Brax could really mean was sending an icy chill down my spine. It was jealousy in its purest form. But I don't think that was even the part bothering me any longer. What bothered me was that jealousy is usually born out of feelings. And I couldn't allow myself to have any kind of feelings for a man like him. At least that was what I kept telling myself though the reality was far more complicated.

I forced myself to control my shaky steps, determined to put on a detached mask as soon as I entered his office. A flimsy defense mechanism, trying to protect me from the man who could break me with the curl of a finger.

"Your guard told me it was okay to come in." I pushed the door open, waiting for his permission before stepping inside.

"Come in. The guards out front already informed me that you were here," Brax said, his tone having trouble concealing a hint of anxiety.

"I didn't realize I was such a celebrity," I tried to sound casual, though my own voice betrayed a slight tremble.

"It isn't every day that someone comes uninvited to invade my space," he said, regaining his usual composure.

"Is that what I'm doing? Invading your space?" I slowly circled the room, trying to avoid his gaze which seemed to be stuck examining every single one of my features. He was looking at me as if this was the first time he saw me. Totally surprised and intrigued at the same time.

"Not for long. I have a meeting in a short while."

"Should I leave, then?" It was a rhetorical question. I might have come at the wrong time, but I was planning on fully availing myself of every available minute.

"What you should do is let me know next time when you're coming. My schedule's insane these days with the election prep."

"How's that going?" Truth was, I hadn't seen Brax in a while. I ran into him a few weeks ago when he was leaving Ferris's mansion but didn't get the chance to talk to him since he basically had his phone glued to his ear. Cole kept me informed about what was going on with the elections and everything else, but I also needed to hear Brax's version—especially since I had the feeling he'd been avoiding me.

"Everything is under control. At least at my end."

"What's that supposed to mean?" I asked, feeling the emphasis in his voice.

"My man is ready to step in and do exactly what we order. It's not him that I'm worried about." *Worry* was a strong word coming from Brax. Something was wrong, and for some reason, Cole kept that part away from me.

"Who are you worried about then? Cole's father?" I seemed to have spoken the magic words since Brax's forehead instantly furrowed with concern.

"It's only a matter of time before he goes back to his old ways and gambles his ass off in some casino. He's just going to be doing it elsewhere. Maybe even another city. But that won't mean he won't jeopardize our plan." Brax seemed pretty involved in *our plan*, and I was beginning to believe it was much more strongly related to his thirst for power rather than to our deal.

"With what money? Does he have access to funds?" I asked.

"Nothing that I don't keep track of. But since I transferred all he lost at my places into Cole's account, he's been asking him for money." Brax seemed to be fed up with Cole's father, and why wouldn't he? Being generous was such a great sacrifice for a man like him, especially since Cole's dad was making his gesture seem to have been for nothing.

I was pretty surprised Cole didn't mention it before, but I figured he didn't want to add to my worry list. He should have done it, though. I keep adding new things to his worry list every day. "What did Cole say?" I asked, knowing Brax had a better grasp of the situation than I did.

Brax's nostrils flared, a sign of his frustration before he could give me a response. "He didn't give his dad a cent. Cold knew what the money was for, and he's not helping him down that path again."

"Cole didn't talk about it with me." For some reason, I let Brax take a sneak peek into my mind and how disappointed I was that Cole had shut me out of this one.

"His dad is a sensitive subject. He was his hero while growing up. It's pretty hard for him to see all his beliefs being demolished that way. I guess I was lucky. I knew exactly who my father was the moment I first opened my eyes."

"Lucky?" I scoffed. Living life by the gun didn't seem so

lucky in my book.

"I was being ironic. I didn't choose this life. This life chose me, and that brings things to a whole different connection." At least Brax felt a connection with something on this planet, even if that something was the handle of his gun.

"Then I'm certainly lucky for the life I have now. Oh, wait. Maybe it isn't luck since I paid for every drop of happiness my family could get." I wore the irony like armor this time.

"Don't sell me that bullshit. We always have a choice. You just chose to change your life. Shit happens every day in the street. People are living in misery, starving, dying. You just chose to do whatever it takes not to let yourself or your family go down that road. Would it feel better if you had a weapon in your hands and went to rob a bank?" He paused to let his questions sink in. "Just don't blame any of us for your choices. We only offered the alternatives. It was you who accepted them."

What hurt most was that he was right. Maybe they did bear some blame for their proposals, but I owned the fault for accepting them.

"What are you doing here anyway, Bea?" The question would be asked at some point. I was surprised we managed to go so far into the convo without addressing the true purpose of my visit.

Still, I deflected. "I haven't seen you around lately."

"I've met with Ferris several times during these last few weeks. I just didn't think I should look for you. Especially since you specifically asked me to leave you alone."

"Yeah, about that... I was still in shock." I had to diminish the impact of his actions so I could get him to buy into my story.

"I already figured that part out. So what, now you've recovered?" He lit himself a cigarette, skepticism etched on his face.

"You could say that... I'm just accepting what you have done *for* me... after what you did *to* me." Fuck, my mouth was getting the best of me again. I shouldn't have let that slip.

I instantly wished he hadn't heard it. But he heard it all right. "Here we go again. What exactly have I *done* to you that wasn't a part of our deal?"

I was a part of the deal for him, and the thought made me want to throw up. I didn't even know if it was in disgust or pain. Willingly or unwillingly, I'd grown attached to him, and being seen as a disposable asset by the man I cared for sent a sharp sting to my heart.

I was no fool. I had no illusion that things could be different. It was just every time I heard him say it, I felt like it was wrecking my soul.

"I didn't come here to fight with you. I came here to thank you. I know you risked your life by breaking into the governor's house." I made an attempt at mending things a little.

Though Brax was the same old Brax I had already gotten accustomed to, maybe even colder than before. "I didn't do it for you. Having you killed, or worse, having the governor on to what we were doing without me taking any measures of precaution would have only jeopardized the plan."

"So, what are you saying? That you did it for the city?" The perspective was amusing to me, and no matter what came out of his mouth, I knew the real reason for which he broke into the governor's house. No one could take that away from me.

"Save the city so I could secure a comfortable seat at ruling it. You were right when you said I wanted a piece of Echo City, and if I remember correctly, that too was a part of our deal."

"So, you're in it for the money?" The perspective began to scare me since I knew what Brax was really capable of. He wasn't exactly the most generous person in the world, much closer to Scrooge than Robin Hood.

"In it for the money... that sounds so bad coming from your mouth. But I guess you could say that. I reckon my wealth will grow considerably, but not for the reasons you may think."

He stirred my curiosity. "What reasons, then?"

"We'll adjust the cash flow between the Hills and Pit. To sum things up, the people in the Pit will live better, therefore, they'll have a lot more money to spend at my establishments." It was all a grand business scheme for him.

It did sound logical, but—"How are you planning on doing that?"

"Simple. I'll have the Elite give up their lush gardens and extra tennis courts that no one uses anyway and have workers from the Pit do agriculture. Almost all zones are lit with artificial light that allows vegetation to grow even without the sun's rays. So why grow grass when you could grow food?"

I had to admit, it sounded like a solid plan, except—"The Elite would never allow you to do that."

"They won't have a choice. If you haven't noticed, I don't really ask for people's permission. Besides, by my calculations, the harvest would surpass by far what our city needs. We could trade the rest for money. Believe me when I say, that filling the Elite pockets would ease things up for this process to happen. It will be a win-win. The Annelids get better jobs and more money, the Elite fatten their bank accounts, and I—"

"You would be the Annelids God," I replied, picking up on his idea.

The thought certainly pleased him. "As I said, win-win for everyone involved."

"And for me?" They were all coming out as winners, while I was the coin that got flipped around to settle *the bills.*

"It depends on what you want." He was getting an idea of where I was going, I also needed some kind of benefit out of this deal. Only it wasn't the kind I was leading him to believe.

I let him wait for a few seconds, then walked straight to the minibar in his office and poured two glasses of his favorite whiskey. "What I want... You tell me what I want."

"Bea, what are you doing here dressed in that same black dress, same make-up, same fucking everything? If I didn't know better, I could say you're trying to stir up some memories, or maybe even more than *memories.*" His absinthe eyes burned into mine as I pried open his fingers to place one of the whiskey glasses in his hand.

"I'm here for the whiskey." I smiled, downing the contents of my glass and setting it on his desk with a loud clunk.

"Are you?" He leaned himself on the corner of the desk, keeping his legs slightly apart to make room for me to join him. "What are you really doing here?" he asked again as soon as I settled against his chest, exactly where he wanted me.

I didn't want to say the words. I think I was afraid that I would sound fake. Or maybe I'd sound too genuine. Either way, I'd only end up losing.

I just let one of my fingers slowly trail the lines of his Italian suit while my eyes remained averted. I was the deer he likes to hunt, this time, spiced up with the drug of irresistible attraction.

"Did you miss me?" he asked, his voice low and teasing.

The exact question I was expecting. I knew sooner or later his arrogance would get the best of him.

I didn't waste useless words on an answer. Instead, I just let my head rest on his shoulder, leaving my gesture to speak for itself. It meant I was admitting defeat, granting him the dominance he needed to assert. I wanted him to think that he had full control over any emotion that ruled me. The same arrogance led him to believe that I could come to bow my head in front of him after what he did. I was much stronger than that, and he should've known it. But his ego overshadowed even his wit.

Catching the upper side of my arms between his hands, he peeled me off him to properly savor his achievement. He was meticulously analyzing every single feature of my face.

So meticulous that I caught a glimpse of the man I had seen that night at the pool. He was there again, blazing through the mask that typically concealed Brax's every studied gesture.

But then the beast took control, and nothing could stop him from claiming my lips as his.
The union was demanding, consuming, and altogether a desperate culmination of a desire that had long been stifled. Strength, the feature that defined him best, was slowly transposing into misery. Though it was impossible for him to fight himself, he continued, attempting to reduce the calling of his soul to mere primal urges. Little did he know that he couldn't remain on that path forever, and with every moment spent together, his body was sending out hints, betraying his real suffering.

There were times I feared I was making a mistake—that this was merely a product of my imagination, born from my own desires and fantasies. But what about his gaze? Those fleeting moments of confusion and unacknowledged sorrow?

There had to be more beneath the surface. And I was betting everything on that.

Patience was never one of his virtues, and Brax's hands rushing to push down the straps of my dress certainly confirmed it. He was even more eager than I expected, and I felt I was reliving one of my previous visits to his office.

He was groaning in satisfaction as his tongue was rolling over the peak of my nipples, while the realization of the time I chose for the visit was getting on his nerves. "You couldn't have said what you wanted the minute you walked through the door?"

At least he bought into my game. He was really under the

impression that I wanted sex from him.

Sure, I couldn't deny that the memories of the night at the pool were still alive in my mind, but never strong enough to ever get me to throw myself at a man.

"Maybe I shouldn't have come wearing clothes at all; that could have saved us the trouble." I giggled, closing my eyes at the same time to savor the way his mouth danced across my melting skin.

"In five minutes, I have a two-hour meeting with some city council board members. I can't fucking postpone it," Brax muttered, his patience wearing thin. Good news from my perspective, not that I would ever let him in on that.

"You have a meeting in the club?" Pretty strange location to bring the city council members, but this was Brax we were talking about after all.

"VIP table and a few lap dances to seal the deal." Great, strippers again; I suddenly recalled how he usually spent his time.

Still, I decided to keep things light. "Are you performing the lap dances?"

"I almost forgot about this mouth of yours." I noticed his lips move to speak again, but he quickly changed his mind. He was trying to hold back all remarks that could have upset me, just to continue from where we'd left off.

He was savoring me like the finest whiskey, taking his time.

Fortunately for me, he hadn't taken a sip of the liquor

just yet. A knock on the door interrupted him sooner than he anticipated. "Come in!" Brax only spoke after he ensured my dress was back in place.

One of the guards I often saw around entered through the door. "Your guests have arrived. I've set them up at the VIP table, but Mr. Harris sounded irritated that you weren't there to greet them."

"Motherfucker," Brax snarled, knowing that he couldn't steal any more minutes before he needed to go. "Let them know I'll be there in a moment. And take a bottle of Macallan to the table along with some Dom Perignon."

"Right away, boss." The man exited as quickly as he had come.

"This is going to take a while." Brax was searching for a way to squeeze me into his life while his evening entertaining the Elite couldn't agree with me more.

"I can wait. I'll be patient, I promise," I whispered on his lips, fully aware that, in fact, he would be the impatient one.

"Fuck, I have an out-of-town meeting tomorrow." He really seemed eager to get *him and me together between the sheets* somehow, despite the pressing schedule. "You could come with me."

"Our last out-of-town meeting didn't end that well, so I'll pass." I gestured a *no thanks* with my hands, recalling how our *last* getaway developed.

This brought a smile to Brax's lips. "I'm not going to be killing anyone."

"I have classes. I've been missing too much anyway." The wait only increased the thrill, and I needed him to reach his breaking point. "How about Thursday?"

"I'll cancel my agenda after 8 pm." He sounded so eager to have me as his again that he couldn't even hide his excitement.

"Perfect." I batted my eyelashes, on my way to the door, not before I slipped in a little detail, just to tease him further—call it the final touch. "Brax, I was thinking we could go to the glass room."

CHAPTER 8

I was back in my room, staring at the ceiling. I had no idea what I was doing anymore. Still, my plans seemed to be coming together. The scheme to rule over the city was on the right track; Brax was getting caught up in my game, and Cole... let's just say that Cole showed all signs of becoming my strongest defender.

And then there was Ferris. My irresistible king of darkness —so unpredictable that one misstep taken alongside him could be my undoing. Good and evil, spiraling to create exquisite madness, always forcing me to use the last of my energy to resist his magnetic pull.

Though this time, I couldn't stay away.

This time, I needed to return to the wolf's den for the last part of my plan involving him.
It was lose or win, or more likely, live or die.

My anxiety level had reached epic proportions as I managed to change my mind at least twenty times before finally deciding to go through with it.

Everything felt like a blur. The university courses, the time spent with my family, and even the school breaks spent attached to Cole's side.

I headed to one of the bars in the mansion, searching for a bottle of red wine to calm my nerves, but the honey-colored liquor Brax favored looked far more appealing.

Just a few sips, I told myself, making the poor decision of taking them directly from the bottle. No Miss Perfection awards would come my way from anyone who'd see me, but then again, I was far from being perfect. More like perfectly broken.

I must've miscalculated the amount of whiskey that went into a glass compared to what ended down my throat. After only what I thought to be two fingers in a cup, I was already feeling tipsy. So tipsy, in fact, that the doorknob seemed to spin on its own as I fumbled to open it.

It was probably for the best. I needed the liquid courage to walk out of the room and follow on my path.

I quickly realized Ferris wasn't inside his room. Unusual for him to be out, especially at that hour, but there was no way of backing down. I lit a few candles to pass the time while waiting for his return. The flickering glow cast shadows on the walls as I soon found myself lazily sprawled on the couch, staring at the ceiling.

Craving some distraction, my eyes wandered around the room until they landed on a bottle of champagne. I couldn't declare myself a fan of the sparkling liquid, but in those moments, anything would do.

After performing a near-disastrous magic trick that almost took out every chandelier in the room, I finally managed to pop the cork. Finally, it was free, and the foam was filling a crystal glass.

To my surprise, I did like that particular champagne. It tasted fruity and sweet—much like the lies I kept feeding myself whenever I tried to find some reasoning behind Brax's or Ferris's behaviors.

I was thinking about the wolves—at least one of them. And right on cue, there he was, walking through the door.

"Bea?" Ferris's tone was laced with surprise to find me there. I could only hope it was a good kind of surprise.

"I hope I'm not imposing," I spoke while refilling my glass for the... hmmm... for the who-knows-how-many-th time.

"You never impose on me." He paused, eyes scanning the room. "Though I must ask, how long have you been in here?"

"Not really sure. Long enough to notice you weren't in," I giggled, a slight playfulness in my voice.

"Yeah... I had a meeting with some bank representatives. Getting things rolling."

I was a bit surprised he'd left the house, although it needed to happen at some point. "You were out?" I asked, sipping from my drink.

"Not exactly. I was downstairs, in one of the conference rooms. I'd asked them to come here." After all, the Ayers name does hold a certain weight. "Still, you haven't answered my question."

"I don't really know... This long ago." I tilted my champagne bottle in front of the fireplace to allow him to see how much of the magic liquid was still left in it. "Enough left to share it with you," I reached for another glass and poured, holding it up for him to clink against mine.

"Are we celebrating something?" he asked, knowing damn well that there was nothing to celebrate... except—

"This." My lips magnetized toward his, making the best of any second we shared.

"I'll have a case of champagne prepared for the next time." He was moving his lips not only to speak but also to respond to my kiss.

"A case sounds nice. It would certainly last until the morning."

"I can make it last until the morning without bringing the case of champagne into the equation," I could feel the corners of his lips raised into a smile without breaking the kiss.

"Men..."

"Maybe you need a sample of my true abilities." He pulled me against his chest, like the perfect prey, falling straight into my trap.

"Maybe I do..." I set my glass on a small table next to me, then shifted to close the distance between us. A smile full of subtext bloomed in the corner of my mouth while my hands glided from the edge of my collar to my breasts. I let them linger there for a moment, gently clutching my fingers until his hungry gaze was apparent with the thought that he wished to replace them with his own.

The black in his eyes blazed with the temperature of a hundred suns, swirling with all wicked thoughts—though none darker than my own. Pressing my palms in the center of his chest, I let them slowly drift away to unravel each rocky shape of his torso. I didn't stop there, letting them drift lower, testing the line of his jeans, letting them slide along the waistband until I could see him swallow the knot forming in his throat, trying to contain the rising tension.

He was hooked, and it was time to finally reel him in.

Despite the anxiety pushing beneath the surface, I was making every effort to show nothing but lust, biting the full volume of my lower lip as I slid lower. His breath hitched in anticipation, it wasn't the metal key of his zipper I was testing, but the depths of his pockets. And no, I wasn't a gold digger, much more of a knife digger.

With a low, throated moan, I drew the cold steal out from his pocket and pressed it in the center of his hand.

Surprise flickered in his eyes, but that didn't stop me from opening the knife's blade with a soft clink, guiding his hand toward the upper part of my nightie.

I moved it further, tracing the sharp metal down my breasts and over the hardened shapes of my nipples. A sigh slipped from my lips, fueled by the rush of adrenaline thrumming in my veins. It was unimaginable tension but also desire.

Though I couldn't show any signs of weakness, only the hunger that pulsed beneath the surface. The challenge wasn't as difficult as I'd feared, especially since the surge of alcohol was still humming through my system, dulling the edges of my anxiety.

I just steered his hand lower, following the path of my nightdress and letting it tear effortlessly through the delicate fabric, stopping at the hem.

"I'm beginning to think I'm going to miss this part.'" The whiskey loosening my tongue, forced me to let out a secret I didn't want to be disclosed.

Fortunately, Ferris didn't ask any questions about it but instantly closed the knife, running his hands along the newly revealed zone, and pushing my panties to the floor. He was leaving me to disintegrate between his fingers. In response, I unbuttoned the hand-sewn buttons of his shirt, one by one. But instead of throwing it somewhere in the room, I draped the shirt over my own shoulders, yearning to be fully bathing in his intoxicating scent.

My plan was falling into place. Ferris lifted me onto a small table, making sure my legs were open wide enough to welcome him. He needed me as badly as I needed him; the only difference was that I also needed to control the game.

Before coming to my senses and grasping what was happening, Ferris kneeled, sending his mouth to join with the silky skin that had been throbbing to have him since the moment he entered the room. The brushes of his tongue found room between my folds, turning my body into a giant ice cream, luring him to savor it as it melted.

My eyes closed, trying to think of what I really needed to do next. Though the darkness only heightened my senses, steering my mind in a single direction—the searing warmth of his tongue dragging me to bathe in rivers of ecstasy. It was unstoppable, like a forest fire spreading to torch my entire being.

I opened my eyes, grasping for something to ground myself before I was lost completely. My *water* was the sparkling liquid hiding in the champagne bottle sitting next to me on the table. I placed it there earlier but never thought it could come so in handy. I tried quenching my thirst with large sips, mixing the perfumed taste with the expert movements of my king. From that moment Ferris would forever taste like champagne to me —effervescent, intoxicating, a mirage of royal charm hiding the darkness beneath. But there was nothing royal about him in those moments as his tongue delved deep inside of me, searching to destroy all balance and make my walls pulse with the power of the pleasure that was about to engulf me.

He loved to own me that way, to have that kind of power over me—so complete that even I was beginning to think that we were nearing the point when his monster would possess the last drops of my soul.

And maybe we were getting too close to that moment.

The beautiful illusions he was creating often made me wish to get lost within them. It would be so simple to abandon myself and at the same time, so complicated for anyone else involved.

When I was with Ferris, I only wanted to be with him, lost in his dream, no matter the consequences. But I felt the same with Cole, and why not face it? With Brax as well.

I took another sip from the bottle and another, until the waves of electric satisfaction were rushing through me in sync with the flow of alcohol in my system. He had crushed me, leaving sweet moans to be vocalized with the rhythm of my heartbeats.

Seconds later, he silenced my moans with his mouth, letting me taste the sweet flavor of my euphoria on his lips. He paused, only for him to trace the lines of his own shirt. I was the one wearing the ivory piece of material, and the view of me being dressed in his clothes was the most powerful aphrodisiac when it came to him. I could see the satisfaction glinting in his eyes, like a signal guiding my next move.

Making sure I still had the bottle of champagne in my possession, I let my body slip from between his arms.

"I'm hot. Don't you feel hot?" I asked him with a hint of madness vibrating in my lungs as soon as I was free.

"I'll put out the fire." His gaze darted toward the fireplace. But before he could take any action, I was heading toward the opposite corner of the room.

I didn't get far. He immediately traced my steps, seeing it as a game of predator and prey. "I have an idea of what could cool you down." Sneaking a hand around the small of my back, he held me tightly in place as he eased the sleeves of his shirt off my shoulders, revealing the round shape of my breasts.

I had no idea how that could ever cool me down instead of setting me on fire. But he was determined to prove a point, taking the champagne bottle out of my hands and dribbling small drops somewhere along my collarbone.

"What are you doing?" I giggled softly, careful not to betray any other intention.

No answer came. At least not with words. Instead, the next

second, his lips melted on the center of my breasts, sipping the liquid that trickled over my nipples.

My mind was instantly blocked, shocked by the sensuality of his gesture, living just for that moment in time, so irreplaceable and so dangerous for my sanity.

Ferris had this way of pushing me over the edge, and that's exactly where I was heading in his presence—past any possible limits.

"Ferris," I whined, my voice filled with an unspoken goodbye.

Instead, he thought it was a calling. That I was calling him back to my lips, when in reality, it was a calling back to normality. No matter what that would mean.

"Not here." I snatched the champagne bottle from his hands and dashed to the balcony.

The instant I pushed the doors open, the cold air hit me, awakening a cruel reality. The passion was swept away with that slightest of breezes. It was only the pain that remained.

It was just a matter of time before he'd need to break me again to fix himself. And I was about to put an end to that cycle of misery.

The sound of my laughter accompanied my steps. It wasn't even fake. It was pure insanity, begging to be pushed to the extreme.

"Come, I want to do it here," I called out to him as my bare feet were leaving dark traces on the frosted pavement.

"Bea, get back inside. It's freezing cold." He hurried through the door, swinging it wide open.

I knew it wasn't the cold he was worried about. He was afraid of not being in control anymore.

And I was about to prove him right. "Since when do you *care*?" I voiced a truth that had me in pain for so long. It wasn't his darkness or his vile thoughts that were hurting me. It was the acknowledgment that he was willing to sacrifice me for a fleeting moment of sick happiness.

Placing my bottle on the ledge, I drove my feet to follow, becoming a tightrope walker exactly where he wanted me—at the border between life and death.

Ferris froze on the spot, visibly clenching his jaw as the image sank into his system. "Bea, get down from there!" His voice was not as menacing as it should be, tinged instead with fear.

"No. Come up here and have me." I was only fulfilling one of his fantasies, after all. It was he who initially wanted to take me on the edge of the world.

As I took a step further, I felt the shirt on my back slipping over my arms. I just let it fall along with the bottle, watching the cloth flutter like a white bird in the dark sky. It was sublime and mesmerizing, the beauty only marred by the horror etched on Ferris's face.

Strangely, the abyss didn't scare me as badly as I initially thought. The idea of being set free blossomed in my mind, along with the thought that I needed just one step to do that. Maybe it was me who was truly the insane one. I felt no fear any longer as if I was willing to let destiny take its course and decide whatever was needed for me. I was numb.

Ferris was speechless, only advancing with cautious steps as if even the slightest breeze from his movement might make me fall. I was the one holding the invisible knife over his throat this time around.

I wasn't sure if his fear was coming from some complex feelings he might have had for me or out of the thought of losing his favorite toy, but it was there, gripping every living cell in his body.

They say you shouldn't look down at this altitude. I neglected that advice deliberately. I hoped I could find something to snap me back to reality, but the dark void below offered nothing. It was far from terrifying me. On the contrary, it sang a siren's call, seducing me toward oblivion.

"Bea!" I could hear Ferris's demanding voice, pleading with me to return. Though it was fading away with each step I took. The effect of that bubbly champagne was beginning to replace my reasoning.

Then it happened, that one wrong step, and my feet slipped on the frost-coated railing.

No flashes of the past raced before my eyes, and no warm memories filled me with comfort.

There was only darkness.

Pitch-black darkness.

And then, a hand.

A hand that refused to let go.

"Hold on to me." It was Ferris's lips that moved, though the words barely registered at that point. I just looked back at him, struggling to make sense of what was going on around me. In his eyes lived fear, horror, and desperation merged together into a wake-up call.

Have I managed to defeat his demons?

I couldn't tell what was real anymore. I was just drifting away over the abyss, while he was struggling to pull me back to safety.

The hoar-frost from the champagne bottle was making my hands slip, but with a quick gesture, Ferris caught my wrist, gripping it so tightly that I was beginning to think it might break. The surge of pain shook through my body, snapping me out of my drunken haze.

Without knowing how or why, I landed, crashing into his secure arms, drained of all my strength.

I remember wanting to disappear, just vanish before the surge of emotions would claim control over the essence of my existence. Though I didn't, and the mix of sensations came flowing in waves, tearing me apart and crushing me against his chest.

"Bea!... Bea, look at me." He pleaded, asking me to acknowledge his presence while I could barely recognize mine anymore. I was at the end of the line, and whether I drowned or was saved was now in his hands.

The inviting warmth of his lips met the top of my head,

finding their way down in search of my own.

Only, a kiss couldn't get me back this time—it had to be more, and he knew it.

I didn't want him to find my lips, especially since he felt so desperate to do that. My selfish ego thrived on exactly that miserable emotion that was ruining him. I just buried my head deeper against his chest, unable to stifle the sound of my anguishing sobs.

"*I'm so sorry*. It's okay. I promise you it's going to be okay," he cast the words to flow toward my ears.

Could I believe him once again?

Was it really over?

I still didn't accept his lips on mine. My nose wouldn't budge from the shape of his chest while my heart still trembled with the effects of what I had just done. A nanosecond and I would have been gone. Ferris was rising up to be not only my destroyer but also my savior. I just needed to know if he could make it last.

"Let me take you inside." He slid his hands beneath my knees and lifted me in his arms.

"I don't want to go inside." I just couldn't return to the same game without knowing if I was at the winner's or the loser's table.

"I don't know what to do. Tell me where I should go." He wasn't referring to where his steps should carry us next. He was referring to his life.

What could he ever do to make things right?

"I feel I'm cursed to destroy everything I touch. I almost did it tonight, with you." His fears were real, fueled by the strength of my gesture. In a way, he was right. He pushed me to climb on the ledge, but he was also the one who saved me. That had to count for something.

"Then stop. Stop living in the past. I can't keep pulling you back all the time. I'm too afraid of the day I fail." Tears couldn't be stopped from burning down my cheeks as I just staked everything on this last wild card. If the near-death experience couldn't keep him with me, nothing could. "Stay... with me. Don't go running or hiding in dark corners. It's safe to share your pain. I'm one of the few people that understand it."

"I see them die... every time a part of me dies with them, slowly but eventually culminating into a road to destruction." He was just stating the truth, though I recognized the path he adopted a long time ago.

And I was pleading to the last remnants of his normality. "But they wouldn't want you to die, would they? They wanted you to live. So why fail them? Just because it would be easier?"

He was so far and yet so close to being a coward.

Similar to what I tried tonight, Ferris was choosing the easy way out. Just play mad until he would be left all alone to pity himself.

"Nothing is easy in my life. Look at what I've done to you," his voice full of sorrow. The warmth of a tear fell on my arm, making me raise my head from the safety of his chest and glance straight at him. His eyes were wide open, and if I didn't know better, I'd have thought the bead of water didn't even come from him. But I could see the salty sparkles in his eyes, even if his countenance was showing no signs of weakness.

"Then stop. It's that easy." This time, my tears were the ones drying on his arms, unable to keep myself together any longer. I wanted so badly to set him free from his pain that I was terrified I had failed and, most importantly, that I had disintegrated in the process.

I felt as lost as he was, chasing only dark shadows in a futile hope that they could ever guide me toward the light.

But then his lips found mine, the same way his soul clung to the last drops of hope. It was a kiss forged in pain and bad dreams, yet it was filled with silent promises—the kiss of a new beginning.

CHAPTER 9

The specter of the moon was shining from beneath purple clouds, setting the sky ablaze with immortal flames. I remained shipwrecked in Ferris's arms without saying a word, just allowing the humming of my pulse to speak for itself.

"Aren't you cold?" He brushed his lips against my ear, nibbling on the skin he found along his way and sending icy tingles dancing down my spine.

Yes, I was cold. The frost of the incoming winter made me shiver, but it also awakened something within me. A will that had been locked away for too long.

I was finally craving the feeling of being alive.

And I wasn't ready to let go of it yet. "I want to stay here," I answered with gentle brushes of our lips, asking him to remain there with me.

It took only that small gesture to tempt him on a quest for more, using the strength of his arms to raise me on his waist. "Your feet are freezing." My savior had come to the rescue.

Something must have been wrong with my lips too, because he decided it was time to warm them up with his own. It felt unhurried at first, like he was trying to heal my soul, gradually bringing it back to life with his kisses. But I could feel the storm brewing beneath the calm surface, fueled by the pathos growing within him.

Soon, he was burning like an erupting volcano, melting away my insecurities with the power of being the Ferris I was dreaming of. He was real this time.

The only question that remained was if he was here to stay.

I guess that was up to me. I was the one who had to play the cards right so that could happen.

For some reason, I was hesitant to leave that balcony, as the warmth of the fireplace could awaken some of his demons. Or perhaps it was because the heat of our bodies pressed together seemed so much *stronger* outdoors. *We* felt so much *stronger* here, under the power of the night—like together we could face anything that might come our way.

Despite my wishes, the passion and yearning dancing between us seemed to be shortening our time on the balcony. His fingers clenched on my ass so tightly that they would leave scarlet imprints—a beautiful mark of his longing.

Suddenly, he began walking toward the room, with me still clutching onto his hips, unable to let him go.

I didn't want to leave the place that finally brought us together just yet. "Don't... Please." I didn't want him to take any wrong step and jeopardize the shimmers of the spell.

Maybe all those *second chances* were catching up with me. Only this time.... this time, it would be the last. I was just having trouble adjusting to that thought.

Ferris probably sensed my restlessness because he only stepped into the room to snatch a blanket off one of the sofas, then returned to the balcony.

He tossed the soft blanket on the ground and gently laid me in the middle, before looming over me, his weight anchoring me beneath him. His presence was so overpowering for a moment that it was shaking the depths of my soul. He was finally focusing so he would remain there with me—for the rest of time.

My lips were trembling with uncontrollable excitement, noticing the manly line of his jaw tensing in futile attempts to somehow control his urges.

I couldn't hold back a whine when his mouth closed on mine, as if he sought to drain the air in my lungs until every breath I would take would occur because of him.

It wasn't seduction; it was passion unleashed, demanding union with the loudest voice of desire. That voice instantly drove Ferris to tug the remains of my nightie up over my waist whilst the buckle of his pants came undone.

He couldn't wait any longer, and I couldn't blame him. Our bodies were calling for each other like the strongest magnets, joining to find their poles.

Our movements soon turned chaotic, our hands roaming each other's bodies like addicts searching for their high as my legs wrapped around his waist, asking him to claim his rightful place. My breath panting, my mind a pure mess, my body on the verge of losing control. As broken as Ferris might have been, he was capable of making me feel emotions I never thought possible. His madness seeped into every cell in my body and strangely, it was making me see things clearer than ever—I needed him. I needed him to do anything he wanted to me—use me, manipulate me, break me. Whatever it took to keep this feeling from slipping away. But the amazing thing was, he was creating this madness out of something else. Something pure this time, a liberation of pain and guilt as he was accepting a warmth that was never there before.

The sensation of his intrusion was rough but so welcome, stretching me to embrace the strength of his arousal. It was assertion, dominance, claiming me the way only a king claims his queen.

I couldn't even feel the freezing chills of the winter's night. Only faint breezes of air blustering against my skin and making his grip on my flesh feel that much more alive. He was warming all my numbed places, getting the blood in my veins to pump so loudly that I was under the impression that he could hear the way it was rushing through my veins.

It was as if the outside atmosphere was being reflected by our beings. Cold and yet set on fire, letting the purple clouds dance under the night's light, the way our bodies shifted to slide over the soft blanket. Friction burns on my back and long red lines on his shoulders from my nails digging into his flesh. His lips joined with mine even stronger than before, clinging onto new drops of hope that we could yet be saved. It might not have been the most thought-through moment to express our feelings, but the juncture of everything around us combined with the need of finding each other again was making it heavenly. Perfect. My moans were drowning into the abyss beneath us, the sky witnessing our joined bodies moving like ocean waves during a storm.

An intense blend of pleasure and pain immobilized me, stripping away any ability to move, even an inch. It was holding me captive to his tantalizing assault, so fluid that he would completely merge with me, flowing through me like water seeps into the soil.

Overwhelmed by unbearable tingles, spreading through every nerve, I listened as his deep groans rippled between his clenched teeth. It went on and on, dissipating the last of my strength until an erupting volcano of pleasure made me squeeze my arms over the tattoos spanning his broad neck.

I was trying to hold on for dear life, hoping that he'd *soon* find satisfaction.

Soon turned out to stretch into eternity until even my short-fractured breath was murmuring his name. I was unraveling, though I was still driven by the raw need coursing between us. Every time I felt myself tighten around him, I thought the pleasure couldn't possibly peak higher. Yet, every time, he proved me wrong.

It was like I'd need to learn how to function all over again after he was finished with me. Never again to be able to function without him.

After my voice became ragged with pleas and whimpers, I finally felt him become rigid, filling me with the liquid evidence of his exhilaration. He roared between his final thrusts, biting onto my lips with primal need, sending the weight of his forehead to rest on mine as if we had become one —body and mind.

His eyes, still dark as the night, glimmering with the

dusty shimmer of stars. His monsters might not have been completely gone, but at least I knew he'd let me be by his side when he had to fight them.

"This time, we *are* going inside. I'm not taking no for an answer." Ferris lifted me off the ground before I had a chance to say even a word. Not that I could complain about his tone of authority.

I was shivering. Probably had been for a long time now, although I could only sense the quivers when the hot air engulfed us.

He immediately tucked me in bed, covering us with every blanket and quilt he could find, stacking them so high I could barely see above them. Not that I needed to see a single thing. I only needed him to be there—with me at the new beginning of our story.

"Let me help you take off your nightie." He disappeared beneath the covers just to resurface with the hem of my dress as he was trying to get it over my head.

"I thought you were supposed to be doing this before, not after." I giggled softly, raising my arms to help him pull the fabric away.

"It's wet." He tossed it somewhere on the floor, then caught me in the most sinful cage—the one of his arms—pulling me tightly to his chest.

"Are you trying to seduce me again?" I let the murmur of my words feather against his Adam's apple.

"Try!... No. I'll go straight in for the kill." He drove his thumb to brush against the contour of my cheek, but the trace of a stray tear stopped him on his path. "What's this?"

What was that indeed?

I thought we'd settled things somehow, although my mind didn't agree. At least not until it heard him actually say it out loud.

Funny, I never needed words before.

I was always a strong believer that no sentence could replace a gesture. But this time around, my sanity was facing its greatest challenge.

And I wasn't sure it fully recovered.

"Nothing," I lied through my teeth, unwilling to admit that I still needed reassurance. I guess that with Ferris, only time could tell where we really stood.

"Crying isn't *nothing*. Did I do something?" he asked as I was managing to confuse him regarding what exactly was going on in my head.

I instantly drove my face to bury it on my pillow.

"Bea." He tried bringing my head to face him, though without any success. I just curled into a ball and sunk deeper into the fluffy cushion.

This time, I was the one having mood swings. Somehow around Ferris, there was no way to prevent my fears from getting the better of me, even if less than an hour before, I was convinced that we were going to make it through.

Though it wasn't some bipolar episode or depression, there

was a hidden reason beneath the crystal tears. Something that had to do with his past.

"Would you talk to me?" he asked.

But I couldn't speak.

I couldn't bring myself to formulate even a word.

It seemed foolish when I thought about it, yet the culmination of everything was finally weighing in on me.

It was like I wanted him to know what was wrong with me without me actually having to say it. A woman's dream, and a man's constant incapacity. The source of all disappointments —men are never mind-readers. Quite the opposite, in fact.

Even so, Ferris managed to surprise me that night. Maybe it had something to do with his attraction to the spiritual side, but he was putting my thoughts into words. "Does this have to do with Vanya? Did she say something to you?"

"Did she have *something* to say to me?" I asked, doubt coating my voice.

"Nothing that would make any difference to what we have." His voice remained soft, despite the weight of my question.

"What we have," I echoed softly.

What did we have?

Everything?.... Or nothing?

"Did you know that when I got shot, I was dead for a couple of minutes?" Ferris decided to finally take a step in *that* direction.

If I was to be honest, I was terrified of the outcome—of what opening up might do to him. And at the same time, this was what could make us invincible.

"I wasn't sure. But I was close enough to understand. I had my own life-and-death experience, and even if I didn't have bullet marks on my chest, I wear the scars in my heart. I tremble every night from the memories." I tried to show him that I understand his pain.

This time, he wouldn't let the past defeat him. "I felt something that night," Ferris continued, throwing his head back on his pillow. "Fuck... this feels impossible to speak about."

"Take your time."

And he did, letting minutes pass in complete silence.

"I felt something beyond pain, helplessness and desperation. I felt a connection to something deeper than all of the above." I could see that he had just made a journey to the bottom of his being, summoning every bit of strength. "It was like I was lost somewhere in the universe, waiting for a sign."

"And then I had it."

"I've searched in empty vessels for so long that I was beginning to doubt its existence. But then you pushed open the door.

"You were the sign I needed.

"A sign that there's life beyond grief. I just didn't know how to deal with everything.

"I was like a clumsy introvert, handed the most expensive gift I'd ever seen.

"So I fucked up.

"Not just once or twice, but with every chance I got. Like someone was betting all their money on my incompetence."

My hand slid through thick strands of his light brown hair, letting them flow between my fingers. "It's okay."

"No, it's not, because I still can't guarantee that I'll ever be the one you want. I don't live in the shadows because I need to; I live in the shadows because I want to.

"The instant I was out of my body, I learned the beauty of darkness. The magic hiding under the spell of night.

"I love the way the fire fits between all of this. How the orange flames bring everything to life, maybe the same way I was brought back to life.

"But you know what I love most?"

"Tell me." I let my head fall on his chest, not breaking eye contact for a second.

"The way that fire brings you to life. How it reflects against your skin. How it connects us..." I knew exactly what he meant. That inexplicable attraction often got me thinking about the day the planets aligned for us to meet. Though I was still in doubt that it was the planets and not his quest for anything that would make him feel human again. And it was leaving me caught somewhere between jumping into whatever this may lead to and total disbelief.

"What about The Pleasure Room?" I asked, hoping to receive an answer that would somehow help me clear my thoughts.

Sure, he was claiming I was special. But was I really the *special one*?

Or the only one who didn't run away?

"You tell me about The Pleasure Room. You're the one that worked there." He gallantly smiled, thinking the seductive curve of his lips would allow him to deflect the question.
It was exactly what I was afraid of—a refusal from him to go down that road. And I couldn't accept splinters of his memories and emotions.

This time I threw everything into the game, and this was it now—all or nothing on both sides. If he didn't know that already, the warning in my tone brought things to a different light. "Ferris..."

"Okay, right. I was trying to defuse things a little." He choked out the words.

"Do *things* need to be defused?" I asked, my tone losing its warmth.

"Probably. Not for me though. For me it means nothing. I'm just not sure if you'll understand what I have to say. At least the way I want you to understand."

I raised my head from his chest to peer straight at him. "Try me." I had a feeling that this would be crucial, and I needed to search for any kind of emotion his gaze might betray.

"Okay... Don't say I didn't warn you.

"I discovered The Pleasure Room around a year ago. It wasn't that I didn't know about the place; it just didn't present any interest until then.

"Alfred was actually the one that asked for my first Pleasure. His sister lives out of town, and once in a while, he leaves the mansion for a few days to go visit.

"I personally used to dread those days. It made me feel alone. Like I could get lost at any time."

"But don't you have other employees, plus the security at the gate?' I asked since I used to see other people around the house. Alfred was indeed the one who coordinated everyone, but the staff around the house could form a small army.

"I do. But he's the only one I talk to. The only one that I'm close to, and I'm pretty sure the only one that cares.

"I like knowing he's around.

"I know it sounds weird, but it's like he's one of the few people that could protect me from myself.

"And since he had to leave, he tried to replace his presence with a distraction.

"I wasn't able to get close to anyone since what happened with my parents. I couldn't bear anyone asking any questions about that night, and any kind of interaction with someone in this city would have brought just that.

"The Pleasure Room was different. No one would ask any

questions. It felt safe, judging from that point." Ferris stopped for a second, filling his lungs with all the air he could get like the oxygen would give him some strength to go on. "Are you sure you want me to go on?"

No, I wasn't sure.

In fact, I wanted him to stop that second, but my conscience would never forgive me for that. "Positive."

"Okay. Just remember you were the one that asked," he warned as if what he had to say next had the potential to change everything.

I nodded. I couldn't do anything else anyway since my body seemed to have frozen waiting for what was coming next.

"Jesus, let's get this over with.

"The first Pleasure was supposed to be company through the night, very similar to what I initially asked from you.

"Fuck, I remember I wanted her so badly to leave, at first.

"I stopped myself countless times from telling her she should go back through the door.

"I made her sit on an armchair for so long that I thought she was also becoming a piece of furniture. That was until she dismissed my initial request and started talking.

"She was bright—not exactly a genius, but I guess being alone for so long had its effect on me.

"We talked about random things. Well, she did most of the talking. That was 'till she made me a proposal.

"She wanted me to add an extra zero to the sum in exchange for... in exchange for her body." He paused, a strange silence set between us, as I suspected what followed. "I didn't say no."

He took another deep breath as if he was expecting me to say something. But there wasn't anything I could say to him at that time. I couldn't judge him, especially since I knew him to be capable of way worse things than that.

"It felt weird. Like I didn't even want her there, but my body needed what she was putting on the table.

"I had sex with her that night.

"100% mechanical and 100% addictive.

"I wasn't addicted to the sex.

"I was addicted to the control.

"To the adrenaline itself.

"I never requested that girl again. But more followed, pushing all boundaries and using them to try and defeat my fears or even test new ones. Until I found myself yearning to take a glimpse at the fear in their own eyes. Like that would bring life into mine—"

"You did that to me too," my voice cut through his sentence, the memories of that time testing my limits.

"Yes." He didn't even try to deny the truth. There was no point in doing it. "I did it to every woman I met."

"So, what was the limit? I mean before me?" I wanted to know how far he would go to satisfy the monsters that ruled him.

"I didn't have any limits. And what scared me most was that I didn't even care what would happen to them." Sadness coated his words.

"Someone from The Pleasure Room told me some of them used to be in love with you." I needed to test that field too. Maybe I was crazy, but I was beginning to think I was also desperate.

"They all saw the fucking prince living in a luxurious castle. I gave them the life they dreamed of, and they gave me themselves. They were in love with what this life meant. That's until I let them take a peek into the dark corners of my mind."

"Did they leave you when they got there?"

"Leave me? Interesting point of view. They broke the deals. I don't see it as any of them leaving me. We were never in relationships. They were transactions."

"As with me..." I murmured, knowing that I fit well into that pattern.

"Not exactly. With you, I felt fear. And I hated that but couldn't control it.

"I was afraid I was never going to see you again, and still, I showed you my monsters from the first second. I wanted you to run because I felt you were so different from any of the previous women. But even though I wanted that, I couldn't let you go.

"With you, I don't want to go back to my old ways. I wanted you to help me find new ones." The probability of him being right was puzzling my mind. He warned me to leave from the start. I just wasn't willing to listen.

I'd always felt like he had managed to get me wrapped up around his fingers, although I was starting to conclude that *I* was the one who got herself wrapped up.

The truth was more painful to handle than I initially anticipated, but I already had an idea of what he might say. I'd come prepared, yet nothing could prepare me for the raw emotion that was dripping from this outcome.

Acceptance.

He was finally accepting his past along with the mistakes that ruled his life.

A monster.

A deceiver.

Even a killer.

But in the end, a man willing to change.

I might have been crazy for believing in him once again. Yes, he hurt me, and yes, he tried to completely break me. Still, he killed for me. He risked his life for me. And if those actions weren't enough to convince me we deserve to give ourselves another chance, the words slowly dripping from his lips did: "They weren't like you. None of the women could ever come close to what you represent. They were just tools that I was using, uselessly trying to fix myself.

"With you, it's all so different.

"With you, *I'm in love.*"

CHAPTER 10

Ferris didn't set me free. I don't think he had it in him to do it. Maybe he was still afraid that I would also leave him, when in fact, I couldn't even imagine the day I ever would.

Whether as lovers, friends, or just broken souls, I'd always be by his side.

I couldn't respond to his confession.

It was because saying it back would make it shockingly real for me, and I still didn't know how to handle him and Cole. I had feelings for both, and if the ones for Cole were blooming with mesmerizing intensity, the ones for Ferris were already deeply rooted in my soul.

I'd been in love with Ferris for a long time before, and having that feeling reciprocated filled me with an unknown strength.

Though nothing could prepare me for what I needed to do next—a final step toward setting my life on track, or maybe throwing it into a speeding rollercoaster.

Meeting Brax in the room with the glass wall was perhaps even a greater dare than stepping on that ledge. He, of all my kings, had the chance to completely break me, and he, of all kings, would be the one who would grasp the opportunity with open arms.

I didn't have any nightmares that night, which made it even harder to abandon Ferris's bed in the morning. But my final year as a student was taking its toll. I needed to get back on track to prepare for exams. Well, as much as I could prepare between the ravaging making-out sessions with Cole and trying to get Jenna to fit in with those who congregated in the upper part of the lobby. It wasn't even about fitting in as much as it was about acceptance. I needed to slowly dissolve the social differences, and I, as the new Queen B, was taking the first steps in that direction by having a protégé from the Herd.

No matter how much I might have dreaded the evening, it didn't fail to come, and the grey sky turned black again as if it was set to hover over all my thoughts.

There was no going forward or backward until the final part of my plan was put into action.

As always, Brax needed special preparations. Failure wasn't an option, and the tight emerald dress along with the matching garter belt and silk lingerie, were setting the scene to ensure my success.

My feet were trembling.

My heart was trembling.

Even the thoughts racing through my mind were shuddering with the knowledge of what I needed to do. But it was the only path to a resolution that I could accept.

I didn't even need to let the guards know that his boss was expecting me. They seemed to have been thoroughly instructed to escort me directly to Brax. The men were acting so carefully that I was surprised they didn't lay down the red carpet.

My king of the underworld was definitely expecting the night I had promised. And it was going to be either a dream come true or a nightmare. My money went into the second option. With my luck, I had every chance of breaking everything apart.

"Hello, Brax." My confidence level was peaking—only on the outside. Inside I was a blubbering wreck.

"You're early." He glanced at his watch, observing that it was showing five minutes to 8 p.m. I wasn't sure if that pleased or infuriated him, but at that precise moment, minutes made no difference. We would either have all the time in the world or none at all.

"Maybe I was anxious to be here." I faked a smile, convinced that I was probably the worst actress ever.

The irony was that I was forced to play the role of my life.

"I didn't realize you missed me that much." He rose from the seat where he had been waiting to take a step toward the liquor table.

The whiskey glass was becoming a ritual in my presence, only this time, he was the one pouring it.

His gesture didn't go by unobserved, especially since he

was never the type to serve. "You must've missed me even more. I don't recall you ever being the one pouring me a drink."

My words struck him like lightning.

He even momentarily had the instinct to place the glasses back on the table. But that gesture would've meant conceding that I was right.

"I decided this is a special occasion." He handed me the glass, trying to make me understand this was a one-time thing. He couldn't risk anyone mistaking him for a normal human being, let alone a gentleman.

"You're probably right. It is a special occasion." I replied with hidden meanings rolling off my tongue.

Brax was never the type to waste his time. He placed the glass in one of my hands and wrapped his arm around my waist until the distance between our bodies was insignificant.

If I had any doubt of it being a special occasion, the closeness cleared it. He felt impossibly eager to start what I came here for, the same way I was impatient for him to ask me to be his.

His movements didn't show anything other than carnal attraction, and that was one of the main reasons for the anxiety that was gradually engulfing my senses. Just one small, hesitant gesture was giving me the confidence I needed to go on. The green color of his eyes flickered as he allowed himself to feel something for a stolen moment. His nostrils flared, filling his lungs with sweet notes of my perfume, drawing it in as if he had waited for too long for the breath of life to comfort his senses.

I just prayed I wasn't confusing my desires with facts because the outcome could be disastrous if it were the case.

I couldn't hide an anxious twitch, feeling his breath graze the surface of my skin, lighting up my nerves. That got him to instantly sober up from the flashing delirium, taking the glass to his lips to drain it. I mirrored his gesture, though I suspected I'd needed the whole bottle to summon my courage.

My lips kept murmuring a prepared speech. I was afraid it came across like I wanted to say something but couldn't. Though, Brax didn't seem to bother, being much more focused on tracing the line of my collarbone with his intoxicating lips. The touch was hypnotic. I secretly craved it for a long time but never dared to let myself realize I could still want the man who tried to break me.

Maybe I was dysfunctional that way. It was what I've been doing lately—returning to all those who had hurt me. Yet, this time, I was coming back on different terms.

"Be patient," I murmured, feeling his hand slip on the contour of my breasts, weighing them as his fingers seemed to be melting to their shape.

"I've been patient long enough." The anxious invitation in his voice was unwillingly disclosing his eagerness, and that was giving me an advantage in the game of love and lust.

"Aren't we waiting for the show to start first?" I was letting him know that, on my part, things were much more relaxed. My lack of urgency was bound to poke at his ego.

"The show is about to start." His gaze pointed toward the glass wall where the dim lights brightened, illuminating the room one by one.

Someone was about to enter. They had to follow the same pattern as before, only this time, I didn't sit by silently, waiting for it to happen. I had a final step in my plan that I needed to accomplish. And it had to be in that second. "What if we were to try something new?" Rehearsed or not, I was playing the role of a lifetime.

Judging from the devious glimmer on his face, the idea seemed to agree with Brax. That's because he couldn't even imagine what my proposal would be.

"What do you have in mind?" His eyebrows arched into a seductive frown, impatient to hear my dark desires.

"I want to go on the other side," I whispered, so seductively that I was one step from convincing myself of my newly discovered kink.

"What do you mean?" His words came out almost frightened. They completely lacked the arousal or the anxiousness a man as cold as himself was striving to display. Instead, his fists clenched, knuckles white as if they were about to break under the pressure as I kept spilling poisonous words directly into his ears.

"I want to switch," I murmured, spotting the brunette I saw last time and an unknown man entering the opposite room. "You said you've had her before. Come on. It'll be exciting." I pressed the curves of my body harder and drove my hand to search for the contour of his length. "I know it'll turn you on. And we can have some fun together after that. If you'll still be up to it." I was setting him up by twisting his arm into agreeing. It was impossible for him to refuse and altogether impossible to accept. But he had a point to prove—I was still an object that he could dispose of at any time.

It was game on, and it only took a nod on his part to advance to level one.

He suddenly turned cold, as if his newfound attitude could force his inner feelings to change at that instant.

Incapable of admitting that he was making a mistake, he picked up his phone and called the brunette to prepare for the switch.

She didn't seem to be bothered at all. Probably screwing the big boss was bringing her some leverage around the place, or maybe even a raise. Whatever her goal was, chances were she was going to see it to an end, no matter the casualties along the way.

"I'll be watching." Brax gave me a nudge by smacking my ass on the way out to the hallway.

He seemed less and less affected by my plan, and as the seconds ticked by my anxiety grew, I was going to fail.

I expected him to have some second thoughts, but he seemed to embrace the idea of different partners. And that was putting things into a whole different perspective.

What the hell was I doing?

It felt like I was walking on thorns. I reckon it was a few meters walk, but it felt like I was carrying my steps for miles, barely dragging my feet to reach the destination. I even stopped in front of the door, having serious thoughts about calling it off. But it was the only chance I had to make a difference.

One way or the other, something had to change that night. It was only a matter of *good* or *worse*.

The nerves rushing through my body were making my hand too unsteady to even catch the doorknob. Before I could do it, the door opened, letting the brunette leave the room so she could take my spot in Brax's arms.

An invisible weight instantly formed in my throat and snuck to the pit of my stomach as the true consequences of my actions began to sink in.

What the fuck had I set in motion?

The thought was much harder to endure than I initially assumed, and that was making the next few minutes almost unbearable.

I closed my eyes in a final attempt to clear my thoughts, dismissing everyone from my mind except myself and the man waiting for me in that room.

I had never seen him before, which made it impossible to foresee his actions. I couldn't tell exactly if that was a good or a bad thing, since everything already seemed to be heading toward disaster.

I faked another smile. I was making a habit of faking things that day—smiles, words, even my attitude.

Contrary to my expectations, the man didn't order me around. Instead, he gallantly stretched out a hand for me to join him. He seemed far less dominant than the other two men I'd previously seen in the room but far more attractive. Making him a double-edged blade.

I always notice the eyes of a man. His were icy blue, the same color the sky used to be in the morning. My mother gave me an old picture of the sky from what felt like a lifetime ago, and his beautiful cyan pools reminded me of that moment. It helped calm me down a little—not for long as the tone of his voice set me back on edge, "First time in a room like this?" He was trying to be nice, probably just because I was his boss's toy.

With that in mind, I still couldn't answer. I simply nodded a couple of times, letting my gaze fall to the ground.

But then a realization made me lift my head, forcing my mouth to gain the courage it needed. "First time, yes."

Brax was watching me, and I didn't need his pity.

That's not what could trigger him.

I needed his jealousy!

"Then I'm going to go easy on you." The tempting promise between his words was warning me that his *easy* didn't mean the same thing for him as it did for me.

"Ready when you are," my lips slowly spoke the words, letting them linger on the tip of my tongue with the most sensual calling.

For anyone watching, I appeared utterly intrigued by the man standing right in front of me, while in my mind, *Please God, don't let me fuck this up,* was becoming the motto of the day.

My answer piqued a strange interest in the man standing in front of me. I was breaking his usual pattern, being very different from the women he would normally put on a show with. This wasn't my job. I was doing it only for fun—or at least that's what I wanted them to think.

"Trust me, you're not ready." He was as arrogant as the rest of the men in my life, throwing me the *I will blow your mind* look while drawing a few fingers through his sun-kissed hair, pushing it back.

I gazed at him like a dumb puppet hanging on thin strings while he brought his hand to the side of my neck, caressing it until his fingers slid over my shoulder, down to my back. He reached for the zipper of my dress, and the moment he pulled it open, the fabric pooled in a green puddle at my feet.

The very sexy piece of lingerie that his gesture revealed got him to arch an eyebrow, visibly impressed by what I was putting on display.

And this was from a man who had seen it all by now.

I must have been doing something right.

That was enough to encourage me to go on, even though with each second that passed, we were speeding to reach the limit of the impossible.

I mirrored his gesture, unhurriedly unbuttoning his shirt, my fingers trailing each inch of his chest along the way. The man was the definition of fit, and I had to admit that the fine display of well-shaped muscles made things easier than I expected. Yet I still felt incredibly awkward, seeing everything as a scene in a play rather than any kind of sexual encounter.

He suddenly disappeared from my sight in a movement that was setting all triggers alive. The man was kneeling in front of me, and no matter how attractive he might have been, I did *not* like where his eye level was at.

I gasped as he came closer, praying that Brax would have some kind of reaction to this proximity.

Yet, he didn't.

And the man came closer and closer, until...

Until I was squeezing my eyelids shut, knowing that I would be unable to fake any kind of satisfaction.

My eyes squeezed so tightly shut, it felt my eyelids would burst open. I was trying to raise my lips to at least fake the shadows of pleasure, though I wasn't sure it was working out too well.

I must've looked like a clown, and I realized that's exactly what I was, as I felt his hands grab my ankle, trying to help me dispose of the dress that had fallen to my feet.

I exhaled so deeply, it felt I'd just escaped some high-security prison.

My moment of freedom was short-lived.

He caught my hand in his, fusing his moist lips with my knuckles.

The gesture felt strangely romantic, but he was just following a routine, raising his mouth back on the path of my body. Though not to my shoulders. He was heading straight to the exposed part of my breasts, carefully attending to the skin that the cup of the bra could not keep hidden.

I suddenly felt sick. Not *lovesick* or even excited. Just sick, as if I'd just eaten something bad, and my gag reflex was piling up in the pit of my stomach, quickly escalating to my throat.

I guess I was sick of what I ended up doing. Of how desperate I'd become to prove a point that was probably wrong from the start.

Brax wasn't even going to lift a finger to stop *us*. Everything I had been hoping for was only in my head. There was never an *us*. He'd been right all along. I was a gullible fool, thinking that I could ever tame a wild beast.

I could hear the man groan, and that only managed to completely terrify me. I knew it wasn't his fault, but the sound seemed so real that it somehow reminded me of my kings.

However, the man standing in front of me was someone completely different. I didn't even know his name. He was just *the man...* the man that I was about to have sex with.

It made me feel cheap, and used, but mostly like a fool to have orchestrated this.

What truly rattled me to the bones was that I was exactly like him—a prisoner of the game, using my body to entertain the audience.

I barely bit back a tear, feeling him reaching the straps of my bra, letting them slip over my shoulders one by one to finally get to the clasp that held the piece of lingerie together.

My body was petrified, clinging to every ounce of strength not to just run out the door. My pulse was racing, and a few tears could not be stopped this time from peaking at the corner of my eyes.

I couldn't even understand why, but this felt so different from what I had with any of my kings. If with them I'd felt constrained by the situation, this time I felt repugnant—even though the man was very far from being repulsive in any way. I think I was the repulsive one, at least for my being, becoming the most toxic version of myself I could be.

Sensing his hands move to unclasp my bra, I felt my balance slipping, but a strangely calm voice brought me back to my senses.

"Get out!"

I wasn't even sure who was speaking. It sounded slightly like Brax but much more out of breath than his usual tone.

I must be hallucinating, I told myself, trying not to focus on the moment my bra would fall and betray any kind of reaction.

But the man that was glued onto me until a second before suddenly let go of the piece of material before it popped open.

With robotic movements, he turned to leave, as if someone had twisted his key and set him on his course.

Was it real?

Was it Brax's voice that I thought I'd heard?

I was too afraid to turn to look at the door and see if it was real or just a trick of my imagination. I just remained motionless, listening to the heavy steps that were closing in on me. Still, nothing could have prepared me for the image of Brax standing in front of me. He didn't even look like himself anymore, so transfigured by rage that I was starting to believe I was more likely face to face with a mad bull.

His nostrils flared with the hot air pumping through his lungs, and before I could even decide if this was a good or a bad thing, he lifted me by the waist and sat me on the edge of the holstered table.

"What do you think you're doing?" I retaliated, trying to look surprised and not like I'd just found an answer to my prayers.

"I'm not going to let you fuck some random guy. You are not a whore!" my king roared so loudly that the glass in the wall shook with the power of his voice.

"Yet, you treat me like one," I muttered, gathering all my strength to stare directly into his emerald eyes.

I was far from intimidating him; it was more like luring him to come closer. "Open your fucking legs." He spread my thighs to find a place between them, crashing my core on the twitching bulge in his pants.

"Exactly what I was saying," I hissed.

"Shut up, Bea. Now listen to me because I'm only going to say this once." He took a second to find the right words. Not that the words he spoke were right in any way. "You're free."

Those were far from the words I had imagined he'd use.

"I release you from the contract. Leave or stay. The choice is yours." Short sentences to determine the course of two destinies.

Typically Brax.

"Are you asking me to stay?" I questioned, knowing that the chances of a real answer were slim.

And I was right. "I'm asking you to do whatever you want."

"I need to know what *you* want." I needed to hear him say something more than half-hearted confessions.

"I came into the room, didn't I?" He was still irritated that his feelings had been exposed—or maybe he was annoyed that he had any kind of feelings at all. But we both knew it was too late for him to back down. The cards were laid face-up on the table. Brax probably realized that I'd just served him a lesson— one that he had nonetheless deserved.

"So what now?" I tried to appear much less affected than I really was, though I guessed it didn't have much point hiding it.

"Now..." He whispered, his breath ghosting over my skin as he grabbed the back of my head to join his lips on mine.

He was about to kiss me. The way all happy endings work. The way they show in all the best movies.

Except, this was real life. And a kiss now wouldn't secure me with a happy ending. It would take much more than just a simple kiss, and denying him of this one was exactly the first brick into building something together.

My lips were numb, not answering his calling. The same way they were the last time we were together in the room with the glass wall. He hopelessly moved against them, trying to coax a response and bring them back to life, harder and more eager until his rhythm slowed down, admitting defeat.

"What's wrong?" His words didn't come out menacingly; on the contrary, they were hindering silent insecurity.

"I don't want this, Brax." And the truth was, I didn't. There was no result coming out of this kiss besides the one I already knew.

I needed more than his jealousy.

I needed his passion—something real, something raw.

"What do you want then?" He pulled back slightly, searching my eyes for the answers he already knew.

"Something real." I finally voiced the truth weighing on my chest. "Something more than sex."

His eyes flashed with the ultimatum I was giving him. It was either the beginning or the end. The choice belonged to him and him alone.

I desperately wished he'd say we'd give it a try. That he'd promise me tomorrow and the day after, and a lifetime beyond.

But that wasn't who Brax was, and I was aware of that all too well. He was as strong and as feared as they come.

Still, my request was far more than he'd ever bargained for. "I need two days." He broke the silence, prolonging my misery, his hand slipping gently through the curtain of my hair. This time, his lips didn't reach for my own but for the soft skin of my cheek. "Let's get you dressed. I'll take you home," his tone warm yet distant, almost clinically detached.

It felt like he was fighting saying goodbye. I could hear the tremor in his voice, as if he was fighting to keep it steady. This wasn't a step toward a happy ending. This was a step toward *the end.*

Picking up my dress from the floor, he helped me off the table, and then to slip back into the emerald gown. No other words wasted, except, "I'll drive you home." An unusual offer coming from him, much more similar to an *I'm sorry* than to *let's start over.*

I gazed at him all the way back to Ferris's mansion in hopes I would find a flicker of emotion. Anything that could give me hope. But he looked more like he'd seen a ghost than someone on the brink of revelation.

He was returning to hide behind his mask, and there was nothing I could do to stop him. Brax was a man of few words— and even fewer visible feelings. No matter what speech I could give him, or what other plan I would come up with, I realized it wouldn't change the outcome.

This was something he needed to settle with himself, to defeat his own demons.

Two days to rewrite the mentality of a lifetime, and the odds were *not* in my favor.

CHAPTER 11

Brax didn't walk me inside, and to be honest, I was surprised he even drove me to the estate himself.

It was a night of change. And speaking of change, as soon as I got out of Brax's car, I headed straight to my room to shed my dress and crawl into bed. Little did I know I had a surprise waiting there. "Cole!" I gasped, flipping on the lights to find him wrinkling my bedsheets in a tangle of lazy limbs and purple cotton.

"Were you expecting someone else?" His question hung between us, and I knew it wasn't entirely rhetorical—because it was a real possibility. That was exactly my problem. I had no idea how to balance my time between all of my kings without everything toppling over. I could only hope things would somehow settle themselves before it all spiraled out of control. Because the alternative was inconceivable. I was far from being able to let any of them go.

"I wasn't expecting you, that's for sure." I shrugged, still surprised by his presence.

Surprised, but not disturbed!

"Do you want me to leave then?" His voice was calm, but there was a challenge in his eyes, like he already knew the answer.

"I never said that. I just need to get changed," I replied, trying to keep my voice steady, even as my mind raced. I slipped into the dressing room, rifling through my clothes to find something else to wear. It just didn't seem right to put on the same outfit I picked especially for Brax, with Cole lying in my bed.

In reality, I was pretty sure he didn't even care. But I cared, and this was one of the mental limits that was making things much more complicated for me. I wanted them all, although I had no idea how I would manage this tangled web I'd spun.

I returned dressed with a loose top and shorts. The seduction was over for the night—at least my attempts to seduce anyone else. Plus, Cole didn't need much seduction anyway. He'd still find me attractive even if I wore a black bin bag as a dress.

"You look so hot in those shorts," he said, as if to prove my point.

I slipped between the sheets, finding a place in his inviting arms. "You think I look hot in anything." I chuckled, giving him a small peck on the corner of his mouth before brushing my lips on the side of his neck as I wrapped my arms around him.

"That's because you do. But I think you look even hotter without clothes." He slid his hands beneath the sheets, searching for the hem of my shirt.

However, my mind was all over the place. "Slow down a little." I needed a moment of time-out to process what I was sure would end in failure—my attempt to win Brax.

"Why? Did you have sex with Brax?" Cole asked as casually as if he was asking for an extra piece of gum.

"Jesus." I jolted upright, pulling away from his arms. "You can't ask me questions like that."

"Yes, I can." He smiled, tilting his head to look at me. There wasn't even a shadow of jealousy lurking in his gaze, and that was leaving me speechless.

I didn't answer, just threw myself back onto the pillows to stare at the ceiling. I had an idea where Cole was going with the conversation. And I wasn't prepared to go into details.

But his intentions were too pushy to be ignored.

He yanked me to cradle against him as his quest to dispose of my top continued.

One of his palms soon found the shape of my stomach. "Did he touch you here?" Cole's question shocked me even more than the previous one. Yet again, there was no hint of resentment in his voice. It was dripping with heated arousal, so sensual that the words seemed to have an effect on me. "Or here?" His hand slid beneath my shirt, cupping the side of one of my breasts, then running his thumb over my nipple, hardening it on the spot.

The movement was so sensual and pleasing that it left me breathless, confused about how exactly I was beginning to fit into this game.

I arched, lit by the tingles that spread across my body, a mix of lust and intriguing curiosity.

My conscience wanted him to stop.

But I didn't.

I wanted him to ask all the inappropriate questions. Anything to fuel the ravaging storm breaking over the horizon.

And the chances of him continuing this game were increasing by the minute.

His eager lips raced to the fine line that marked the upper side of my shorts. "Did he kiss you here?" He traced a line straight to my navel, making me capture his head between my arms as I instinctively turned into a human ball.

Brax didn't get to any kind of kissing, he never made it this far. Still, I couldn't bring myself to shatter the electrifying mood. I was probably as fucked up as Cole was. But I was also living for every twisted moment.

Surprisingly, he managed to turn my spirit a hundred eighty degrees around, only being his devious self.

"How about here?" he continued, nibbling on the silky skin beneath my breasts, testing each level of arousal.

"Mmmm," was all I could say, willingly falling prey to his dark fantasies.

Yet fate didn't seem to agree with our moment of intimacy. Something broke the spell for an instant—a vibrating sound as my phone was coming to life on the nightstand.

I ignored it at first.

Then another buzz broke the silence.

Another text.

What if it was Brax?

I needed to know. Maybe he'd figured things out sooner than I expected.

"Cole..." I pleaded with him to slow down so I could reach the phone, but he was far more focused on driving my body to a boiling point than on any kind of socializing.

I had no choice but to crawl through waves of incoming ecstasy in a thwarted attempt to get to my phone.

"This might be important," I tried once again, though my words seemed to fall on deaf ears.

I finally managed to reach the nightstand just as he decided my pants had to go. With a hasty movement, he tried to remove the unwanted piece of clothing, but his grip loosened, and I seized the moment, lunging for my phone.

"Where do you think you're going?" He pulled me back into his arms, pinning me to face the sheets as he sank his teeth into one of my ass cheeks.

"Ouch." His revenge for my disobedience hurt yet excited me at the same time. The sensation was so intense that I was having trouble even remembering the access code for my phone.

"That was for trying to escape me. And this is... Well, this is just for fun." He sank his teeth again, biting on my other cheek until a heated coil flashed straight to my pussy.

It was going to be a long night.

But definitely *not* in the way I anticipated.

Another coil managed to sneak its way down my spine. Unfortunately, this one had nothing to do with Cole.

The texts flashed on my phone's screen, making everything cease around me.

We all pay for our mistakes.

Your turn is coming, Bea.

The letters began spinning randomly in my head, making Cole's lips dissipate somewhere else in the universe.

It was just me and dreaded memories, fighting to get away from the monsters that were closing in to haunt me.

I had no idea who wrote the texts. It could have been anyone, but the governor's image appeared in front of my eyes once again.

Stiff as a corpse—that's the only way a person could have described me in those moments. My body went rigid as my sickened heart ceased to function for a second. I was far away from the warm bed or Cole's arms. I was just wandering to a distant place, where the force of the blows made my body writhe in unbearable pain.

"Bea! Bea!" Cole roared while securing my temples between his large hands, in an attempt to capture my attention and snap me out of it.

What had happened?

The question spun in my mind while my body twisted, trying to escape Cole's touch.

I could hear Ferris banging on the door so loudly that it was moments away from falling apart though Cole couldn't leave my side. That was until Ferris's nerves reached their limit, and the door was thrown in the middle of the room.

That gave me enough time to jerk the sheets off the bed and curl into a ball in the darkest corner I could find.

"Not going to let you go there." Ferris appeared in front of me, trying to pull me back on my feet. "Get up."

I just couldn't follow his command. The images in my mind began dissipating, but my body was far from being under my control.

Ferris probably noticed I was much more similar to a lifeless doll than a human at that moment.

Without wasting a second more, he slipped an arm under my knees, and carried me back to bed.

Both he and Cole sat next to me, trying to decipher the mysteries that cast a shadow on my mind.

Ferris finally broke the silence only after he observed my heart had come to a more normal pace. "What happened?"

Cole was equally as confused as Ferris about my behavior. "I have no idea. We were playing around, and she suddenly began trembling."

I could remember exactly what triggered this madness. My eyes locked onto the phone lying right next to Cole, half-hiding between the messy sheets.

He hadn't even realized it at first, and I was in no shape to speak yet. But as he tried to adjust my feet to a more comfortable position, he ran across the lit screen.

"Fuck!" he snarled, clutching his hand on the phone so hard that the screen was almost about to break.

The cobalt blue in his eyes was gone, being replaced by a much darker shade. The color of anger and hate. His beautiful jawline sharpened with the sound of his grinding teeth, his reaction eerily similar to one that Brax might have had. "Who sent this?" he asked with a hitched breath, barely holding himself together so I wouldn't be totally freaked out.

"I don't know," I mumbled, seeing Ferris snatching the phone from Cole's hands to see what this was all about.

"Bea, it's going to be okay." Ferris kept a much calmer tone, locking his gaze with my own, assuring me that no matter what, they would be there to protect me.

But who was to protect me from my nightmares?

"Double the guards." A press of a button from Ferris made the place Alcatraz secured. Though it couldn't dispel the fear that had infiltrated my system, nor the concern shadowing their eyes.

"I'm going to get you something to calm down." Ferris left and returned with a pill and a glass of water.

Like my anxiety level wasn't high enough... I was supposed to accept a drink from Ferris, who I knew had the bad habit of occasionally drugging me.

"It's okay. It will help you sleep, nothing more." He rolled his eyes, noticing the insistent stare coming from both Cole and me.

Things didn't turn out that great last time I had a combination of Ferris and pills.

It was a matter of trust, and for us to have any kind of future, I owed him the benefit of the doubt. I just prayed he wouldn't fail me. Failure at a time like this would completely break me.

I took the pill and cuddled back on the pillow to try and sleep my anxieties away.

If things could only be that easy...

And if it wasn't complicated enough, Cole's body snuck behind me while Ferris was finding a place beneath the sheets to soothe me within the safety of his embrace.

Sure, I felt protected. Nothing could get to me in those moments.

Messages.

Monsters.

Nightmares.

But I also felt panic settling in.

My anxiety level was at its peak, and at the same time, I was immersed in an intoxicating sensation. I was protected and loved, and... and despite everything that was going on, I was utterly aroused by the combined feeling of their hands securing my body.

And that was leading me to one conclusion: *I was in deep fucking trouble!*

The morning found me with Ferris's arms wrapped around my waist, my back molded to the form of his chest, while Cole's face was buried in the front part of my shirt. No surprise at all; on the contrary, it made me smile—typical Cole.

With everything going on, I hadn't expected to get a moment of sleep, yet strangely, it was the best sleep I'd had in a very, very long time.

I blamed it on the pill because the alternative seemed highly improbable.

I couldn't have slept that well just because I had my kings with me.

Could I?

Ferris was also starting to wake up, and the sensual moistness of his lips was coming alive on my shoulder. "Do you feel better?" he murmured, observing my head falling backward to make room for him to continue his voyage on my skin.

"Yes." I nodded. I did feel a *lot* better.

"I'll ask Alfred to send up breakfast then." The kisses stopped as Ferris was preparing to get out of bed.

Yet, that wasn't what I had in mind. "Please, don't go," I begged him, not prepared yet to be separated from his embrace. I just wanted to prolong the moment. Nothing could hurt me there. Nothing could reach me.

I could almost call it perfection, except I didn't have all of my kings. I might never because I was missing Brax.

Cole was still asleep.

That was until he let the blue color of his eyes flicker, looking up at me.

He didn't disturb the atmosphere with even a sound, just stretched like a lazy cat and buried his nose against my chest for ten more minutes. Or at least that's what he claimed. Though when we finally woke up, it was noon.

"They're going to kick me out if I don't start attending classes soon," I whimpered, realizing that the day of lectures was wasted.

"No, they won't," Ferris assured me with the calmest voice. He probably owned the university—teachers and all. And even if there was any part that he didn't possess, it probably belonged to one of my other kings.

But it didn't give me much comfort. I wanted to know I'd made it on my own.

"We should inform Brax about the texts." Cole decided to speak, forcing me to lose any hope that I could ever dismiss my mobster's presence, even for a second. There would always be something reminding me of him. And that scared me the most, especially since I was becoming certain that he would choose the ways of his past over any kind of a new beginning.

Knowing there was no point in fighting Cole's will, I didn't oppose it. It was probably for the best because if anyone could get to the bottom of things, Brax was the perfect man for the job.

It wasn't long before we were all seated on the living room sofa, and the doors were trembling with uncontained wrath as my King of the Underworld was making his way to join us.

"Give me the fucking phone!" he barked, causing even Ferris to jolt from his seat. "Who the fuck dared to do this?" He was out of control, unable to stop his jaw from tightening as he processed the information he had just received.

No matter what was going on between us, I was under his protection. Coming after me meant a direct attack on him. And in his world, there was only one result for such a foolish mistake—death. On the streets, it was kill or be killed, and since Brax was standing imposingly in front of us, it was easy to know who was always the winner.

"Calm down." Ferris was as close to the voice of reason as it got, but not even he could reach my mobster in those moments. Brax was lost somewhere between brilliance and madness, trying to figure out all possibilities.

Was it someone close to the mayor?

Was it related to the governor?

Maybe someone from The Pleasure Room?

He couldn't figure out an answer. And that was sending him spiraling into the worst level of paranoia, to the point that he pulled the curtains open to stare into the yard.

We couldn't tell if he was thinking about something or just verifying that we weren't under attack, but the murderous intent blooming in his eyes was making my skin crawl.

"Why didn't you call me earlier? These texts are from last night!" His anger came spilling over us.

We didn't know exactly who the question was aimed at, but no one seemed to dare tell him that we slept until noon.

Cole took the initiative of explaining things through. "Bea was in shock. We needed to focus on her at that time. Plus, Ferris doubled the guards, so the place is safe."

"I'm the one who gets to say if the place is safe or not," Brax, the security expert, was severely disturbed that any decision had been made without his involvement.

And if I knew him well enough—which I did, that mistake wouldn't be repeated.

"I want to talk to the head of the guards. And Ferris, tell Alfred to prepare me a room. I think it would be best if I were to stay here for a while. You know, so that things like this won't repeat themselves."

At that point, I didn't know what pissed him off more—the

texts or the fact that he didn't receive a call about them the second I got them.

Maybe we did make a mistake leaving him on the outside, but when it came to mistakes, I was sure the list of his own was endless.

"Are these the only texts? Or have there been more?" Brax asked while Ferris left the room to search for the people he needed to find.

"Just these. I would have told you last night if there had been more." I crossed my arms, peering straight through him. I was visibly annoyed that he came thundering and roaring into the room but didn't stop for a second to even ask if I was okay.

Which I wasn't.

I was scared and hurt, but mostly I was unsure about what the future held for us.

He was definitely not making things better as his attitude was getting colder by the minute, haunted by the thought of failure. He blamed himself for leaving a loose end even though he couldn't tell exactly what he did wrong.

"I want her guarded 24/7, understood?" he growled toward Cole, like he was the one to blame. "And I'm starting to think you should also have a guard, at least until we figure things out."

"I don't need a guard. I'm not five." Cole laughed at Brax's paranoid nature, although things were as serious as it got.

"If this has something to do with the governor, you too need a guard. And anyone else involved. Including Nat and

Seb."

Hearing my siblings' names was only worrying me more. The chances were, if someone came after me, they would try to get me through them. That made me reluctant to oppose even a single word Brax said.

Until we figured out what was happening, personal guards were our best defense against the unknown.

"I agree." I couldn't believe I was saying it out loud, but Brax was right. We needed some kind of protection, not only for us but for the future of Echo City.

"I'm glad we see eye to eye. Now I will ask you to go talk to Seb and Nat. I need to say something to the guys." Brax was sending me away. Apparently, I didn't belong in their little chit-chat, or worse, I was the main subject that they were going to talk about.

I just agreed with him on something, and he was already ordering me around like he owned me.

"I thought you said I was free of the deal." I put on a frown, trying to figure out how exactly he thought this was going to work.

"You are, but that doesn't mean you're free to commit suicide. You got me into this *ruling the city* thing. Now deal with it. I can't run my businesses, deal with the elections, and have to worry about everyone in this house. That's not how things work," Brax's patience was reaching the end of the line fast.

I never considered things from that perspective. Probably because he always seemed so powerful that it led me to believe he could juggle everything without much difficulty.

What if I was wrong?

Was I putting too much of a burden on a single man?

And what did he mean by *that's not how things work*?

Was he beginning to consider me as an obligation he needed to look after?

I couldn't answer any of those questions. And I couldn't be there either. Everything felt too confusing in those moments, as if the threatening message hadn't panicked me enough.

Brax's determination to keep us under supervision at all times made me fear I would end up a prisoner in a golden cage just as I had gotten my freedom—my partial freedom, since Ferris still couldn't let go. But I had a feeling that he wasn't going to use his prerogatives anymore either.

Convincing Nat and Seb that they would both need guards was far more difficult than I imagined, especially since I had no chance on this earth to avoid an avalanche of mind-wrecking questions. They could range from '*Are we secret royals?*' all the way to '*Is there an alien invasion?*'. Like a few bodyguards would save us from that.

My nerves were at their max when I returned to the living room. If that wasn't enough, the guys turned silent, as though I had interrupted some secret gathering, transforming me into a barrel of gunpowder waiting to blow.

"I'm going to the university in the morning, and I don't want to hear a word about it," I warned them, hoping that it would be the match that would start up the flame.

Yet not a single one of them dared to contradict me.

They were a lot calmer than when I left them—Brax included.

"I have an interview in an hour. I need to get ready." Ferris, my king of darkness, was finally stepping into the spotlight, and I had completely forgotten about it.

Maybe *I* was the villain in this story after all.

"And I have a meeting to bribe another Annelid leader. I suggest we take a vote soon if we should keep paying them or if I should just shoot a few of them. It would save us a lot of money and trouble." Brax tilted his head from one shoulder to the other until he heard that satisfying crack that eased the final signs of his tension. "See you tomorrow." I knew exactly who he was referring to.

And I dreaded that *tomorrow*.

The rest of the day wasn't about me. My problems could wait. I needed to step up and help Ferris get through the interview. The task was close to impossible for a man with his trauma, and he needed me to be there, helping him not to get thrown straight back into his past.

I was the one who got him into this mess, and I would be the one who would aid him set forth into a new world.

CHAPTER 12

Cole helped me cut the reporter's enthusiastic questions short since Ferris's interview could lead to certain disaster. No past, no drama, or hints of his hospitalization. Just presenting himself as the perfect candidate to occupy the empty seat.

A check that slipped into the right pocket did the trick. It was the way the world worked. We weren't going to play angels when the devils lurked in every corner.

A change was needed, and we were the voice of that change.

I spent the night in Nat's room. Falling asleep while talking to her—more likely escaping to clear my thoughts.

Anyone in my position would consider herself lucky to have both Cole and Ferris in their lives, but my heart couldn't feel whole. An invisible weight burdened my soul, and that scared me even more than the letters of the text ever could. I just needed to clear my thoughts, which prolonged throughout the day at school. Classes and lectures were a must, but breaks weren't. I managed to sneak my way around the university, mostly hiding in the bathroom to avoid anyone approaching me.

Cole had to leave early anyway to attend a press statement given by his father. I was out of the woods—at least until I needed to return home. Well, not completely out of the woods, I felt suffocated by a bodyguard who was following me around as if I were a prisoner. I've had guards before, but they always came around in a second car, keeping a fair distance. Most of the time, I didn't even know they were there, but my current six foot five gorilla was pretty hard to miss.

Luckily, he didn't raise too many questions among the other students. I was living in the land of the rich and famous, so a personal guard was as common as a phone.

The feeling that I needed to do something—anything—to ease the wait was killing me, Brax's silence was filling me with stressful tension.

His answer would be *silence,* and I was slowly preparing to accept it.

Still, the pathetic old me hoped to see one of his cars parked in front of Ferris's mansion—it wasn't. I even dreamed of him waiting for me in my room. Of course, that was empty too.

To prolong my torment, none of the guys were home either. They were too busy saving the world. I turned them into superheroes, and I was the one paying the price.

When the clock struck 8 p.m., I knew all chances of seeing Brax that night were gone. He would usually send at least a text by then to meet him somewhere or a demanding one of *my car is picking you up at 8 p.m.*

That was it. A date with a glass of wine in the armchair next to the window awaited me, and the invitation I made to myself grew more tempting by the minute. At least that's what I wanted to believe, so I wouldn't let the lame side of the disappointment I felt rule my evening.

I just needed to take a shower first and change into some fluffy pajamas. I had a specific picture of how my evening should be, and I needed to get at least that part of the day right.

The warm water did me good. Perhaps because I shed a few tears between the crystal drops that were falling on my skin, in the last attempt to relieve some of the stress tormenting me. I was still unable to let go of Brax.

I needed that wine ASAP. But I also needed a pair of fluffy socks to make my dream scene complete. I had forgotten to pick them up from the dressing room, so a second later, I was heading there to grab them.

I rifled through the fourth drawer, still searching for that specific pair I had in mind when I heard something move in my room.

I instantly wanted to scream for help, but the sound of footsteps closing in petrified me. My eyes scanned the room for anything I could utilize as a weapon.

Nothing that I could use was in my field of vision.

Nothing except a few pairs of stilettos.

That would need to do.

I was prepared.

Armed and... not so dangerous—just in time for the assailant to reveal himself.

"I'd say you're either a psychic and were already searching for something to wear, or you were just about to Gucci me to death." The man my heart had lost all hope of seeing stood in front of me.

Brax was holding a large white box, very similar to the one he had sent me through his driver a couple of months ago.

"What are you doing here?" I knew that was probably the dumbest question a person could ask. But my mind was blank at that moment, surprising myself I could even speak.

"Do you want me to leave?" I guess my foolish question deserved an equally absurd response.

I could only shake my head as a *no*.

But he already knew the answer. "I take that as a no." He smiled with a charm I never noticed before. It wasn't rehearsed, and it wasn't hindered by any masks. On the contrary, it was coming from a place I never thought would be revealed—his real self. "Do you want to trade weapons?" He slowly extended the box in return for the pair of stilettos.

A fair trade, since both objects could indeed be used as weapons of some sort. While my heels could be used as a means of self-defense, his present was the weapon that was leaving my heart defenseless.

A silvery cocktail dress and a matching pair of heels—a gift that was setting the grounds for a new beginning.

My stomach quaked with emotions, yet I was never too good at showing the true intensity of my feelings—kind of like him.

"You have a thing for gifting me dresses." I finally said between the tremors that were making my voice shake.

A hint of frustration flashed on his face as if I had just blown his cover. "I'm no match for Ferris in this avenue, but I try. Let's help you put it on."

"Now?" I was caught off guard, completely unprepared for any plan he had in mind.

"Unless you want me to take you out looking like a polar bear." He shrugged, looking at me from head to toe.

Damn, I forgot all about my sleeping outfit. I always imagined that in a moment like this, I would be wearing some silk dress, and my hair and makeup would be styled to perfection. In reality, I looked like a snowball, and my perfect hair was replaced by a messy bun. I couldn't even get started on the makeup unless reddened eyes from tears could be considered a new fashion statement.

"Where are we going?" I hated to ruin the surprise, but I wasn't exactly sure I liked the kind of surprises Brax could come up with.

"Raise your arms." He gripped the hem of my hoodie, pulling it up over my head, making my heart race at the unexpected intimacy of the gesture.

My question went unanswered, but that wasn't actually what troubled me most at that time. I had no bra on, and Brax's touch made me instinctively try and cover myself.

Seeing my shyness, followed by a certain clumsiness as I kept trying to keep myself together, raised a smile on his lips.

He was probably right to be amused. I didn't even know what I was embarrassed about. He'd seen me naked on so many occasions that it shouldn't even matter. But somehow, it did. It felt like I was standing in front of a brand-new Brax, and every single one of his actions reinforced my thoughts.

"I'll play your game if that's what you want." He was amused by my behavior, and I couldn't deny that he was probably right. Still, I couldn't help myself. It was who I was, and not even King Brax could change that.

Without warning, he started to push my pants down, pulling the dress from the box and letting it cradle at my feet, ready for me to slip right into it.

He was dressing me in the sexiest way possible, his fingertips trailing up my skin, sending goosebumps from my toes to the back of my neck as the fabric followed his touch.

It was certainly a whole different Brax. One who possessed an undeniable skill for seduction. On the contrary, he seemed to have doubled down on that specific leverage.

"Turn." He guided me to face the full-size mirror that was reflecting an earth-shattering image. The dress was superb, no doubt about it, but it paled in comparison to the sight of us together. The imposing presence of my king of crime, bowing his lips to rest them on my shoulder while I still held on tightly to the cups of my dress. I believe he was supposed to tie it together, though, in reality, I had no idea what was going to happen next.

His plan was to go out, while mine was currently to *drop the dress on the floor.*

Luckily, he saved me from myself, raising the zipper that secured my dress, then arranging the final straps over my shoulders.

Except, I wasn't just dressed. I was wet, throbbing with an uncontrollable need for him.

"Never thought dressing you could pose such a challenge," he whispered in the back of my ear, stealing the pin that held my bun together. Long, chocolate strands tumbled over my shoulders, cascading all the way to my breasts, preparing me in just a second for a perfect night out.

"I need to... put on some makeup," I babbled, bewitched and overwhelmed by the mood he was setting. Brax of all kings had a special kind of power over me. He was leaving me speechless and breathless at the same time, making longing replace all reason.

"I'll be out on the balcony having a smoke." He was giving me a few minutes to get myself together.

The reality was, I needed at least a few hours to get ready for that kind of date, and he was asking me to compact all of that into just a few ephemeral moments.

Eyeshadows, blushes, perfumes, and hairspray were leaping across the room as I was making a turn-the-table transformation. I knew better than to keep him waiting, and I didn't want to test his patience on day one, so five... ten minutes later, I was returning to my room.

Brax was still on the balcony, probably enjoying his second pack of smokes by then. Yet, that wasn't the first thing I noticed as I walked out of the dressing room. A sweet scent instantly caught my attention, and my eyes turned to an extra-large bouquet standing on my nightstand. I couldn't even count the number of pink roses, carefully arranged by an exquisite florist into a silent declaration of emotions. I couldn't tell what kind of feelings Brax really hid, but it was the first time he was showing signs of being willing to take a step forward, even if that would happen in his own unique way.

"I see you're ready. Let's go." He opened the terrace door, gesturing for me to walk to the lobby while I was still sinking my nose into the bouquet, drinking in the beautiful scent of the roses.

He didn't even look my way, let alone at the flowers, as if he had no idea where they came from or how they *magically* ended up in my room.

I mused, abandoning the roses and following his lead. It was all baby steps when it came to Brax, but at least they were steps in a direction we were to follow together.

One of his limousines was waiting for us in front of the mansion—nothing too uncommon about that. But the *driver* opening the door, following each step of proper etiquette, snatched a giggle out of me.

The chances were that Brax instructed one of his men to act like a pro. His position didn't leave room for errors, so being on the road unguarded—especially after those texts—wasn't an option for either of us.

"You still haven't told me where we are going." I searched

his gaze for even a small hint that would reveal his surprise. But it was Brax we were talking about; I had a better chance of getting information from talking to the car than I had from asking him.

"Are you always this impatient? I didn't notice that about you." I could feel the irony hiding in his voice.

How could I ever be impatient around him when, in the past, most of the time, all I ever wanted was to run away?

I must've received too many blows in the head because I still couldn't figure out how it was that my heart twisted in pain to be with him. After all that he'd done! I couldn't dictate my soul no matter how hard I tried, and having him change for me was opening the door of hope again.

"You would've strangled the driver for information by now." I shrugged, knowing I was the last person to talk about impatience. He was always like an active volcano when it came to making him wait, if only for a minute.

At least this time, he was admitting it. "You're probably right. Though not tonight. I'm planning to keep my calm this evening."

"Special event?" I stuck my tongue out at him.

And he was playing into my game. "You could say that.'

"Let me guess... celebrating the elections or... hmmm... maybe a special date."

"I haven't been on a date since I was still forced into gym class... so, if the first in adulthood is special, then so be it." He seemed honest about it, and I didn't think he needed too many dates with every soul entering his clubs throwing themselves at his feet.

"Who's the lucky woman?"

"Someone who talks way too much, asks too many questions, and who will be in her flannel pajamas back home in the next ten minutes if she doesn't shut up." The old Brax wasn't completely gone. It would take some *time* to chisel him into something closer to a gentleman. I just hoped that *time* would mean during this life*time*.

In response, I just pouted, turning my back on him to look out the window. I thought I could succeed in getting to him that way, when in fact, I was providing him with what he wanted. One of his arms ran down my waist, pulling me against his chest, where I remained, in silence, for the rest of the ride.

We ended up in the Pit again, at a location I'd never seen before. The building seemed to be the oldest around, judging from the architecture, yet it had been renovated to a state of majestic glamour. It reminded me much more of the Hills than the bottomless pit we were in, and I was surprised I hadn't noticed it earlier, during the months I lived there.

Taking another look around me, I finally recognized the place. I used to pass by it every day on my way to the university, but I could've sworn that the building wasn't there before—or at least, it never caught my attention.

I expected a few rusty vehicles and some cabs at best, but the sidewalks were crowded with luxury cars and even a few limousines like the one we were in.

Incredibly strange for the Pit.

"This is our stop," Brax announced, helping me out of the car and straight onto a red carpet.

"What's this?" I asked, noticing a few paparazzi rushing to take pictures of us.

"The grand opening," his tone too casual for the event.

Brax's half-sentences were leaving me even more confused, as usual. "Grand opening to what?"

"My new club," he answered just as we walked inside, stepping into a whole different world. Glamorous chandeliers and mahogany-covered walls convinced me that the place was the setting for The Great Gatsby.

"This is so different from anything else in the Pit," I exclaimed, marveling at the architectural wonders I was discovering.

"That's because I wanted to bring the Hills to the Pit."

"Why would you want that?" I asked, knowing that the two social classes didn't mix well. After all, we were trying to prevent the Elite from making a fence to keep the Annelids away. That alone says something about the interactions between the two.

But Brax seemed to have other plans. "To make their money flow this way. If this thing works, a few fancy shops will spring up here and there. That means workplaces for the Annelids and more money into the Pit. That's how you create a new ecosystem and unbalance the old one."

Brax had a special sense for business; I always knew that,

though this plan was pure brilliance. Of course, it would bring money into his pocket, but it would also save who knows how many lives from sheer misery.

"I still don't understand how you got the Elite to *demean* themselves and come down into the Pit." I didn't even get to finish my sentence as a part of the answer revealed itself with astonishing glory. Vintage, elegant tables were displayed in an atrium shape right in front of a stage, carefully arranged to attend the incoming show.

I just hoped the *show* wasn't the kind I usually attended with Brax. I wouldn't put anything past him. "What's the stage for?" I asked with exactly *that* tone.

Instantly, he turned his head to look my way, bursting into delicious laughter. "It's a piano recital. Relax." He couldn't stop laughing as he kissed my cheek. It's not like I didn't have reasons to be worried—so many reasons that I didn't even notice the grand piano on stage. Paranoia, here I come.

"And as for the Elite," Brax continued our discussion. "This is an oasis of freedom. They're escaping the stuck-up society clubs, coming to a very similar environment. The exception is no one judges them here." He showed me to a central table.

"What does *no one judges* mean?" I arched an eyebrow, knowing him all too well.

A devious smile tugged at the corners of his lips. "A casino upstairs and some luxury entertainment for the guests."

"Jesus!" I muttered, it seemed I wasn't that paranoid after all...

"What? I'm doing this my way. Besides, the Elite are

my most loyal customers anyway. Now, I'm just extending the services. High-end entertainment in this very room, fine dining, and a well-stocked bar. I'll make an all-inclusive resort out of this place pretty soon."

"You're awful," I muttered, knowing damn well not a single good intention resided in his body.

"Am I, Bea?" He caught my hand between his, capturing my full attention.

Yes, he was awful and wicked and... and so seductive that I felt I was going to melt under the table.

I was in serious need of therapy. "You are full of surprises. I never know what to expect from you. And yes, you are awful at times."

"Perhaps you're right. I'm usually awfully determined to get what I want."

"Don't I know it," I mumbled, reminding myself of our past.

"A bottle of Krug." He gestured to the waiter, pointedly ignoring my remark. He wasn't going to let anything ruin our evening, including my big mouth.

"I loved the flowers." I was extending an olive branch, trying to tune up to his mood. But my words only got him to stiffen like he had made an error and softened up too much. He simply shifted his gaze to the stage, where the piano recital was about to start. Chopin, The Preludes—the same classical music that had played in his house on the day of my first visit. Coincidence or not, it sent me back down memory lane, only this time, we were writing a different destiny.

The ending of the concert seemed to have washed all questions away. The flowers were forgotten; at least that's what I let him believe so he could relax back to his earlier mood.

Dinner was served, along with a second bottle of French champagne. Though it wasn't just any dinner. It was something divine, every bite making my taste buds explode with joy. He wasn't kidding when he said the place catered to the Elite. Judging by the chef's skills, he could easily host any kind of royalty.

Deducing from the presence of the champagne, we were celebrating something. Maybe the grand opening.

Or maybe not.

I liked to think we were celebrating *us*. Though I never asked, knowing that if that were the case, a question would only ruin everything.

Sometimes you don't even need questions to know the answers.

His fingers intertwined with mine, remaining so for the rest of the evening, despite the distinguished clients who came to greet him.

Except for that night out of town, where the mission required it, I was becoming sure he didn't usually display any kind of public affection. At least that's what the stunned gazes of his guards were telling me. Maybe he had shown lust, sexual attraction, but no sentiments were ever involved.

To my utter surprise, he didn't even show any kind of sexually charged gesture. No hand under the table, no naughty remark, not even the intention of a kiss.

I wasn't even sure if I was pleased, shocked, or even a little angry that he was depriving me of any sign that would feed my womanly ego, but the new Brax was turning into a monk. Though not for long, I would bet all my money on that. He couldn't escape his old ways completely, and I wasn't even sure I wanted him to. Not *the glass wall room* way, but the raw, crashing attraction that pulsed in his veins.

The evening had an unusual vibe that was gradually sneaking into my soul. It was the first of what I hoped would be many, and most importantly, the first night when he was introducing me to his world. We weren't hiding behind closed doors. On the contrary, we were the central pieces of attraction, and more strangely, I was becoming Queen Bea of the underworld. You'd think I'd be used to it by now, but this step was taking my life to a whole different level. I just needed to be ready for the challenges it would bring along—and the extra guards that would be breathing down my neck for a very long while.

"Let's get you back home," he said after the crowd began to scatter, leading me back to the limousine.

I had no idea what that meant. Did his words contain a hidden threat, maybe even a promise? I hated myself for being extra anxious to find out. By some twisted magic, he was reversing the roles, and I was turning into him. My mouth was dry from peeping at the alluring way the fine Italian shirt had wrapped around his torso. And those pants... I could write a novel about how the fine lines hugged his frame perfectly, disappearing over his tantalizing ass.

I couldn't even get to describe the absinthe in his eyes as each time I tried, I was falling prey to their allure.

My heart jolted seeing him dismissing the limo driver and following me through the steps of the mansion, but I quickly remembered he was living there too.

My head was a mess.

I had won—or at least that's what I assumed, given how unpredictable Brax was. Still, I felt angry at myself for being unable to withstand that impossible attraction I felt toward him.

I kept counting the paces as we were heading down the lobby that would set our paths apart.
Though when we finally reached the crossroads, he didn't stop, just walked forward with heavy steps, breaking the silence.

Small beads of sweat were blooming on my skin at the thought of *him and me* throwing away the key to my room.

I was a sinner, and he was the devil who would take me to a perfect hell.

At least that's what I was hoping for, but I would never have asked.

We stopped.

I didn't even realize we had arrived, like I didn't even recognize my own room, blinded only by my insanely charming king.

A smile appeared, wickedly tugging at the edge of his lips as he leaned toward me.

He was going to kiss me. Then he was going to say some

cheesy line, and I was going to fall prey to his masterful skills of seduction.

Yes, that was perfect!

That was the plan.

"Bea, are you okay?" He was bringing me back to earth, as he recognized exactly what effect he had on me.

I was such a fool!

"Y...yes," I mumbled, still waiting for him to make a move—anything to make me *fall* for him.

I was so willing to fall.

"I know I said two days." He leaned even closer. "And I think you got your answer." He pressed his lips to mine in slow motion, asking my own lips for permission to move against them.

This was so untypically Brax that it completely took me by surprise. I kept waiting for him to speed up the pace and do some magic trick. Lift me on the wall, break the door open, and heal the scars that he caused with hundreds of tormenting kisses. Instead, I could see his eyes opening as he was slowing down the rhythm, preparing to stop. "Goodnight, Bea. I'll see you tomorrow."

What in God's name was he doing?

I watched him turn and walk back to where he came from, leaving me to stare at his shadow disappearing down the hall.

He was taking *doing the right thing* literally, and it seemed that no matter what I did, I always ended up losing in front of him.

He was giving me a lesson in manners as my greatest curse came alive—I'd somehow turned Brax into a gentleman.

CHAPTER 13

Torment—that's all I could say about that night since all my thoughts were leading me to Brax's chamber.

I knew there wasn't a chance in hell I'd go there. It would be a huge setback at a time when I couldn't allow any mistakes, especially since I just crossed the finish line—at least the one regarding my kings, because when it came to ruling the city, we still had a long road ahead.

If over the previous days, I'd managed to avoid all interactions at the university, it was time to face the world again.

I only took comfort that I wasn't alone. Jenna seemed to be eager to greet me the second I set foot out of the limo. "Who is this?" She waved a newspaper in front of me.

I don't even remember when I last saw a newspaper. Everyone in the Hills had phones these days.

"Where did you even buy that?" I asked, amused and intrigued by what the piece of paper may hold.

"We still have a few newspaper stands in the Pit. You know not everyone has a phone there, but gossip is gossip; we have to keep entertained somehow. I spent my allowance for the day on it," she let out an involuntary truth, the words slipping out before she could stop them. Her money situation hadn't improved, but she was too proud to accept any more help from me. I didn't have much money myself. Ferris usually ensured I had everything I needed, but I could still find a way to help her out—if she'd let me.

"Let me see that." I snatched the newspaper to find a familiar face right on the front page.

I... well, Brax and I, stepping on the red carpet together.

One of the paparazzi from last night must've sold it to the newspaper. Just what I needed, even more unwanted attention pointed at me.

"You have to tell me all about it." Jenna seemed way more excited than I was about that level of exposure. "Who is he?"

"You don't know who this is?" A voice from behind me seemed surprised at how out-of-the-loop she was with the tabloids.

"Well, of course, I know who this is. It's written here in the newspaper—an important Pit entrepreneur, known as Brax." Jenna turned to scold Thomas since he was the one who had crept up behind us.

"Yeah, right, *entrepreneur*," he cackled, "In the mafia enterprise." Thomas probably considered himself funny.

But I wasn't going to let him talk about Brax like that, truth or not. "Watch your mouth!" I never thought I'd need to pull rank on my friends, yet Brax's reputation seemed to be known worldwide.

"Hey, don't shoot the messenger. Everyone knows who he is. He used to be king around here before Cole," Thomas tried to explain, triggering some of Jenna's memories.

"Oh My God, you're right. He and... I can't remember... there was another guy who used to rule the school." Jenna kept trying to jog her memory, though it didn't seem to be working.

"Ferris," I grumbled, knowing I'd just invited Hell into my life.

"Yesss, Ferris," she gasped, like she'd just had a revelation. "Wait. Ferris, as in..." She instantly clamped her hands over her mouth, remaining stunned for a minute. "Thomas, bye, we need to leave." Her senses kicked in, dragging me by the hand toward a secluded corner of the hallway where no one could hear us. "Talk," she ordered, arms crossed like she knew I'd been holding out on her.

Well, I had *been* holding out on her, but I wasn't expecting to be exposed.

Besides, where should I even begin?

Cole, Ferris, or Brax?

"And say what?" I shrugged, thinking it was pointless to go through all the details.

Pointless to me...

"Everything. I want to know what and when and how," she

demanded. By her tone, I knew that she wasn't going to let it go before I gave her some answers.

"Okay, okay. This is hard for me to explain." The truth was that I couldn't fully put into words what I shared with the guys. I had no idea how someone could justify three boyfriends—or whatever my kings were. "You know Cole…"

Jenna nodded, waiting for me to go on even though I had no idea where exactly I was going with this.

"And you seem to know Brax," I added. "And Ferris…"

"Would you tell me already?" She was clearly losing her patience, hoping I'd speak before we turned fifty.

It was unfair of me to keep my relationship with them hidden from her, considering she let me into every single detail of her life.

"I'm with all three of them." The words just blurted out of my mouth before I could stop them. The band-aid had been ripped off—and it was one hell of a band-aid.

"You're with them? What does that even mean? Like you're sleeping with all of them?" Jenna blinked repetitively like she was having difficulty processing the information.

It was a lot to take in, I admit.

I was beginning to think she saw me as a tramp who used them for my personal gain, when in fact, we couldn't be further from that.

Yet the news hit Jenna differently than I expected. Pressing her palms together she finally blurted, "Teach me, master."

Was she actually begging me, or just making fun of me?

I couldn't tell for sure, but the second plea convinced me she was serious. "You're my new mentor. I wanna be just like you when I grow up."

"And you're insane." I chuckled.

There was no shutting down Jenna. "I'm intrigued! I want to know more. I want to know everything! How on earth did you end up with three extremely hot men?"

"Three extremely hot men, Mouse? You're shameless!" Cole's voice echoed from down the hallway. He was walking straight toward us, probably having overheard everything.

Jenna and her big mouth.

At least now, she'd clam up, staring dumbfounded at Cole, who stopped right in front of me.

"I'll punish you for that." He cast a sinful smile, crashing his perfectly carved mouth over my lips. "I mean it."

"We'll talk about it later." I wasn't about to let Cole go into too many details, especially with Jenna standing there.

Though it seemed I didn't have a choice. "We'll talk about it later, at dinner with my mom. That should be interesting." He bit my lip before I could pull away.

"What *dinner with your mom*?" I stuttered. I didn't remember making any kind of dinner plans.

"This smells like trouble." Jenna practically ran off before either of us could squeeze in a word. I guess she'd learned her lesson.

"We're having dinner with my parents at 7. Now get to class before you're late." Cole seemed to abandon me too, leaving the second he finished his sentence.

"Since when do you even care about my classes?" I called out after him, uselessly trying to get his attention.

I did have an idea or two of what could get his attention, but we were still in a public place, and neither idea seemed like a good decision at the time, especially with all the extra sets of eyes looking our way.

For the first time in weeks, I managed to attend all my lectures and labs—and actually pay attention to most of them. All of that between a lunch break interrogation from Jenna and a few stolen moments with Cole in the courtyard.

"Ready?" My king snatched the notebooks I was carrying, to help me with *the burden* of fifty paper sheets.

Not that I could complain.

His gesture was sweet, yet so unlike him. And that didn't go without being noticed.

"Oh, Cole baby, would you carry my undies for me?" Jason caught up from behind us, matching our pace.

"Shut the fuck up," Cole barked, trying not to pay too much attention to him.

But it felt as if Jason was deliberately trying to piss him off. "Okay, baby, but don't forget to get me some tampons on your way home."

There would be trouble. I could feel it in every pulsing vein in Cole's neck.

Reaching for his hand, I attempted to get him to keep his composure, but I was beginning to think that *Cole* and *composure* didn't belong in the same sentence. I barely managed to grab the tip of his fingers before his body jerked in Jason's direction, slamming him against the wall.

"What the fuck is your problem?" Cole growled like a beast, ready to rip his friend apart.

"N...nothing." Jason was backing out of the fight as if he wasn't the one who was looking for it in the first place.

Not that the king of the ECU was going to let things slide. "Speak!" Cole barked, sensing something was wrong with Jason for a couple of weeks. He'd mentioned it right before I returned to the university, but between politics and taking care of me, he never got the chance to do anything about it.

"There's nothing to say. I was just clowning around." Jason's voice cracked with fear. He knew all too well what Cole was capable of, and crossing him was a bad decision at any time, no matter the reason.

"I said *speak*." Cole's hand tightened around Jason's throat, preventing his friend from doing just that.

I needed to act before this turned into one of his usual bloodbaths. Jason wasn't exactly on my favorites list, but I felt responsible for breaking their circle and the tension between them. I was beginning to think Jason's attitude had everything to do with my interference in their lives.

"Ease up on him." I tried pulling Cole away from his friend, though my best efforts didn't seem to get him to budge even an inch.

"Back off, Bea. Remember what happened last time you tried to get me off someone." He was steaming mad, reminding me of the same scene with Ace.

And that was exactly the problem—Ace.

I realized that as Jason groaned, trying to get away. "Don't you see what she's doing to us? You fucking sent Ace into exile because of her."

Strangely, Cole seemed to be amused. "Don't be a fucking drama queen. *Exile?*" He started laughing. "I didn't send him to become a monk. I just cut him out of our circle."

Jason's gaze shifted toward me. "Because of her."

"Because of him." Cole's tone grew more aggravated with every breath he took. "You're free to join him if you want. I'm not keeping anyone here by force." He was perfectly aware that Jason would never choose to be an outcast over the power his current position provided. He just needed to knock some sense back into him.

Though Cole had a strange way of making people see reason.

Not sure if brute force was suited for such a task. But a punch sent Jason's head crashing into the brick wall behind him, leaving him more unconscious than awake.

Still, Cole wasn't leaving without clearing things up

though. "Bea wasn't the only reason I ditched Ace, and you know it! He was waiting for the first wrong move to take my place. And now it seems you're trying to do the same."

"Noo." Jason uttered, knowing what Cole was capable of, and any kind of threat to his kingdom would have ended in blood. "I was just angry that you don't hang out with us anymore. It's either Bea or who knows what you do after classes."

"Man the fuck up. I don't owe you my time. When you fucking dated that Lizzie bitch we didn't see you for a month. Just get a hobby, a girlfriend, whatever. I have more important things to do these days than to babysit you."

Jason just nodded, realizing that he was acting like a spoiled little girl—or worse, a ditched ex-girlfriend. He just seemed so disappointed that even Cole felt he should say something to soothe him. "I'm not ditching you two. I just have other priorities at the moment. And you should too. The world is changing, and we're not going to be in college forever. This will all end sooner or later."

Listening to Cole, I realized he'd understood an important lesson—we should be the change we want to see in the world. And he was just taking his first real steps in that direction.

"Let's go, Mouse." He glanced at his watch while releasing the grip from Jason's neck. "Just in time for some food poisoning."

"Are you okay?" I had to ask, seeing him rushing through the corridor. He was definitely not running away from Jason —more like running away from his temper before he'd do something he'd regret.

With a swift move, he pushed the entrance door open, shoving a few students to get out of his way as he raced to find the cold air of the winter. "I just need some air."

I couldn't catch up with him. My wounds weren't entirely healed yet, and running still posed some difficulty.

Not that Cole could notice. His temper prevented him from seeing anything but flaming red in those seconds—including me.

He only realized that I was behind by the time he reached his car.

"For fucks sake, why didn't you call out for me?" He retraced his steps until our roads met halfway.

I gained some resistance standing up, even at rejoining my usual activities, but fast walking still seemed to give me trouble. "I'm okay. I just walk slower than usual."

"I didn't realize. I was just..." he trailed off, still fuming.

"Steaming mad?" I teased with a small laugh.

I could instantly see a slight smile blooming on his face. "Why is it every time I want to take you home, I get into a fight?"

"Maybe I jinx it. I do have some trouble with the idea of family." I didn't mean it as a reproach; it was more like a regret that life didn't seem to offer me the full joys of a complete family. My father's greed and envy didn't leave us with too much family time. When my mother died, I hopelessly tried to keep the bits and cracks together, but there was nothing there to start with.

"You don't jinx it. Stop talking like that." Cole's anger seemed to have turned into something completely different— a protective need was subduing his rage, diffusing his usual selfishness so he could focus on me. "Get in." He opened the car door, helping me to get in like I was a cripple.

"I'm fine. I just got a little tired." I chuckled, remembering how different he was acting the first time I met him. Quite a change from the man whose sole goal was to make me fear him.

"Do you want me to take you back home? I can postpone the dinner." Cole was making me an offer I could hardly refuse.

But I refused it anyway.

He wouldn't have asked me in the first place if it wasn't important to him, and after everything he'd done for me lately, I wasn't about to let him down. "I want to come to dinner, really. I'm not tired. Besides, I like your mom's cooking."

"My mom's cooking is a lottery. She never does a meal the same way twice. So, always prepare for a surprise." He laughed, starting up the engine and driving off. "Don't worry; we'll have some takeout in my room if she completely messes things up."

"Did you want us to stay over? If so, I should text Nat," I said, opening my purse to reach for my phone.

"Yeah, I already talked to Brax, he's going to have a few extra men watching the house tonight. The bodyguards would only freak out my mom." It seemed Cole already had everything figured out.

"Oh, I see you were extra thoughtful."

"I just like knowing you're in my room," he confessed, a devious gaze glinting in his two blue orbs.

"Hmmm... just knowing I'm there?" I asked, sensing there was much more than just *knowing I'm there.*

"Okay. Knowing you are naked in my room." He slowed down the car. "Moaning, screaming, begging..."

I instantly held up my hands in a back-off gesture. "Jesus, remind me next time to stop before I ask something that could have the slightest kind of connotation."

"Okay, Ms. Prude," he teased.

"That prude thing again..." I rolled my eyes, annoyed he wasn't giving me a break about that. And knowing him, the chances were he never would.

"Then tell me your darkest fantasies," he pressed.

I wasn't going to fall into that trap again, especially since I had no idea what that even meant anymore.

Was it something related to his thirst for testing the limits of public exposure?

Perhaps something to do with Ferris's near-death experiences?

Or maybe Brax's games in the glass room?

What worried me most was that it could be something that

had to do with all three of those.

No matter what my thoughts were, I wasn't going to let the conversation with Cole degenerate into anything that could increase his sexual appetite. We were on our way to having dinner with his parents, and I wasn't going to be a part of some under-the-table sex party.

That didn't mean I couldn't have some fun with him. "My darkest fantasies... hmmm let's see. My darkest fantasies involve something hot... and something creamy." I paused, watching his pupils flare. "Something creamy poured on a steaming hot surface. And then it hardens." I moved my tongue across my lips, noticing him swallowing the lump in his throat. "And then you flip it, turning it bottoms up."

"Flip who?" He asked, his patience clearly wearing thin.

"Not who. What. The pancake, you flip the pancake, then you pour some chocolate syrup and ice cream over it. Talk about dark fantasies. That dessert's a caloric bomb," I winked at him, sticking out my tongue.

"You should write erotic books. You're giving me blue balls with that description," he said, his tone a little exasperated.

I was just replying to his request, although I was doing it my way. "You're the one that asked."

"I meant another kind of dark fantasy." He tried to steer me in the direction he wanted. "It could still involve the chocolate syrup and ice cream."

But I wouldn't play his game. "No, it can't. I don't want your mother to get the wrong impression."

"She saw you sneaking into my room at three in the morning. Any impression she needed, she got." Great. That just made me not want to go to his parents' house anymore.

"Take me back home," I whined, knowing that any chance of escape had already vanished.

"Relax. You'll get a 'no babies until graduation' at most from my mom," Cole shrugged as if that was no big deal.

"Do you think jumping out of a moving car would kill me? I don't want to risk surviving this." I asked, making him burst into laughter.

"You're going to be fine. Nothing can hurt you as long as you're with me. I promise." I knew he meant those words.

But little did I know what those words would come to mean.

"Home sweet home," he said, ironically, as he parked the car, and then came to my assistance so I didn't slip on the ice that formed on the steps leading to the front door.

His mother seemed ecstatic to see us, immediately rushing to stuff us with appetizers and home-baked cookies.

But my king didn't seem so thrilled about it. "Since we needed to let go of our cook, my mother has turned into a chef. I told her we could get a new one, but she decided she should continue to torture us."

"Watch your mouth, or I'll have you grounded." Mrs. Clayborne was actually scolding him like a kid.

Pretty fun to watch if you ask me.

"Don't you think I'm too old for you to ground me? Besides, at this point, my room would be a blessing." He spat out a nutshell from one of the cookies he'd just tasted. "Though I'm starting to think you'll be sending me to the dentist and not my room."

"You're not going anywhere. Dinner will be ready soon." She stopped for a second as if something was upsetting her. "I also wanted to wait for your father, but he's not answering his phone."

"What do you mean he's not answering his phone?" Cole's countenance didn't show off any kind of worry, despite the tension brewing in the city. It showed anger.

An almost composed outrage that got him to instantly head toward the door. "Bea, I have to go out for a moment. I'll be right back," he excused himself. Abandoning me again with his mother, he stormed through the door, racing to his car.

I knew it wasn't polite to interfere, yet I couldn't help but ask Mrs. Clayborne. "What happened?"

Her gaze dropped to the floor. "I'm not sure, but it looks like we're having dinner together. Just the two of us."

"Cole said he'd be back."

"If he went after his father, it may take a while. My husband is having some troubles lately." I already knew—gambling troubles—though I couldn't tell her I knew.

I just nodded and helped her set the table, waiting for a few more minutes for dinner to be ready.

"You should come by more often, now that you feel better." Her words struck me like lightning.

How much did she know?

I felt I should've gone through some kind of instruction before paying a home visit to Cole's residence.

"He told you I was in the hospital?" I was surprised that he'd talk about me with his mother.

"Well, I didn't see him for almost a week, so he was forced to," she smiled, knowing she still had the power to make him confess anything.

An awkward pause followed. I wasn't sure exactly what Cole had told her, because I doubted he'd confessed everything.

Did he make something up, or did he tell her what really happened?

My doubt made me look like a fool. I could barely open my mouth to talk, tripping over my words, "I'm... I'm sorry he made you worry about him."

Her eyes suddenly gained a warmth only a mother could show. "I was also worried about you. Your pneumonia seemed serious."

Pneumonia... phew, that's what it was.

"My son slept at the hospital every night," she continued, unknowingly exposing all her *son's* deepest secrets. "Despite appearances, Cole is an introvert."

"An introvert?" I burst into laughter.

What part makes him an introvert?

Being king of the entire university?

Public exposure?

Or perhaps the dirty talk he enjoyed so much?

"I know he doesn't show it." Mrs. Clayborne interrupted my thoughts, cutting through my amusement. "Cole very rarely bonds with people, but when he does, he's like a wolf. He does it for life. He's very careful when it comes to the ones close to him, and even though he's always surrounded by a lot of so-called friends, he doesn't let anyone in." She reached for my hand, giving it a little squeeze. "But you got in, haven't you?"

Maybe she was right, and he was an introvert from certain points of view. Not as much of an introvert as Ferris, but still one in his own way. Just because people were around him didn't make them a part of his life.

Hearing her talk about the hospital took me back to the day I first woke up there. I didn't like to think of that moment, but there was something I was forgetting about that day—Cole's face. His beautiful cobalt eyes were rimmed with exhaustion, barely able to stay open. The dark circles beneath them betrayed all the sleepless nights.

That made me special.

That made me *his.*

The sacrifice he made to look after me was making his

mother's words true. I got into the very depths of his soul.

Mrs. Clayborne was right, Cole didn't return until evening, and when he finally did, he was practically carrying a very intoxicated man on his shoulders—his father.

"I'll put him in the guest room," Cole muttered, dragging Mr. Clayborne a few feet down the hallway before helping him get on the bed.

"I'll take it from here." His mother hurried to follow in his steps and take care of her husband. "Cole, go ahead and have dinner; you must be starving."

"I'm not hungry," he groaned, returning to the living room and throwing himself on the couch in a hopeless attempt to find some relief.

I settled onto the floor beside him. "Are you okay?"

I wanted to know what was wrong. And mostly, I wanted to help him fix whatever it may be.

He ran his hands over his forehead as if trying to sort through the chaos. "I'm okay. I just need a second."

I had an idea about what was going on but couldn't tell for sure. Odds were, his father was gambling again.

"Fucking bastard," he barked a few minutes later, then quickly flashed me an uncomfortable look, like he even forgot I was there. Maybe it was best to leave, but I knew he'd never abandon me that way if the situation was reversed.

Cole needed me, even if he wouldn't say it. And I wasn't going to let him down.

With gentle moves, I lifted my body to hover over him, catching him in an embrace. An embrace that turned into a trip to the couch.

Cole's arms lifted me to join him, keeping me tightly fused to his taut chest.

"Want to talk about it?" I asked, half-expecting silence. Cole wasn't one to open up easily, especially about this.

Yet once again, he surprised me, and his words began spilling, each one heavy with the weight of his pain. "What's there to say? It's always the same story. The same person dragging us down—my father."

"What did he do?" I asked, my voice low and comforting, trying not to push too hard.

"Nothing, except ruin us. I found him using a fake ID in one of Brax's casinos."

"A fake ID? I'm pretty sure he's over twenty-one." I tried to make fun of the circumstances since I couldn't understand why he would fake his identity.

"Brax gave a gambling interdiction on my father's name in all of his casinos. So my dad—brilliant as ever—got a fake ID. I found him wasted, without a single dime in his pockets. Not that he had much money to begin with. But that's not the problem. The problem is that he can't help himself. And that endangers both our family and our plan," Cole's voice was tight with frustration.

"Is there anything you could do about it?" I asked, though I already knew it wasn't that simple.

Cole pushed his head further into the cushions, "First of all, I need to stop Brax from killing him. He was fuming when he found out."

"He won't kill him. More like keep him under supervision. The highly guarded facility type." I tried comforting him, although I wasn't sure I was doing the best job at it. All the time spent around Brax was making me an expert on how he operated. Besides, Cole was his friend, and we still needed his father—at least until Ferris took office. That kept Mr. Clayborne out of the woods for the time being.

Cole let a frown appear on his forehead, his frustration deepening. "Well, he needs as much supervision as he can get. I can't deal with him anymore. I would end up killing him myself."

"Don't talk like that. You'll end up regretting it."

"How is it that he never ends up regretting losing the family money? He got drunk and gambled the money for the utility bills—just because that's only what I took out of my bank account. Fucking idiot. I'm not going back to how I was two months ago. And I'm sure as hell not putting my mother through that again."

I knew exactly what he was talking about. The thought of going back to struggle for a crumb of food sometimes kept me up at night. That's what drove me on and pushed me further to finish my studies. And that's what gave me strength for my plans. "No, you're not going back there. Because you will always be around to stop him from self-destructing."

Cole sighed. "I thought that a public position would bring him to his senses, that this kind of responsibility would get him to wake up. Now he's only one step away from messing this up for us."

"He's not going to mess things up. We're not going to let him. Besides, Ferris will take the lead soon. I'm more afraid of him messing this up for us." I laughed, but the truth beneath my words hung heavy between us.

Cole nodded, a grim agreement in his eyes. "You're probably right. Ferris is going to be difficult to deal with until he gets used to society again. We'll have two *troubles* on our backs."

"We'll handle both of them. One at a time," I said, catching his hand, gently squeezing it. He wasn't alone in this anymore. Neither of us were.

"I still feel I screwed things up with my father being involved in all of this..." he trailed off, feeling responsible for his father's failures.

"You're a good son, Cole. Don't let anyone tell you otherwise. You won't mess things up." We were a team now, ready to support each other.

"I still don't get how things ended up like this. He used to be my fucking hero. I used to believe in him."

"Now it's your turn to be the hero. *I* believe in you." I tightened my arms harder around his chest while his fingers wove through the chocolate strands of my hair. He was transforming from devil to hero, and I was committed to remaining by his side each step of the way.

The night slipped by, leaving us to sleep on the oversized sofa in the embrace of safety and strength. I felt safe in the comfort of his arms while he was drawing from me the energy he needed to keep going.

We'd traveled so far from just lust or just sexual cravings. Sure, those remained as strong as ever, but now, we were building something together. We were building trust, and support, a feeling so indestructible that it was all the fuel we needed to conquer the world.

We were building a future.

CHAPTER 14

I didn't stay for breakfast. Even though supporting Cole was my main priority, I didn't feel that I belonged in the conversations that were to follow between him and his father. Besides, it was bad enough that the ECU would miss its king for a day. It also didn't need to be deprived of its queen, especially with Jason slipping into the enemy corner.

Despite what I was expecting, things were calm back at the university. I was slowly helping Jenna integrate into my end of the lobby. My strategy was to pick a few of the other marginalized girls from the Herd and bring them into the Elite's corner. I needed to start dissolving the hierarchies before my time at ECU would be up, and I wasn't in the habit of giving up on my plans.

I wasn't sure Cole fully agreed with me regarding the necessity of making a difference at the university. But he didn't disagree either, and that was fine by me. He acknowledged that the world we lived in needed a change, and was ready to give up one crown for another. The years of ruling over the students of ECU would soon be over. Ruling beside Ferris and Brax was waiting for him—if we could pull it off.

My lectures were done, and so was I. The night spent in Cole's arms had healed me at an emotional level, but the couch sleepover had ruined my back. Every bone in my body seemed to be aching, and there was only one thing that I could think of to ease my suffering—an afternoon nap in the comfort of my welcoming bed.

There was only one problem. The definition of afternoon *slipped* my mind, and when I finally opened my eyes to wake up, it was 7 p.m.

Who knows for how long I would have slept if a knock on the door hadn't pulled me out of my haze and I realized it was dark outside?

Alfred was the one who kept knocking at my door until I finally answered. "Good evening, Mr. Brax asked you to join him at his villa. He said, and I quote 'Tell her to wear the black dress with crystals'. I'm not sure what he meant by that."

I knew exactly the dress he meant—his first gift. I'd thought he hated that dress along with the mistake he had made by gifting me the gown.

The request felt pretty strange in my opinion, but it was Brax after all. Everything could happen with that man. I just needed to be always on my guard.

"Thank you, Alfred." I bowed my head, realizing that I was daydreaming while keeping the poor man in my doorway. Besides, I had big plans. I wanted to take Brax's breath away —that, without the aid of a knife or gun. I needed to play the seduction card for the night, especially since lately, I felt that I was losing ground in front of him in that category.

As if in a repeat of the night he came to *abduct* me from my dressing room, makeup products, perfumes, and scented lotions were flying all over the place, just in a much more calculated manner. I wanted, whatever this invitation was, to be perfect. It was about time fate would spare a moment for just the two of us.

I couldn't tell exactly why, but I was even more nervous than on our previous date. Maybe because now he wasn't in the room with me, bringing the rush of longing to mix with my anxiety.

Strangely for him, he hadn't given me an exact time to be ready. He probably didn't want me to disappoint him again and be late. I knew all too well how a five-minute delay could get Brax to lose his temper. So, there won't be any five minutes if I don't have an exact time to meet him.

I was finally ready. Well, not ready-ready, more like physically ready, because emotionally, I was a mess. Alfred said Brax was waiting for me at his *villa,* and things didn't work out too well the last two times I paid him a house call. It felt like walking straight into the lion's den; only I turned out to be the tamer—at least that's what I hoped for.

The night was unlike any other. It was well below zero outside, yet somehow the atmosphere was sublime. It had that chilling cold that freezes everything solid, making you long to cuddle beneath extra-fluffy blankets in front of the fireplace. Although, I guess I should have stayed in with Ferris for that because Brax was far from the cuddling type.

The car ride blurred into a dreamlike haze. Images of my kings spun through my mind, and all sorts of emotions were sneaking up to surprise me. I was missing Ferris, eager to get to

Brax, and worrying about Cole, who I was trying to reach but wasn't picking up or returning any of my calls.

I didn't even know how I ended up in front of Brax's door, but there I was, ringing the bell and taking another step into the new part of our lives.

I held out no hope that he would be the one answering— which he didn't. One of his guards let me in, then quickly made sure he could disappear before his boss would decide he was intruding.

With steady steps, I made my way to the living room, trying to take a peek and locate my mobster.

It didn't take long before I found him, sitting on the sofa, eyes fixed on his phone. At least this time, the screen was lit because, if I remember correctly, last time, he was staring at a blank TV.

The scene mirrored the first time I'd come to his house. And that was sending a cold chill down my spine.

Despite the memories flooding my mind, my feet dragged me further across the room until I ended up inches away from Brax, just for him to ignore me completely.

He knew all too well I was there, but the cat-and-mouse game was still coursing through his cells. The pulsing neck vein was betraying his inner turmoil until it could no longer be contained. He eventually stood, acknowledging my presence. No kiss, but no sign of a *you're late* tantrum, so, if I was to translate his gestures, we were on good terms.

"This," he murmured, his eyes darkening as they roamed over me, "was exactly what I imagined when I picked out this dress." He took my hand, spinning me slowly so he could get a better image of how the fine material was arranging itself around my curves.

"So, are you saying that last time it didn't look that good on me?" I chuckled, hoping he would realize that I was only messing around, teasing him. I never knew how far I could push his sense of humor, and I didn't want to end up on the bad side of the radar.

"I can't even remember the *last time.*" He let out a panty-melting smile, then snuck an arm around my waist while his gaze flicked in the opposite corner of the room. "Lucia, you can serve dinner."

I immediately recognized what he was looking at. The same round table for two. Only this time, it didn't lay strewn across the floor with plates and glasses shattered all around it. The crockery was carefully arranged, waiting for dinner to be served.

We'd returned back in time, putting into play a moment that our mistakes let go to waste. Second chances do exist after all, and Brax was asking for just that—maybe not with words, but with actions.

We'd both deprived ourselves of that particular moment, and we were going to make sure it wouldn't slip away again.

Still keeping my hand prisoner in his, he walked me to the table, pulling out my chair so I could take a seat. He was so different from the man I met all those months ago that I was starting to ask myself which was indeed the mask Brax was wearing—the one of the cold-hearted mobster or the one of a tempter, aiming straight to steal my soul.

The atmosphere was so thick, pressing down on me, that I could feel the sting of unshed tears at the back of my throat. I had no idea if it was because of the madness he was creating, restoring a moment we lost, or because I was afraid of the consequences if we should also fail to live it this time around.

"Is this all for me?" I asked, fumbling for words. I was even clumsier than my usual self when it came to Brax, and starting a conversation was by far one of my weak points.

"No, it's only for show. We're actually having Chinese takeout in the back of one of my vans." It seemed Brax had a sense of humor, after all, even though it hid in his sarcasm.

"Such a waste of a dress then." I teased, smoothing its folds with a playful touch.

"Don't worry, the dress will be somewhere on the front seats of the van before we even have time to unwrap the chopsticks," he said, his voice low as he opened a bottle of white wine, and poured us two glasses.

"Hmmm. I see you don't waste any time." I was playing into his game which sounded tempting enough to be explored.

Though it seemed Brax's patience had enough of games. "I've wasted enough time." His words flowed like a river of liquid emotions within my ears, sneaking down my spine, stirring a fluttery sensation in the pit of my stomach.

He immediately froze, like the music had suddenly stopped and only his voice remained, hanging heavy between us. The revelation of the present capturing us in an immortal moment had left us breathless, acknowledging with the magnetic vibrations of our hearts what no words could ever describe.

"Your dinner." A voice that was just background noise to me cut through the moment, saving Brax from himself, returning a drop of the calculated man I used to know back into the room. Lucia was the one who interrupted us, placing two seafood platters on our dinner table. "I put them into the wok for two minutes, just as you said." The woman took a few steps away from where we were seated.

"That will be all for the night, Lucia." Brax gestured for her to leave for home, probably so we could have some privacy and he could offer me his *complete* attention. "Dinner is served." He turned his head toward the plates, ensuring everything looked perfect.

Except I didn't like seafood... It wasn't like I got to eat it every day to get used to it.

The seafood had become scarce because of overfishing and pollution, making it too expensive for anyone living in the Pit.

The first time I had seafood was with Ferris. I couldn't say I liked the taste, so I couldn't understand how someone could pay an Annelid's monthly wage for a single plate of food.

As usual, Brax's sharp observation kicked in, noticing my hesitation. "You don't like it?" he asked with a disappointment that was so uncharacteristic of him.

"It's not that I don't like it. It's just that I don't think I've ever eaten something like this before." I didn't even know why I was so reticent about it. I mean, I've put worse things in my mouth than that.

"You haven't even tried it. Seafood cocktail, herbs, and wine sauce. I guarantee it's delicious." He looked straight my way, waiting for me to take even a bite and see my reaction.

But I had a feeling it wasn't just that. "Did you make it?" I asked, as the revelation just ran through my mind.

And he confirmed my suspicion. "Would it be that impossible?"

"N...no..." I stammered.

Well, yes... as improbable as winning the lottery or the sky opening up and angels singing.

Brax cooking—the thought made me chuckle as I imagined him with an apron and a frying pan... wearing a pair of jeans and a casual shirt. *Or better yet, shirtless?*

Fuck, the thought was making me sweat, not laugh.

"It helps me relax." His voice shattered the image forming in my mind. And it was for the best. I was just about to melt under the table.

"So, are you *relaxed* now?" I murmured, every sinful bone in my body coming alive.

But this was Brax I was talking to—always expect the unpredictable. This time, he didn't play along. "Not really. I'm never relaxed. Just not as tense as usual."

I shared the guilt for a part of that tension. The pressure I'd put on his shoulders weighed even more heavily on him than his own businesses, keeping him always on guard.

I'd better start eating, I thought to myself. Not wanting to put myself in a position where it would seem I would make fun of the effort he put into tonight.

"Just don't think about business tonight." I arranged the food on my plate, preparing the perfect bite.

"Believe me, I won't." A smile that hid a thousand different meanings was shining on his lips while he was paying attention to see if I was enjoying my dish or not.

I just needed to not throw up, and was putting all my effort into it.

I finally took the first bite. A mental cheer played in my head, hoping it could help me eat it with more ease, but it turned out I didn't need it to start with. The dish was amazing. The flavor awakened my senses, stirring an insatiable appetite —just like the man who cooked it.

The dinner conversation dripped with sexual tension, testing our patience and spreading the heated waves of yearning to course through our bodies.

The food was delicious indeed, but I could hardly recall its flavor as his gaze seemed to burn through me, devouring me instead of the meal he'd prepared.

A strange silence set upon the room the instant our forks were set on the plates.

A silence that screamed with the tension between our bodies.

"We also have dessert." He suddenly stood up to walk to what I assumed to be the kitchen.

"I'll help you." I followed him to... well, *help him carry the desert*. Like that could ever be a plausible excuse.

We did end up in the kitchen. The room was large enough to cater to an entire restaurant. Though I didn't have much time to look around as I followed Brax's steps to a side-by-side refrigerator.

"Frozen creamy mocha." He pulled two frosted ice cream cups from the freezer. "And no, I didn't make these."

"I was just about to ask." I giggled. "But caffeine at this hour?"

I'd had a severe coffee addiction before the incident at the governor's house, but the more slowed-down rhythm I had adopted lately got me to quit the crazy amounts of caffeine.

However, Brax seemed to think I would need it. "Caffeine is good. I plan to keep you up for a while." Threat or promise, his words rushed straight to that throbbing place below my waist, igniting it to the very limits of my resistance.

Of course, I said nothing in return. None of my neurons seemed to be firing at that moment. I just turned my attention to the TV that was on, from where some slow tune was playing.

"Lucia probably left that on." Brax immediately observed the direction of my focus.

"I love this song. Such a shame no one is dancing to it."

"Is it, now?" He abandoned what he was doing, clasping my waist until my fragile arms snuck around his broad neck.

The lyrics were moving us with dreamlike steps, melting the world around us.

I never knew I was alive until I met you,

I never knew the eternal night could end somehow.

"I never..." I started laughing since I was about to complete the song's lyrics. "I never thought you could be so romantic."

"Don't tell anyone, or I'll have to kill you." He didn't stop dancing, just tilted his head toward my own so he could crash his lips on mine. "And by the way... I'm done with the romance." His palms passionately grasped my waist, pulling me so close to his body that I could feel the effect this evening was having on him. The bulge in his pants was threatening to break the material free, pressing against me with a calling that raised unbearable anguish below my waist.

I didn't have the chance to react before he swept me off my feet, lifted me to wrap my legs around his waist, and carried me to the real lion's den—his bedroom.

The power of his steps as he was walking raised something unknown within me. It was primal, born of basic instincts, and shaped by all lessons we had learned along the way. He was the modern caveman, finally claiming his woman.

I landed between fluffy pillows, floating on the bed that smelled like him, his presence enveloping all my senses. He soon found his place, towering over me, caging my body between the strong pillars of his arms.

Moments had passed, yet he didn't continue, stealing the stealth of the night and glancing at me through the darkness. I could still feel his inner turmoil. The fight was far from being over, as the sounds of the battle were still echoing in his mind. Yet this time, I held the ultimate weapon. I offered a second chance of the purest happiness in a world where that particular essence was scarcer than gold.

He growled, biting on my lower lip, as his lips crashed to mine while he was searching for my dress zipper, causing my outfit to slip off the bed.

He was staring again, although, in the black of the night, it was almost impossible to distinguish anything.

Maybe that's exactly why he turned on the dim lamp beside his bed.

"What's wrong?" I quivered, convinced that I'd done or said something wrong, making our past return to haunt him.

"Nothing, just stay still." He kissed the words onto my lips, moving his hands to unclasp the straps of my bra.

I was naked to the waist while his mouth abandoned me again, and he came to rest on one arm, studying every inch of my body.

I suddenly felt too exposed, like he was looking at much more than my flesh, glancing straight into the depths of my soul.

A single gesture changed the dynamic of everything.

His hand didn't mold on my breasts but traveled somewhere below my left one, beneath my heart.

I recognized the place he was searching for. It was the spot where I had one of the largest cuts on my body. I couldn't remember what caused it, but I could remember the pain it had provoked.

"I recall this one. I kept my hand on it to stop it from bleeding." There was a silent agony in his voice as he spoke, while his eyes couldn't stop roaming my skin. "Your bruises are almost gone. But the scars remain." His fingers glided over my skin, seeking to ease my pain.

I wanted to cover myself, embarrassed that he was paying more attention to my scars than to the moment we were sharing.

Was I that ugly, tattooed with the violet marks that told the story of my dauntlessness?

"It's okay, Bea. I just need to see that all wounds are gone. I guess my mind needs to convince itself. You suffered so many injuries before I could get to you that I didn't think you would make it." His head tilted so his lips would melt against the side of my stomach. "I just need to feel they're gone," he continued, ascending to kiss the places I'd been hurt.

To my surprise, he remembered perfectly the map of my skin, tracing each cut and each former bruise to the point I was beginning to think I should inflict some injuries on myself just so he could do it all over again.

The moment was sublime, bonding the strength of our connection to unimaginable limits.
The urges of our bodies could no longer be controlled, and his need to heal me had to be replaced with more sensual gestures. He was heading toward *other* ways of caring for me. I quickly realized that as my panties disappeared and his head lost itself between my thighs.

I immediately arched against the bed, dazzled by the sheer force he was pushing my hips to open with. He was right; we had no time to waste, so with a primal snarl, his lips found *mine.*

I couldn't help myself other than to allow my fingers to slide through the raven strands of his hair, grasping them with the strength that was reflecting each one of his movements.

He was doing something unnatural to my body. I had no idea what, but I felt like I was exploding and fainting at the same time. A circular movement, combined with the gentle nipping of my clit with his teeth, made me purr his name as I gathered the sheets around me in a useless attempt to withstand him. I didn't stand a chance against him. He was too strong, and I, too weak to stop the inevitable.

I felt that coil of tormenting heat flowing straight to my core as he was drilling me with the magical power of his tongue. He danced across the sensitive bundle of nerves, making them shudder in an unrelenting surge of waves of ecstasy.

I was lost, falling prey to the spasms ravaging my body. I was floating somewhere in the room, eyes tightly closed, hoping that there was a way to endure a full night with him.

I was still fighting the remains of my orgasm when I felt him easing himself into me with his throbbing cock. The gesture left me eyes-wide-open to look straight into the dark green shade of his own as he leaned to hover over me.

The light was gone, though I had no idea how or when it happened. I was just trying to discover him through the darkness until all shadows cleared, and he was left as the only silhouette that could ever make sense to me.

It was so much more than body on body. It was destiny

crushing against destiny, with each thrust, changing the perspective of our worlds. He wasn't holding back—not from seeking the pleasure of my flesh, but in living the moment to its full extent. Nothing mechanical, just passion-driven movements meant to convey every unspoken word between us.

We were losing ourselves between kisses and moans, gliding through the sheets as we were transforming them in the sparkles of a firestorm.

It was astonishing... until he stopped.

His eyes were tightly closed like he was fighting off the demons that were still demanding total freedom. He wasn't a man who could be tied in any way to someone.

A moment of panic flew through me, knowing too well what that meant. I was losing him.
He was slipping back into the shadows.

My fingers clenched into his arms as if I could do anything to prevent him from leaving.

I would have given a piece of my heart to prevent him from leaving. Though if he was to have gone through with it, he would have taken my heart along with him as well.

But then his eyes opened. A golden ring framed the absinthe green, making it shine in the darkness of the night.

"Look at me," he breathed, even if his words had no use. I was already subdued to his spell, glancing straight into the magic of his emerald orbs.

His gaze was so incredibly different than before. He wanted

me to look at him so I would know that he was there. That every gesture held so much more than animalistic pleasure.

Yes, it was dominance.

Yes, he was claiming me.

But his reasons were completely different this time around. I wasn't just a piece of his collection anymore. I was the piece he couldn't live without.

While on the other hand, I was investing so much in him.

Submission.

Faith.

Love.

If he still wanted to crush me, he would succeed this time around. My soul was as vulnerable as my body. Grasping at his back, neck, arms; with the last remnants of my strength to keep my body as close to his as he claimed my soul.

Loud groans were being ripped from his lungs as the bed seemed one step away from disintegrating, every nut and bolt threatening to snap under the force of his hips digging into mine. Pleasure built up with every grind across my channel while one of his hands slid between us to capture the all too treacherous part of my body—my clit. Tingles of something unreal ignited at the first brush of his finger, need bursting through my entire nervous system as I felt that if he wouldn't stop circling that damn nub, I would faint beneath him. I wanted to beg him to stop, but the conflict within me made his touch too good to give up. Every movement sent me closer to a place I yearned to be, even if my arrival would mean I'd fall into bits and pieces.

I felt myself tightening around him while the intensity of his kisses increased alongside the force of his thrusts. Harder and harder, until my whimpers began drowning down his throat, mingling with the sweetest misery I had ever known.

Acknowledging my distress, he slowed down for a split second, allowing me time to breathe, only so he could take my breath away the next moment.

He pulled me against him so tightly that I was beginning to think I would break when one of his hands slid to grasp the nape of my neck. The intrusion of my senses continued in a show-off of strength and skills, moving so deeply that I was under the impression he was reaching for the pit of my stomach.

He was consuming the moment, and he was consuming me with such eros that no mask could ever find its way between us.

My groans betrayed my impending release, his free hand ran to intertwine with my chocolate locks. He was close as well, and the signs of his hitched breath only managed to increase my heartbeats.

I wanted to see that pleasure run through him. The unhindered passion he pushed back for too long.

Though before he could succumb to ecstasy, my body took me by surprise, giving up on me. I was shuddering again while every single one of his muscles tensed only to roar a few throated groans of his release.

Brax never broke the kiss. He didn't let me slip away from

his arms either, just pulled me beside him as if I were a snowflake nestled against his chest.

"Are you sleeping here with me?" The foolish girl, full of insecurities, had to ask. No matter how hard I tried, I couldn't mask that thought, especially since I knew he didn't like sharing a bed.

Maybe I needed a vocal confirmation that I wasn't dreaming, or maybe I was just hurt for so long that I could no longer tell real feelings from illusion.

"Why would I not?" Brax asked, though he knew too damn well the answer to that question.

"I don't want this to be like the pool." My greatest fear slipped out, leaving me defenseless at his mercy... just so he could wipe all anxiety away.

"It won't. You have my word." His confession imprinted itself in my brain, writing the last page of my kings' path to redemption. "I won't let you go."

We remained in silence. Any other words felt useless. I knew who I was, and I finally knew who he was. Final pieces that were completing a much larger puzzle.

I had felt betrayed by my kings for so long that I once thought I could never recover. But they weren't betraying me. They were only betraying their own souls.

All masks had fallen. It was time for a new destiny to unfold.

They were fucking gods. And they had just made me their goddess.

CHAPTER 15

No matter how much we wished to stop time for a few more hours, the night had passed, and so did the morning. Brax refused to get out of bed or even let me slip through the sheets and stray away from him. But the world wasn't going to wait for us, and his phone caught a life of its own, making the nightstand vibrate with incoming calls and texts.

"Fuck..." he muttered, struggling to open his eyes. "Reality..." He let a large arm fall over me like a lazy bear waking from hibernation, somehow managing to pick up his phone along the way.

He just swiped to unlock it, glancing over my shoulder to see who dared to bother him. And it looked like absolutely everyone—guards, a few officials, even Ferris had called him.

"I have to..." For the first time, he was trying to explain himself to me.

Things had changed!

"I know." And I did know how difficult it must've been to

walk in his shoes every single day. He wasn't leaving because he wanted to. He was leaving because he needed to.

That made all the difference in the world.

"You can stay for as long as you want." He fused his lips to my shoulder blade, probably already regretting the moment he would walk out the door.

But I had an agenda of my own. "I need to go too. I want to check up on Cole. He wasn't answering my calls last night."

"Another issue on my to-do list," Brax snarled, attempting to summon enough courage to get out of bed.

With a swift move, he stood up, but so did I. The only difference was I remained in the middle of the bed, dressed in just a sheet.

That made Brax instantly arch an eyebrow, lifting the corner of his mouth into a smile. "You're not helping."

"You do need to be punished for your past actions." I let the bed sheet fall, then slowly—and I mean *slowly*—went on to search for my dress.

"Don't tempt me. I've never been one to follow orders. So, your chances of success are pretty low. While mine—"

"Yours are to get dressed and go to work." I pressed a soft kiss on the cheek. He might not know it yet, but I had every chance of succeeding.

"You're only safe because I'm pretty sure something's gonna catch on fire if I don't leave right now. But that doesn't mean I'm done with you. I'll make you pay." His threat was arousing me much more than frightening me.

"If my payment will be a repeat of last evening, then I can't wait." I wrapped my arms around the black ink of his shoulders, rushing to give him a make-up kiss.

I couldn't afford to have a mafia boss angry at me, could I?

"There will be many of *last evening,* and many more *last nights.* You have my word." I knew what that meant. His word weighed more than money in our world. It was about the one thing he valued most—honor.

We both needed to leave and if my intention was to look for Cole, the moment I arrived back at Ferris's mansion, I understood I would have to look no further. His car was parked outside, and I found him in the main room on the first floor, apparently entertaining himself.

"I've been worrying about you, and you've been here all along?" I muttered, spotting him and Ferris playing on the PlayStation.

"Brax told me you were going to see him. I didn't want to ruin your evening." Cole stopped the game, tossing his controller onto the couch beside him.

That seemed to also ruin Ferris's game. "It couldn't wait one minute? I was kicking his ass," he muttered, visibly displeased that he didn't get a chance to win.

"The fuck you were." Cole turned off the TV, throwing the remote control next to the controller and letting his head fall on the couch's backrest.

He was not in good form, and I didn't exactly know how to

handle the situation.

Luckily, Ferris decided to save the day. "Can you go and see if Sebastian still wants to go to the auto show?" he asked, grabbing his phone.

"Shit, I forgot all about that." Between everything that was going on, I was neglecting my family.

"Don't worry, I got you covered." Ferris gave me a wink, insisting on playing hero.

"You're going outside the mansion?" I was a little shocked that he'd willingly leave the estate without a blade hanging over his head.

He let a gallant smile tug at the corner of his lips, as he turned the TV back on. "I don't need to go outside the mansion to do that."

I'd completely forgotten about his private auto collection.

"Rematch." Ferris threw the control back to Cole as I left to prepare my brother for the grand garage tour.

While Seb was getting ready, I also showered and changed. The black dress I still had on from my dinner with Brax was a little too much for a normal night, even for Ferris's chateau.

I changed my outfit, a baby-doll dark violet dress. I already felt like I was suffocating since there was a slight chance I would find a solution to Cole's problems. I felt constrained enough that I couldn't do much to help him, so I didn't want to also feel constrained by any clothes.

Ferris and Cole were in the same room when I returned

with Sebastian. They were just finishing off another video game, although it was much more similar to a game of supremacy than just simple entertainment.

"Eat shit, sucker. The Coleminator is ruling this show." Cole couldn't resist rubbing the victory in Ferris's face.

And my king of darkness didn't seem to take defeat lightly. "You only fucking won because my mind was occupied thinking about taking Sebastian to the garage."

Cole powered off the console with a smirk. "Fuck off, you're just a sore loser."

"I'm going to let this slip just because I know you're having a bad day." Ferris wasn't the type to ever be defeated, and neither was Cole. That's what you get when putting two alpha males into a room. Luckily, Brax wasn't here too—it would have turned into a full-blown massacre.

"I'm out of here. Let's go, Seb." Ferris didn't wait for a reaction from Cole; he just grabbed my brother and headed for the door.

Cole and I were left to drift in a burdening silence, looking at each other and expecting the other to speak first.

I knew damn well that he wouldn't be the one to start the conversation, especially with his nerves still wound tight.

"Mind if I sit?" I asked, stepping closer to the sofa.

"Is that even a question? Come here." He extended his arms, guiding me to land straight into his lap instead of the couch.

"You seemed kind of angry a few minutes ago," I observed, following his request and sitting where he indicated.

"I'm never angry when it comes to you." He cast off a smile but it was more bitter than sweet.

"Said the man who thrived on my terror." I was reminding him of the past at the worst possible time. "How are things with your dad?"

"Except for the fact that he's an idiot, I have everything under control. I just wished I didn't need to watch his back with every step he takes. It should have been the other way around. You know?"

My head came to rest against his chest. "Yea, I do." I knew too well what he was saying, and in my case, the scenario was much worse than his when it came to the male parental figures.

"Shit, of course, you do." He forgot all about my own father for a second.

"That's okay. I got used to the idea a while ago."

"Still, I could see that it bothered you. And that's the last thing that I want. Let's just not talk about it anymore. At least for the night. I've had enough of my father as is." Without giving me a heads up, he lifted me off his waist until my feet landed to straddle him between my thighs. "I just want you to be with me."

"I *am* with you." I shrugged, surprised he still didn't understand that I'd be with him every single step of the way.

But I was starting to think he did understand after all...

He raised an eyebrow, making it clear that *being with him* meant something entirely different than what I first assumed.

"You mean h... here?" I babbled.

Did he want to have sex on the couch?

He clasped his hands on my waist, positioning me directly on top of his throbbing cock. "Here, Mouse."

I pouted slightly, knowing exactly where this was headed. "I thought you needed to talk."

"I don't need to talk. I need to feel." His hands glided beneath my dress, advancing upwards on my thighs.

"Is that so? You think sex will make all your problems disappear?" I asked, my tone edged with displeasure.

"They won't disappear. But they'll tone down. You'll heal me with your magic puss." His hand rushed to draw a straight line in the middle of my panties, down to the center of my core.

"Jesus, Cole!" I gasped, unprepared for what he wanted of me.

Not that he took my reticence seriously. "You'll be saying *Jesus*, all right."

"Can you stop?" I tried to get up but without any success.

"I'm just getting started." I felt his hand running to unbuckle his belt, freeing his length to press against my panties. Maybe sex would get his mind off things after all. So, how could I resist helping him out?

The atmosphere was quickly escalating, his burning gaze was the fuel needed to make me burst into flames. It hid devastating lust, but beneath that, it held a tormenting need. He needed to forget, if only for just a second, and I was going to help him do just that.

The full size of his lower lip disappeared between his teeth the moment he felt me move on top of him, lifting myself slightly so he could find room to sneak his hand between my thighs.

With expert precision, he tugged my lace panties aside, sending two of his fingers to glide through the slick evidence of my arousal.

"So fucking wet," he growled, jolting his lips toward mine while his fingers kept roaming the sensitive skin of my folds.

It took only a swift move for him to slip himself inside me, grinding on my walls to a painful limit.

My body tensed instinctively, overwhelmed by the sudden intrusion, but as soon as the sharp pangs subsided, I began moving against him with unrestrained urgency.

I wanted to feel him in every way possible. I wanted him to submerge in the depths of my core, the same way I wanted him to find peace in the depths of my soul.

My hips found a life of their own, grinding against him to coax each delightful groan from his lungs. I yearned to watch his breath falter, to know that from this moment on, his every thought would be of me.

Searching for the round shape of my nipple, he tugged down the upper part of my dress until his mouth found its prize.

Like a dragon, his warm breath melted my skin while one of his hands slipped to the small of my back, guiding me to close the distance between us.

I let him sink deeper and deeper, my hips swaying against him in slow, rhythmic movements, finding the exact pace I needed to lead me to ecstasy. And if that wasn't enough, one of his hands slid back beneath my dress, reaching directly for my clit.

For a second, I froze, unable to keep moving on top of him and utterly incapable of withstanding the overwhelming sensation of his touch.

Cole noticed, and secured me even tighter with his free hand, continuing to move my body with the force of his muscles. I was his puppet in a tantalizing show. A puppet that he was determined to drive to scream in pleasure.

His plan succeeded, and before I realized what was happening, I was biting his shoulder, trying to make as little noise as possible.

"Take that hand out of there, or I will kill you." I was making a direct threat, feeling his fingers relentlessly rubbing on my already tortured clit.

Although my warning made Cole burst into laughter, my threat seemed to have worked, and his hand left to secure itself on the free side of my waist.

With even stronger moves, he was crashing me against him, drawing out the last remains of my ecstasy. My vision blurry, the pressure in my body so intense I thought I was about to pop a vessel. Yet *the torture* felt so incredibly amazing.

I was clenching onto his neck as if my life depended on it when he finally found his release.

I think I was probably more dead than alive, barely able to move, let alone stand.

But no time for cuddling or sweet words.

Ferris's voice shattered the newly settled silence, making me shudder from within.

"How is it that I'm always the only one that only gets to watch?" His tone hovered between amusement and irritation. But it was soon left only with the amused part, as he noticed me shaking from all joints, struggling to rearrange my dress.

"Where... where's Seb?" I asked, frightened that he also might be around.

"Alfred needed to go into town for some parts for my cars, so I let them take the Bugatti for a spin," Ferris replied, a hint of pride lurking in his voice for showing my brother such a good time.

And he wasn't the only one having a good time. "Just them?" I asked, still rearranging my clothes while Cole was doing who knows what behind me.

"Them, and an army of my bodyguards. Relax... and don't change the subject." Ferris said, his tone carrying a slight warning. This conversation was about to get interesting.

"The subject?" I quivered, completely unprepared to discuss anything about *the subject.*

"You seem to be in trouble, Mouse." Cole had an amused tone. I didn't get to ask why he found this so funny—he just kissed the side of my neck and made his way to the door.

"You're leaving?" I called out, my nerves ready to explode.

"You're in good hands. I guarantee it. Just scream if you need help." I could hear the seductive vibe in Cole's voice while I had no idea what he was talking about.

We just had sex, and he was leaving me all alone to deal with all the rest!

Was he?

I guess he was, because the next thing I knew, the door closed behind him, leaving me alone with the prince of darkness—Ferris.

I couldn't even begin to explain what I was feeling.

Anger.

Embarrassment.

But mostly, a strange tingle running through the back of my neck straight to the aching need between my thighs. I couldn't exactly tell if Ferris's face reflected irritation or impatience. One thing was for sure. It was reflecting lust.

The same lust I felt still flowing through my body. There

was something seriously wrong with me.

"Cole seems to be feeling better." Ferris's observation brought a fiery red color to flush my cheeks.

How in the world could I respond to that?

My gaze dropped to the ground, hoping it would open somehow and swallow me whole.

Yet, Ferris wasn't willing to cut me any slack on this one. "Is it his father you were talking about?"

"He didn't want to talk about his father," I managed to mumble.

"It looked to me like he didn't want to talk at all." The devious arch of his eyebrow was letting me know exactly what he meant.

"I should go back to my room." I tried excusing myself to get out of there as quickly as possible.

Although Ferris begged to differ. "No, you shouldn't." He was throwing the words at me like pointed arrows.

There was no doubt that I was in trouble.

I just didn't know how much trouble I was in.

And Cole... he was going to pay for abandoning me there to deal alone with the nerve-wracking humiliation alone.

"Come here, Bea." Ferris rested one of his hands on the fireplace mantle and turned his gaze to look at the orange flames.

My initial instinct was to run—to just crawl under my bed where I could die of embarrassment.

But I couldn't ignore his calling, especially since I had guilt written all over me.

With shaky steps, I made my way to where he stood.

He didn't move an inch. Just stood there watching the dancing flames while my heart began to pound so loudly that I was beginning to think he might hear it.

Was I being punished, or maybe just teased? I couldn't tell any longer, but his attitude was instilling a nervous tremor to run deep within my veins.

Mimicking his stance, I stopped to watch the fluid movement of the flames. They were mesmerizing, alluring, seducing me with their demonic grace—immortal, devastating yet altogether indispensable.

The strongest characters are forged in the strength of the flames; Ferris was forged in the strength of the flames. I could feel his unearthly connection with the fire, and it was exactly that connection that drew us together.

I felt one of his hands coil around the small of my back with snakelike movements, his entire form towering behind me.

He didn't even feel human.

He was as mystical as the flickering of the flames we were admiring.

An uncontained groan betrayed his distress, and I could feel the tip of his nose nuzzle through the curtain of my hair, just like an insatiable wolf sniffs out his prey.

My thighs squeezed together as an unhindered response to his gesture, waiting breathlessly for his next move. I expected something suave, something gentle, like the lips that just found their way over the curve of my neck. Instead, his hand wrapped around the full volume of my hair, grabbing it into a tight ponytail. Driven by pure lust, he pulled my head back, pressing me against a black skull that was majestically illustrated on his shoulder.

"I'm not sure what to make of what I just witnessed," he said as I felt the passion of his mouth roaming the side of my neck. "But I'm sure I need a closer look." His free hand lunged straight below my waist, gripping my pussy so forcefully that I almost lost balance.

It bordered on pain, yet was far closer to euphoria.

"What are you doing?" I quivered, afraid that he might lose it again. Although he wasn't anywhere near letting himself run back to his demons.

This time, he had full control of his actions, and I was just about to find out how that specific control would manifest itself on me.

"What does it look like I'm doing?" His hand clenched harder on my flesh until I felt my knees melt into a pool of anguishing need. His body gave me the support I needed to still stand, yet the dangerous closeness found the throbbing shape of his longing.

I knew exactly what he was doing.

He wanted me.

He wanted me right there, in the same room where I just had sex with Cole.

Maybe he was mad, or maybe it was a power play between my kings, but my body was already waiting for him.

"What does it look like I'm doing, Bea?" He repeated the question, assuring himself that I'd answer this time.

"You want revenge?" I wasn't even sure why I said it, but there was a grey shadow hovering over each one of his gestures.

"I don't want revenge." He lifted my dress over my waist, pushing down my panties over my knees. "I just want you to purr for me as you did for Cole." I could feel the tip of his cock slipping through Cole's and I's combined release. "Think you could do that?" He slipped inside in just one move, jabbing himself as far as he could go.

I couldn't hold back a gasp as he withdrew completely, only to thrust back in, stretching me in painful pleasure. And then he did it again, and again, until I felt the movement somehow raw, animalistic, trying to take everything I had to give.

A shattering vibration reverberated throughout my body, driving me to seek support against the fireplace.

I needed to hold on to something. Anything to withstand him.

My palms braced against the mantel while he still kept a grip on my hair, drawing my head so far back that I could look him in the eyes.

A kiss took me by surprise as I'd become so arched that I thought my spine was about to crack under the pressure.

It was the perfect kind of pain, soothed by the tantalizing assault of his lips.

I had no idea if it was a punishment or if he was just having fun. Either way, whatever I did to get there, needed to be repeated.

I barely held my ground as I was propelled toward the fire. But the lightening of delirium flashing through me made me break the kiss and let my head fall forward, eyes staring into the flames. They seemed to have escaped the fireplace and snuck straight inside my body, lighting me up in futile attempts to grind against my king.

Seeking ultimate pleasure, he reached to expose my breasts, catching one of them in his palm and squeezing so forcefully that it made me cry out. I was ravaged by vicious rapture as the blend of his thrusts, the silent pain, and the warmth of the flames caressing my free breast made all contact unbearably intense. The rapture crept over me, igniting my every cell as if I was about to transform into something unearthly.

I felt myself clasping around him so tightly that I was under the impression I was about to break him, and if I had any doubts, the roar of pleasure escaping his lungs assured me he was moments away from his own ecstasy.

His grip on my hair tightened again, turning my head to the side so he could sneak his tongue inside my mouth as his thrusts gained an incredible velocity. The kiss was as fierce as the act itself, his tongue piercing clinking against my teeth at the same pace his cock was pounding inside of me.

It was all too much. The fire was leaving me defenseless, while Ferris's relentless intrusion wasn't allowing me even a single moment to unwind, constantly needing to fight the explosions devastating my body.

Stripping me of all strength seemed to be his ultimate goal.

I thought we were going to tear the chimney apart—until I couldn't even hold on to it. I felt myself slipping away, being supported only by the power of his arms. The orgasm almost brought me to my knees, and as much as Ferris might have liked that position, I could barely stay conscious.

The room started spinning, and I was on the verge of blacking out when, with a few more thrusts, I felt him coating my inner walls between loud growls.

"Did you faint on me back there?" The arrogant satisfaction he was feeling couldn't be withheld as he turned me to face him.

"I slipped." I knew I was lying, and he knew I was lying, but I wasn't going to admit to anything.

Maybe Cole was right—I was a prude.

"How about after dinner, I take you to my bedroom and make you *slip* a couple of times more?" He tilted his head to gently merge his lips with mine. But that didn't excuse his arrogance or the fact that he made me die of embarrassment after he saw me with Cole.

"Hold that thought... for a *couple of days more.* Jenna is coming here later for a sleepover."
That definitely burst his bubble.

He cursed something beneath his breath, biting my lip to show off his wrath on my treacherous plans. Still, he didn't break off the kiss, keeping me wrapped in his arms until Alfred made his way into the room to announce dinner.

It was a hell of a merry-go-round I had jumped myself into, but Cole's adrenaline rush, Ferris's pain mixed with beautiful darkness, and Brax's unmatched emotions would never let me return to a normal life.

And who gets to say what's normal or not, anyway?

For me, this was normality.

For me, this was perfection.

CHAPTER 16

A sleepover with Jenna.

A little white lie to tone down Ferris's ego.

I guess that was the problem with my kings—their unmatchable egos and uncontested will to always have things done their way.

Ferris wasn't going to receive any bedtime from me for the day, so calling Jenna to ask her over actually seemed like a good idea.

It was a little last-minute, but she couldn't say no to some girl time, especially since we didn't have the chance to talk in what seemed like forever.

I sent a cab to retrieve her from her home and bring her to the base of the Hills, where the limo Ferris put at my disposal picked her up. I couldn't send the limo directly to the Pit—it would have brought too much attention to her place, and attention down there can get you in trouble. Still, I wanted her to travel in style, at least for as long as it was possible, especially since I knew she loved the limo rides we used to share.

"What happened?" was the first thing she asked as she entered the main door.

"Well, hello to you too." I walked over to her and caught her fragile body in a hug.

"Sorry, I thought something was wrong. It felt a little last-minute for a sleepover," she said, extending her arms to respond to my embrace.

"I have to admit it was a bit of a last-minute thing. Wasn't sure you'd come," I smiled, a little embarrassed for using her as an excuse to escape Ferris, although it wasn't just that. I also wanted to spend time with her.

"What do you mean? What are best friends for?"

"Don't really know. Never had one before you." I was being honest. I never had true friends. More like acquaintances.

"Well, you have one now." The kindness in her voice was letting me know she was honest. It wasn't about money, or me living in the Hills. It was purely about friendship, and since I was enjoying a better life now, so would she.

"I know... let's go into the kitchen and get ourselves something to eat." I wasn't good at sharing emotions. Even when I knew how I felt, getting the words out was difficult. My trust issues kept me from expressing myself, but sometimes gestures meant more than words.

"I thought you were having dinner when you texted me."

"I didn't get to eat that much." The truth was, I held back at dinner because I knew Jenna wouldn't want to eat alone. "Come on, it's Greek night. You wouldn't believe the moussaka the chef made. None of my clothes are going to fit if I keep this up."

"Hahaha, you don't have to worry; I'll take that burden off your hands. Not sure my whole house would be enough to fit your clothes, though," Jenna chuckled.

"Or you could take one for the team and eat my portion too." I shrugged, pushing the kitchen double doors open.

Jenna looked straight at the rotating display of cakes and chocolates that greeted anyone who walked through the doors. "Jesus, no wonder you're afraid of putting on a few pounds."

"I try not to look at them, or else I'd be tempted to live in here. Come on, dessert after dinner. That moussaka has to be around here somewhere." I was searching the countertops to figure out where Alfred hid the rest. "Ahh, the oven." I finally found the lost treasure.

No need to mention that we stuffed our faces until we could barely walk back to my room. Jenna decided to bring along some of her new cake friends from the rotating display, just in case. There was a slim chance we could have a few more bites without fainting.

I was just searching my dressing room for a new set of pajamas for her to wear when a knock on the door interrupted me.

My first instinct was to tell Jenna to open the door and let whoever it was in, but if she could handle Cole and even

Ferris, with Brax, it was a whole different story.

"Come in." I rushed out of the dressing room to see who was visiting me. "Ferris!" I couldn't hide my surprise, especially since he knew Jenna was going to be here and he didn't like interacting with other people, except for his close circle of friends.

Maybe that changed somehow. "Guess what I brought you two," he said, without bothering to introduce himself while keeping both hands behind his back.

"I'm a little nervous when it comes to your gifts," I whispered, with a laugh as I remembered how he gifted me the phone and, a few days later, the little vibrating *thingy.*

"This one is innocent. I promise. Not sure about the next one though." He chuckled, bringing his hands to the front, along with a brown paper bag.

"I recognize that bag! But how?" I was surprised he remembered the small cake shop we visited during our road trip in the Pit.

"I went to the Pit, to one of Brax's clubs. He needed some cash for... you know." *Paying off the Annelids leaders to keep low and let my kings take power.* I got the message even if he couldn't say the rest of the sentence out loud with Jenna there. Best friend or not, it was something too important to risk.

"Brax's clubs?" My mind raced straight to the room with a glass wall. The thought of Ferris going there was having an unwanted effect on me.

It must've shown on my face because he quickly moved to clarify. "I know what you're thinking. I didn't go to the basement."

Ferris was a mind reader, after all.

"Now open it. I got the best ones." He waved the bag teasingly in front of my now hungry eyes.

"I'm surprised there's even anything left in the bag." I laughed, snatching the paper bag to see what he'd brought us.

"Let's just call it bag number four." Ferris rolled his eyes. "Alfred and Cole were also on my list."

"There's still one unaccounted for." I laughed again, knowing exactly where those cakes went.

"I lost that on the way to my car." He wasn't even putting in the effort to properly lie to me.

"You still have some strawberry frosting on your nose." I was only fooling around, but that didn't mean he didn't check, wiping his face, just in case. "Gotcha!"

"You think you're funny? Just wait until I get you alone." He was making a threat. One that I couldn't help but look forward to.

Unfortunately, his teasing made Jenna feel uncomfortable. "I don't want to be imposing."

"You're not imposing," he rushed to explain himself. "As a matter of fact, I wanted to talk to you about something."

"To me?" Jenna was stuttering. She seemed confused about what Ferris had to say. And so was I.

"Yes, to you. Bea told me your father lost his job."

"Yes... the company where he used to work shut down." I could still read the sorrow in her eyes as she spoke. Life had weighed on her so heavily, she'd come to accept it as a daily routine.

"Maybe I could fix that somehow. Call him, tell him to go to Ayers Enterprises in the morning—the HR department. I'm pretty sure they'll find something for him there," Ferris said in a certain tone, as if this was already a done deal.

"You would do that?" The surprise in Jenna's voice betrayed the fact that life didn't give her many opportunities like the one Ferris was presenting.

"Just make sure he votes for the right man." Ferris cast off a benevolent smile, trying to make her think that it was a trade, not an act of charity.

But I knew better than that. And that's exactly why I threw my arms around his neck to merge my lips with his. "You're a good man," I whispered, meaning every word.

"No, I'm not. I'm actually expecting *you* to pay me back for my good deed," he teased, biting my lower lip.

"All these threats, Mr. Ayers... I'll need to see them put into practice," I whispered back, not ready to let go.

He gave me a few more pecks on the lips while blaming me for my own misery. "You're... the one" *kiss* "who decided" *kiss* "not to see them acted on tonight." *Kiss* "Your loss."

"Well, it wouldn't have given you the chance to do the

good deed I'm now supposed to pay for, would it?" I was twisting his words only to tease him.

"I was bound to remember about Jenna's dad at some point. I wanted to tell you from the day I first found out. Just had a lot on my mind... you know I wasn't feeling well," his voice was saddened, the weight of what he'd put me through evident.

"I know." I snuck in one last kiss on his cheek, getting ready to return to the real world... especially since I had company.

Ferris was also preparing to go back to his den. "I should get going. I don't want to take up your girl time. And one last thing... I'm open to loans without interest. Just don't sell any of the diamonds for the price of second-quality glass again." He must've thought he was funny, yet Jenna couldn't help but feel embarrassed. I could see the most awkward expression forming on her face.

"It's okay. He's just kidding about the diamonds." I tried to comfort her since she probably couldn't make out the difference between when Ferris was serious and when he was joking. Not that he had chosen the right subject to be joking about. "Let's resume the pajama hunt. I think there's a bottom shelf I haven't devastated yet."

I led her back to the dressing room to continue our pajama search.

"I can sleep in any old T-shirt and shorts if you can't find the pajamas. I'm not really picky." Jenna giggled, taking a seat on a small footstool to wait for me to find the needle in a haystack.

"Got it." A new pajama set caught my eye.

Though I didn't get to speak another word as another knock on the door interrupted me.

"What now?" I muttered, heading back to the room to answer.

"*What now?*" Brax raised an annoyed eyebrow the second I opened the door.

He overheard me.

"I thought it was someone else,"—the dumbest apology I could come up with.

"Someone else? Were you expecting *someone else?*"

"Ferris was just here." I shrugged. It wasn't like Ferris and I had anything to hide.

"I'm changed." Jenna walked out of the dressing room, just to turn around and walk right back in the very next second. "Sorry."

"It's okay, you can come out." I called out to her.

Brax might be the big bad wolf, but I'd managed to tame him a bit over the last week or so.

"This is my friend, Jenna." I tried to make some introductions, but the next second, Brax pulled me out in the lobby and shut the door behind us. "Well, that was rude," I mumbled.

No answer.

Just a snarl right before he crashed me on the wall, driving his mouth to join mine like a tidal wave crashing on the rocks on the shore. He was asking for so much more than just the few seconds I had to spare, and if I had any doubts, he decided to vocalize his desires. "I had plans for us tonight." A certain level of annoyance mingled with the need dripping from his words.

"I'm sorry, I didn't know." I apologized, even though I had nothing to apologize for.
Call it the Brax effect.

He had a special way in which he claimed not only my body and soul but also my time. Like I still owed him something for getting him involved in my plan and in my life.

"I'll make sure to be all alone tomorrow night." I promised, kissing him with every vibrating cell humming within, in the hopes of easing his wait, at least until the following night.

"I don't like to be kept waiting." The features that defined his position of superiority were strongly reasserting itself, especially after realizing the impossibility of things going his way.

I let the corner of my lip curve into a smile. "Sometimes the prize might be worth it."

"Am I getting some special treatment? Or what exactly should I get out of this?" he asked, testing the limits.

And I was playing along. "We'll see. Depends on how you play your cards tonight."

"Oh, Bea, I always play my cards right." He slid his hand beneath my dress, reaching for my already damp panties.

This man would be the death of me.

"What are you doing?" I quivered, worried that Jenna would open the door at any second and be a witness to our indiscretions.

"Nothing." He ran a finger along the smoothness of my sensitive pussy, doing absolutely *nothing* more.

He was really doing *nothing,* yet somehow making me crave for *everything.*

"I still have a few phone calls I have to make. You go back and enjoy the evening with your friend. And, Bea... think about me when you go to bed." An evil smirk blossomed on his face as he turned to leave, abandoning me right in front of my doorway.

He was right, I was going to think of him from the moment the sheets would be covering my body for the night. The most sinful thoughts a person could have, crowned with the memory of that wicked curve of his lips.

And to top it off, I didn't have just one king to think about. I had three.

"If I'm bothering you, I can go home." Jenna tried excusing her presence the second I set foot back into the room. "I don't want to intrude."

"Intrude? I'm the one who asked you over. Besides, I don't usually get so many nocturnal visits. I don't know what's with the guys tonight."

"Guys are just like spoiled little kids. They want all the attention they can get."

"Trust me, it's not just attention they're after." I giggled, knowing each one of my kings had an ulterior reason besides me giving them just mere attention. They all craved the kind of *attention* received when clothes and inhibitions fell away.

"I want details." My friend was going from the shy girl, afraid of intruding, to the one avid for steamy gossip. "Who's better?"

"Better?" I echoed, surprised by her question.

That made her try to explain it to me—explicitly. "You know... who has the nicest moves? Who makes you wanna climb the walls?"

"We are not talking about this." I tried to stop her from going off track, but things weren't that easy when it came to Jenna.

"What else do you want me to talk about? Economics? Advanced math? Chemistry?" She rolled her eyes to the back of her head like I was the abnormal one between us two.

Truth be told, I had no idea where I stood and what was normal or not anymore, especially since my new normality could be called an abomination by so many voices.

"My money is on the mobster guy... the one who just left." She was still trying to stir things up and get some indiscreet answers.

And I couldn't resist throwing her a few juicy tidbits. "They're all different, okay? One is more intense, another more passionate, and the third...," I trailed off, glancing toward the dressing room. "Come on, I just remembered—I forgot something in there." I basically ran away from her.

"Noo... and the other? How is the other?

"And who is who?

"Don't leave me hanging like that!

"I'll start guessing."

"No, you won't. Come on, let's get you something to wear for the morning. I don't want to wake up at 5 a.m. to pick out outfits." I tried deflecting.

And it seemed to be working. "You know how to shut me up. Clothes over gossip." She instantly ran to the walk-in dressing room. "Just tell me what you want me to wear."

"Pick whatever you like." I shrugged. I was never the materialistic type, and aside from a few pieces of clothing, like the dresses Brax gave me, she could choose whatever she wanted.

And that was exactly what she did. "Can I borrow this black skirt?"

"Whatever you want," I encouraged her to keep looking through the shelves.

"Okay. I think the black one's gonna get me a new boyfriend. Time to put this sexy body to use." She swayed her hips, making a little show-off of what she was preparing for the rest of the world.

"Wow, remind me not to let you into my dressing room ever again. I don't want to hear what you have to say when we get to the lingerie section."

"I'm surprised you even wear lingerie. I mean, what's the point?" Jenna chuckled, rushing toward the coat rack. "Hey, can I borrow this one?" She picked up a red winter coat. "I've seen it on you a couple of times, and I love it."

She was right; I'd worn that coat more than a couple of times. In fact, it was one of my favorites, and I wanted her to wear it with all my heart.

A dear object for a dear person.

No one would bat an eye. It was a custom, even in high society, to share luxury clothes. So, her getting to wear something they knew was mine could only be a reinforcement of our friendship. Not that either of us needed confirmation, but a little extra for the Elite couldn't hurt.

"It's yours." I helped her take it off the hanger, and put it on, doing a fashion show spin in front of the mirror.

"Thank you! I'll give it back after classes," she said, gratitude lighting up her face.

"No, you don't get it. It's yours. And so are the other clothes."

"I can't." She hesitated, trying to back down.

But I wouldn't let her. "You can and you will." I knew

Ferris wasn't going to get upset over this. He bought me so many clothes that if I were to wear a different outfit each day of the year, I would still have some left with unremoved labels. "Now, let's see what I'll wear." I quickly went through some blouses and pants, taking out exactly some of those with labels still on.

Next thing, we headed to bed. It had been a long and tiring day, and I couldn't imagine having even more things to do before I got a chance to rest my feet.

Or at least that's what I thought.

But fate seemed to always try and make fun of me.

Just as I got on the bed, another knock on the door made me jump to my feet.

There was only one person left.

"Come in, Cole." I sat back down on the bed as soon as I realized it was him who had come for the third visit of the evening.

"Jenna, so you're the one occupying my spot tonight." He observed, as soon as he entered my bedroom.

Although it wasn't exactly his place for the night, he'd have to wait his turn.

"Why do I feel like the fifth wheel every ten minutes?" Jenna complained from behind me, dragging the sheets over her head.

Not that Cole had anything against her visit. "I'll share beds. I used to go to summer camp." He was *kind* enough to offer.

"I'm pretty sure the Elite summer camp is made of villas and not bunk beds." I intervened, cutting in before Cole would actually get in bed with us. "I see you're feeling better."

"A certain someone healed my pain." He nudged me over to slip next to me onto the pillow.

I whirled my body in his direction to look at him. "What exactly do you think you're doing?"

"No one said three's a crowd." Cole pulled the quilt over himself, as he settled in to sleep.

"*I* say three is a crowd." I yanked the quilt off, shoving him to the edge of the bed.

I knew what him sleeping here meant, and I also knew how he wouldn't be able to keep his hands to himself. And this sleepover wasn't turning into some new torture he would use against me. Been there, done that, I'd had enough.

"Okay... okay. I'm leaving, don't get your panties in a twist." It was more like he'd get my panties in a twist if he stayed.

"Your appetite is never satisfied," I whispered, giving him a good night kiss, hoping he'd be the last of my evening visitors.

"How could it ever be, Mouse? I want you every minute and second of the day." Although he was confessing exactly the opposite, Cole knew it was time to leave, so he didn't make things even more difficult for himself. Besides, I was certain that he'd find a way to make up for the lost time during our time at school in the morning.

"I really need to take notes." Jenna broke the silence that followed after Cole had closed the door.

"They'd drive you crazy. Imagine three guys with anger management issues," I muttered.

"Well, I could use at least one. I haven't had a boyfriend in ages," she said, frustration creeping into her voice.

"Trust me; you don't need one."

"I can't get one. At least not a decent one. Hey, don't any of your guys have some insanely hot friends?" Her question amused me. But it was also a theme to think about. Ferris was off the list from the start, Brax was certainly a loner—except for Ferris and Cole—while my king of ECU seemed to be surrounded by dickheads. None of his friends from the university could fit on a list of possible boyfriends for her, nor any other acquaintances he might have. Camden was living proof of that.

"Their friends are mostly psychos. And I think I'm saying it in the nicest way possible. You're better off without, trust me on that."

But Jenna was seeing things much more theatrically. "I'm going to adopt ten cats and live the rest of my life locked in my apartment."

"Don't be so dramatic. You'd still have to get out, and get a job so you can feed them." I started laughing, making fun of her misery. "Chill, I'm pretty sure there has to be a nice guy out there waiting for you."

"I just hope he finds me before my pussy grows spider webs."

"You worry way too much. Let's just focus on graduating," *and avoiding a civil war*—though I felt I needed to leave that part out. "I promise you'll find someone nice who isn't related to you."

"Hey... that cousin thing was one time. Besides, we're *distant* relatives."

Yeah... sure.

We kept chatting and giggling about everything until dawn.

I'd never felt friendship so deeply rooted within me before. And along with that came responsibility. I felt responsible for her. I was going to help her reach every single one of her goals, even if I had the feeling that my work was cut out for me.

For Jenna, things were a bit more complicated. Sure, she was pretty, but that wasn't enough to make up for the fact that she used to be an outcast at the university, or her Pit origins.

Maybe I was lucky when it came to that. Not that I could ever call it luck. It was suffering and sacrifice taken to the extreme, but my actions didn't just allow me to help my family. I was helping many others, and Ferris's promise to hire Jenna's dad was proof to me that it was just the beginning of the real change.

I'd set the wheels in motion, and from there on, the sky was the limit.

Little did I know how dark the sky could get.

The night passed, and after a healthy breakfast—well, as healthy as bacon and eggs could be—Jenna and I got inside the limo and headed toward our destination for the day—school.

It wasn't the first time she got a ride in the limo, but this time around, she seemed to enjoy it more than usual. Probably because of the red coat she wore so proudly the second she stepped foot on the ground.

I smiled, giving her the confidence boost she needed. Maybe she would find her Prince Charming after all. In so many ways, she was just like me. Same background, same type of introvert, and similar evolution—a girl from the Pit dressed in shiny new clothes, ready to face the world.

Her ginger hair was darker in the winter, almost by a couple of shades, making Alfred confuse us from behind earlier in the morning—especially with her wearing my clothes. We looked so similar, we could be sisters. I was sure that there was already gossip floating around the university that probably my mother had some sort of fling with her father. People around here watch far too many soap operas.

Not that I cared.

We just needed to get to class in time, but Jenna ran into Thomas and decided to spare a few more minutes to chat with him. He'd been avoiding us since we migrated to the other end of the lobby, and despite my efforts in getting him to join us, he decided to keep his distance.

I was preparing to go to Economics, Jenna and I shared the class. I kept thinking about how I should convince her to come with me so we didn't miss it.

I never got the chance.

A heavy thump sent the dried leaves quivering with the sounds of crows screeching into the sky. The noise had frozen the very blood in my veins, petrifying me on the spot as I tried to make sense of it.

It was something terrible. That I knew for sure.

But there was a strange silence that followed the seconds after.

Everyone stood frozen, waiting to see what was really going on, like wolves sniffing out the air.

Out of all possible outcomes, there was one I never saw coming.

The white snow beneath my feet quickly turned fiery red.

A pool of red liquid covered the soil as screams erupted all around us.

The moment diluted with the horror flooding my soul as I felt my bodyguard shoving me to the ground. "Get down!" He threw himself over me, becoming my human shield against the danger.

Though I wasn't the one that needed saving.

My best friend was lying motionless on the ground, her body eerily still. I reached out to her, but no matter how far I stretched, I couldn't follow her to the place she was heading.

And I couldn't make her stay with me either.

"Jenna…"

CHAPTER 17

For a few seconds, all I could hear was a terrifying roar. Yet, it was just background noise compared to the thundering in my heart.

I felt like I couldn't breathe, and it wasn't because of the body weight of the guard that was squashing me to the ground. It was because I was staring into Jenna's eyes as they were losing the last flickers of life. They looked exactly like Ferris's candles, losing the final battle and making room for the darkness to settle in.

"Let me go," I screamed, my lungs burning as I fought against the guard, desperate to check if my friend still had a pulse.

I sensed him move and, at that very instant, jerked myself from his grip to reach Jenna. But I didn't seem to be going anywhere close to her. On the contrary, I began moving in the opposite direction, being dragged away by the guard securing my protection.

"Nooo!" I tried kicking him off, but there wasn't too much room for negotiations when it came to a man like him.

He only obeyed direct orders. Those came from Brax and not me.

I kept kicking and screaming to be set free, but even if I had the slightest possibility of succeeding, Cole's voice coming from somewhere behind me crushed any hope I had left. "Get her out of here. Now!" he roared, rushing toward Jenna while his own goon was following close behind, assuring his protection.

I was a fair distance away when I saw him leaning over her body to search for a pulse, and in the few seconds he remained listening for any sign of a heartbeat, I still had a shadow of hope. But then his head moved, slowly raising his gaze from the ground until it finally reached mine. It was devastatingly painful, not only because of what he was witnessing but because he knew the effect it would have on me.

She was dead.

My friend hadn't survived.

It all went blank from there on. Just shadows moving in my field of sight. Scared students running to their homes, cops flashing their red and blue lights like their presence could ever solve anything. And then there was Cole, securing me tightly against the defined shapes of his chest in useless attempts to protect me.

Things were clear.

Death comes when you least expect it.

Death doesn't care about age, ethnicity, or innocence. It just comes to claim its toll, grabbing any soul in its way.

Red and blue lights began flashing somewhere in the distance as the apocalyptical humming was announcing the irrefutable end.

Even the birds had fallen silent—or maybe just vanished completely, leaving us prey to painful tranquility.

For a moment, the world itself felt dead.

As dead as my friend who was lying on the cold pavement.

But just for a second, because the sound of the rescue units broke through the stillness.
Though what were they coming to save when there was nothing worth saving any longer?

Madness began.

Ambulances and police cars swarmed the scene as my tears made them just blurred clouds of color.

It all felt surreal.

Nothing made sense any longer, just like I'd been transported into a parallel universe where no one could reach me.

No one, except Brax.

I remember his voice breaking through the crowd of people gathered in front of me—so many that I couldn't even see Jenna anymore.

It felt like he was pulling me back from the depths,

reaching for the surface with its last remaining strength. Though I was choking, like something so evil was zoning in on me so that I could never recover.

"Bea." Brax's call was a distant echo, drifting in the noise in my mind as his hands kept roaming my body like he was searching for something. "Are you okay?"

He was searching to see if I'd been hurt. His hands kept moving frantically over me, searching for some unseen wound. But I couldn't answer. My lips couldn't move to murmur even a word, frozen in front of everything that was happening around me.

"Was she hurt?" I could hear Brax roar, ready to rip Cole's head off like he had something to do with any of it. My king of ECU was just there to protect me, pulling me so close to his chest that I thought I was going to suffocate.

"She's all right," Cole tried to reassure him, although it was a lie.

I wasn't all right.

I was so far from being all right that it was scaring me to the bone.

"Who did this?" Brax roared more than asked my bodyguard, who was paler than the snow blanketing the ground.

He knew all too well who Brax was and what could be the consequences of failure. "The police don't know shit," the guard grumbled, trying to keep focus and retell the events as they happened. "No threats. Not any kind of conflict. All we could hear was a shot being fired. I saw a man running at

9 o'clock, but I didn't try to pursue him. My objective was protecting the girl."

"What did the man look like?" Brax was continuing his interrogation, while it was the first time I was finding out what had happened.

"I couldn't see his face; he had a hood pulled over his eyes. But from what I could ascertain, he was Caucasian, around 5'8" tall, athletic figure."

"You just described a quarter of Echo City's male population. Fuck." Brax was obviously recognizing what had happened as a direct threat to our security. "Cole, keep an eye on her. I'm going to talk to the police." My king of the underworld signaled his man to join him as I was just starting to realize that the incident had every chance of having something to do with me.

"Cole, was I the target?" I turned to face him, uneasy about what his answer might be.

"I don't know yet, Mouse... I just don't know." He pulled me even tighter to his chest, trying to take away my worries. "I will always protect you. Always!" He kissed the words onto my lips so slowly that I began to think they would infiltrate my being.

"She was wearing my coat," I whispered as soon as Brax returned, my voice barely audible, as if saying it out loud would make the horror real. I was still trying to make sense of what had just happened.

"Do you think the attacker could have mistaken her for you?" Brax arched an eyebrow, trying to put two and two together, although I was beginning to think he was already suspecting what I had just told him. "The police don't know shit. Not that I am surprised about that." He seemed even more pissed off than before—if that was even possible. But Brax's words soon became just random noises as a familiar face made its way through the crowd and headed straight for the police-closed area.

A man in his forties broke through the students gathered around the yellow crime scene tape, ignoring all warnings and threats as he plummeted straight on top of the white sheet that covered Jenna's body. He looked so much like her, even though his face seemed transfigured by pain. A heartbreaking image that would be forever etched somewhere in the back of my mind.

I looked at the nametag that hung on his jacket.

Ayers Enterprises.

I did that. I made that tag happen.

Just as I made his daughter lying dead on the ground happen.

Ferris's miracle was just dust in the wind compared to the tragedy that had struck their family.

Ferris... "I need Ferris," I murmured with a final cry as the feeling that the world I knew was about to come to an end was starting to haunt my mind.

"Cole, can you take her home?" Brax asked, probably knowing that when it came to feelings and that kind of emotion, he was the worst man for the job.

Though life didn't always agree with him.

"The police asked me to make a statement. I can't leave right now. They didn't say anything about Bea, so at least she can go."

"Okay. I'll take her then." Brax nodded, looking straight at me. "Just keep an eye on things and try to see if you can find out anything more. I'll have my men check the streets after I take Bea home. Someone has to know something."

I could read the anxiety etched in his expression. He was futilely trying to hide it beneath that mask of anger he usually put on. I knew better than to believe in his facade ever again. He was concerned about me being the main target.

"Cole, call me if anything shows up." Brax gestured to one of his guards to bring the car around, then watched me like a hawk until I got into the vehicle.

I couldn't say a word through the tears, and I had a feeling Brax didn't want me to speak either. I knew that he was never good at sharing emotions, yet was so perfectly flawed in so many other different ways.

His comfort didn't come with well-thought-out phrases but with a gesture that outshone any other consolation someone could offer me. With gentle motions, he reached for my hand, then tugged it between the collar of his jacket and straight over his heart. He was probably never going to say it, but he was showing me in the most genuine manner he could.

I owned his heart.

Perhaps my reaction wasn't what he anticipated. The raw emotion only amplified my tears, placing extra pressure on my already burdened soul. I couldn't help but press my ear next to my fingers, which were spread across his chest, in a desperate attempt to ease my pain. The electrifying sounds of his heartbeats brought as much life as they could back into my being. His hand—which had just moved to secure my head to his chest, helped me breathe properly for the first time that day. He was going to be there for me. His unspoken promise washed over me, a current of silent commitment to always protect me.

Yet, he couldn't fully understand me. Not the way Ferris did. And Brax knew that. He would probably be able to help me with my pain. But he would never be able to feel the devastating emotions by my side.

"I'll be back later to check up on you." He kissed me goodbye so he could return to what he did best—keeping us informed. Information is power, and it has always been a starting point for all of our actions. We needed to know what we were up against, and there was no man better for the job than Brax.

To my surprise, Ferris was waiting for me on the steps of his mansion, rushing toward the car the second it pulled to a stop.

I was in his arms before I realized it, though I couldn't take my eyes off Brax. There was something inside of him breaking because he couldn't take care of me the way Ferris could.

Brax was the hunter, and Ferris the healer. That was the way our world functioned and how it would continue to work from there on. And then there was Cole. He was the right man in the right place, constantly helping me handle every fucked-up thing in my life, while I could only try to do the same for him.

Ferris didn't ask if I was okay or not. He knew the answer to that question better than I did, sensing the burden my soul carried without me having to say anything at all. Locking his eyes on mine, he drew me closer, intoxicating me with the spicy scent of his cologne. The same scent that used to drive my senses wild now soothed them as I found it to be bringing me a feeling of home.

I was home.

No matter how fucked up it may seem, Ferris's mansion had become my home, not because of the material nature of the bricks lying around me, but because of the people living within. My kings lived there now, and whether I liked it or not, *they* were my home.

Not a sound was wasted before Ferris imprinted the shape of his lips on mine, lifting me from the ground and helping me to become just a grain of dust between his arms. Like he knew the exact place I needed to be, he gently laid me on the sofa in his room and cocooned me in an extra fluffy blanket, hiding me far away from the rest of the world.

I wished that could make me feel safe.

I thought that could make me feel safe.

But a devastating feeling of guilt canceled every single one of his attempts to get me to recover.

I couldn't overcome the thought that I was wrapped up in warm blankets while my best friend lay cold on the M.E.'s table.

"I want to see her." I stood up abruptly, ready to leave.

It didn't seem fair for her to be there all alone, even though I knew all that was left of her was an empty shell that used to shelter a beautiful soul.

"You're not bringing her back if you get yourself killed. Believe me, I know." Ferris said with the pain I knew so well coating his words. "Just don't move. I'm going to get you a drink."

Without wasting any time, he rushed to the bar and poured me an extra-large glass of whiskey. He probably thought it would last me through the night, though without giving it a single thought, I drained it in a swallow. "Refill it, please."

"You know I'm not going to do that. It's not a drinking marathon." He took the glass away, probably regretting he even thought a drink could possibly be a solution. I knew he was only trying to help me relax, but I was in self-destruction mode, heading straight to the edge of a cliff again.

I immediately turned my back on him, sinking into the darkness moments away from engulfing me completely. "This is my fault," I barely forced myself to murmur. "There's blood on my hands. Blood on my hands and an excruciating pain tearing through my soul."

"Why would there be blood on your hands?" Ferris asked, his voice low and comforting.

"Because I wanted this. All of this madness. I stopped at nothing to achieve it, including selling my body and my spirit. I caused her death. I can feel it." My words came out heavy between tears.

"You can't know for sure that it had something to do

with you." Ferris tried to diminish the ravaging effects Jenna's death was having on me, though I knew he didn't believe his own words either.

"I know for sure. She was wearing my clothes. That's what got her killed." The certainty in my voice warned him that I couldn't handle any attempt to lie to me. I might have still been in shock, but I recognized facts from hallucinations.

The only thing I didn't know was the reason behind it.

My list of suspects was far greater than I could really think of since anyone in the city could have been responsible. What we were trying to do usually pissed off the wrong kind of men. Even Brax's influence and network of information proved to be insufficient in front of the hidden threat looming over us.

This assassination attempt had something to do with the texts I received that night. Still, none of us even had a clue who the author was.

All I knew was that only the mere thought of ever finding the one responsible sent dark thoughts racing through my mind.

"What does it feel like to take a life?" The words just blurted out from my mouth as a result of every second of that day, culminating in a type of rage I'd never felt before. For the first time, I was considering killing another human, becoming the criminal myself. I wanted whoever ended Jenna's life to pay. The person responsible for her death didn't deserve to live.

"I'm fucked up in every sense of the word. I don't think I'm the right person to be asked that question." Ferris was trying to dodge the subject as well as he could, although no signs of regret were actually reflecting on his face.

"I want to see the person responsible for this to pay." My blood was boiling, blinded by the thought of revenge. I needed to know justice would be served since that same morning, I witnessed the greatest injustice I could imagine. An innocent life had been ended for no reason whatsoever.

"I'm not going to let you have that on your hands." Ferris's sober voice echoed with something so dark that it brought me straight back from the place of utter desperation I was sinking into. "But I do promise that when we find the one responsible, I will give you the revenge you need." I could feel that there was no shadow of a doubt he would do it. He would give me my revenge even if it would cost him the last part of his soul. And I didn't want that. He couldn't be doomed because of me.

"No, you can't do that. This didn't happen because of you. It happened because I set things off balance."

All I wanted was to save him, not to push him further over the edge, yet somehow I knew it wasn't up to me anymore. He'd made up his mind, and there would be nothing stopping him. "Things were already off-balance; we're just setting a new course. You're not the problem, Bea, but you might be the solution." Ferris was trying to comfort me—maybe even comfort himself. No matter how much good our plan might bring to the city, we couldn't ignore the victims along the way.

"And what if we're not the solution?" I doubted even the air I was breathing in those moments, though it seemed I wasn't seeing the whole picture.

"You are my solution for everything. That has to count for something," Ferris whispered in my ear, making room on the couch beside me and lifting me to place my head on top of his chest.

His emotions made a jolt of pain run across my heart.

A perfectly beautiful pain, forged in the fire of pure feelings.

We needed each other so much it hurt. Every crippled piece of our souls was completing a circle—I was his salvation, and he, the keeper of my essence.

I tried to close my eyes and sleep.

Useless.

Vicious guilt didn't stop tormenting me even for a second while endless questions roamed through my mind. "She did nothing wrong. Why did this happen?" My trembling voice could not be controlled, bringing to the surface all my regrets and uncertainties.

"It's life, Bea." His arm slipped from my back to rest upon the scars on his chest. "Do you think my parents deserved to die?"

"Ferris, I didn't mean to..."

"It's okay. As I said, it's just life. I finally understand that. It doesn't mean it makes anything easier or that it has any sense at all, but you can't change your destiny, and you can't alter fate. Things happen for a reason, even if sometimes we have no clue where these moments might lead.

"I know that what I'm going to say will sound horrible, but I believe she was there to save your life. She died so you could live.

"I'm not saying, as an individual, your life would be worth more than hers. Sure, for Cole, Brax, or me, it means everything. What I'm saying is, what if this happened to serve a greater purpose?

"What if you're still alive so we can really make the difference we're planning?

"Everything would fall apart if anything happened to you, and you know it."

"I can't live with that guilt," I sobbed, the tears almost preventing me from saying a word.

"You don't have to. It's not your fault. You weren't the one who pulled the trigger." Though no matter what Ferris would say to me, the desperate pain still lingered—a somber mixture of grief and culpability in a poisonous cocktail of emotion. "Come, let's get you in bed. You're uncomfortable on the couch. That's why you can't sleep."

Without asking permission, Ferris lifted me in his arms and slipped me between the black silky sheets I loved so much.

I was safe in a place where so many pivotal moments had shaped me.

I was safe in the place where I almost died a few days before.

Maybe that was what Ferris was talking about—life works in mysterious ways, and the place that I thought would be my destruction was becoming my ultimate salvation.

I kept staring out the window while he removed my top, only to replace it with one of his loose T-shirts. He was trying to make me feel as comfortable as possible; the only problem was I didn't even feel I was in the room with him anymore. I was drifting between memories, hoping to immortalize the moments spent with the first person who showed me any evidence of humanity when I first came to Echo City—my friend Jenna.

Somehow, Ferris managed to change my clothes completely. I only came to my senses when I was already carefully placed on fluffy pillows, and he was settling into his spot on the bed next to me again.

The sound of the bedroom door opening made me jump, though I already had an idea about who it was.

No one would dare to enter without even knocking.

No one except for Brax.

"How is she?" he asked in a hushed voice, thinking I was sleeping.

"Miserable," I answered before Ferris got a chance to say a word. Not that he could describe my feelings better than I would.

"You're awake?" Brax walked around the king-size bed to reach my side and take a proper look at me.

Funny how the normal awkwardness of being in bed with Ferris while Brax was in the same room didn't bother me. On the contrary. Seeing him sent me straight back to a few hours before when the disappointment of him not being able to comfort me was etched on his face. Yet, he was helping me in so many different ways.

"I can't sleep." There was no need for me to share the motives for why my eyes refused to remain closed. He already knew how I felt, and was ready to finally be there when I needed him.

My hand ran over the sheet next to me in an unspoken invitation to be by my side. And he didn't hesitate to answer my unspoken call.

Throwing his jacket on a chair, he came to occupy the free side of the bed, claiming my hand to intertwine his fingers between my own. I wasn't expecting any words. Ferris was the master of things to be said, while Brax was the master of body language. No matter how hard he tried to deny it in the past, the reactions of his body always betrayed what was smoldering in his heart.

"Did you find out anything?" It was Ferris who asked the question that had been on my mind as well.

"We will, soon. My men are on the streets. We have a vague description but nothing more. The man was wearing a hood over his face."

"Ask your men to bring him in alive. I want to end him." Ferris *cared* to let Brax be aware of his plans.

"Ferris, it isn't your call," I objected, unable to agree with him.

"It will be." My *royal origins* king traced the line of my cheek with the back of his fingers, caressing my face. Like that would be the ticket that could grant him access to pursue revenge.

Surprisingly, Brax was the one who called for calm this time around. "That's enough. We'll decide when the time is right and when we can all see things clearly."

"Who said four's a crowd?" Cole's voice echoed from the other end of the room, taking all of us by surprise.

"Doesn't anyone knock in this house?" I was the one protesting about the intrusion and not Ferris, the rightful owner of the room. He didn't even seem to care, just saw Cole's presence as natural as me being there.

"It's not like I could stumble onto something that would shock me." Cole flashed a wicked smile. "More like something I could join."

I couldn't go there with the conversation, especially at a time like this, and he quickly realized it. Yet that didn't stop him from finding a place between my legs. Following Brax's lead, he tossed his jacket on a chair and crawled onto the bed, nudging my thighs apart.

"What do you think you're doing?" I snapped, irritation rising. I assumed his gesture had a different intent—not that I wouldn't have normally enjoyed it, but it was the worst possible time and place.

"Relax, Mouse. I'm only searching for a pillow." He pushed my legs further apart, then rested his head on the inside of my thigh as if he truly meant to sleep.

I didn't really know how to react but let him claim his rightful place as the final piece that was making me whole.

Each of them were a part of me in their specific ways.

Ferris was making me understand how life works.

Brax was giving me strength.

And Cole was making my every single cell shudder with the pure feeling of living.

Together, they made me feel complete. It felt like I'd finally found a place of my own, even if that would be an illusion, even if it would last only for an ephemeral moment, and even if the dawn would pull me straight back to crushing reality.

That's how I managed to fall asleep, protected by my three kings, drifting into a treacherous safety, because one truth remained—*you never know what tomorrow brings*.

CHAPTER 18

I didn't want to open my eyes and acknowledge it was morning.

In fact, I think I didn't want to acknowledge that the outside world still existed. I wanted it to be as lost as I was, swallowed by the same suffocating darkness.

It seemed I was in bed only with Cole, who had somehow advanced onto Ferris's pillow and made sure I was tightly caged between his arms. The heavy inhales and exhales moving his chest were letting me know he was still sleeping. No matter how much I hated the thought of bothering him, I just couldn't stay in bed any longer. I felt utterly trapped, struggling to breathe, like even Ferris's massive chamber was too small to accommodate what I was feeling.

Fear.

Pain.

Regret.

Empathy.

Guilt.

All smothering me so fiercely that I couldn't remain between the sheets one second longer.

I jumped out of bed without any idea why or what I was going to do next. I just needed to do something. Anything to get my mind, even for a second, from what had happened.

"Where are you going?" Cole's groggy voice stopped me before I could reach the door.

"I was just going to have a look around. I can't be in bed." The truth was, I was just drifting like a paper plane, praying that the thoughts haunting my mind would come to an end.

"I'm coming with you... to have a look around." Although Cole wasn't saying it directly, he was worried that I could do something stupid. I couldn't blame him because my mind was spiraling with all sorts of absurd thoughts.

I wanted revenge, and at the same time, I wanted to take her place in the immortal silence.

With or without my will, Cole was my shadow through the dark hallways as I was still trying to figure out what to do next.

I wasn't truly prepared to face Sebastian or Natalia. It didn't seem fair to bring the burden of my pain on them; therefore, my steps carried me away from their section of the mansion. That meant I ended up back with my kings, just when Brax was trying to figure out what to do next. "The chief inspector called. They found a weapon thrown in a trashcan a few streets away from the university. They're trying to trace it, but it has its serial number scratched off. I've sent a few of my men to look into it. They have much more chance of succeeding than the police. I just need to decide if I'm going to burn the town down until I find the one responsible for the assassination or if I should keep things low so I don't scare him."

"Keep it low for a few days." Ferris rubbed a hand over his chin like he had the most important information to process. "If that doesn't work, you can turn every corner of the town upside down. It represents an immediate threat, and we're not going to sit around doing nothing as long as Bea is in potential danger."

"I can't stand the thought of more people getting hurt because of me." I couldn't help but betray my presence.

"I'll try to keep things as civilized as I can." Brax was making an effort to comfort me. I felt that he would have done anything for me in those moments. Any of my kings would have, though the problem was there wasn't much anyone could really do. It was up to me to deal with the pain, to grieve my friend—no one else could carry that weight. It just seemed I wasn't ready for any of that yet. I still needed time to get used to the idea, as the severity of what happened had shaken my existence to the ground.

"Do you want to eat something?" It was Ferris who was trying to achieve the impossible, although he knew that his question didn't make any sense.

"No. I just..." I guess it was time to admit the truth to everyone, including myself. I actually left the room to get away from Cole, but overheard their conversation instead. "I don't even know what I'm doing here. *I just want to be alone.*"

Those were the last words I spoke to my kings that day... and for the days to come. The silence felt safer than facing them.

My own room became my refuge, or more likely the place where I was hiding from the rest of the world, trying to figure out a way to live with the burden that I might have played a part in my best friend's death.

Alfred helped Jenna's parents to take care of everything needed for the funeral, sparing me from the details I couldn't bear to face. Money wasn't an issue when it came to Ferris, but him personally handling everything that was needed at the church could have brought back anguishing memories of his parents.

Cole managed to drag me out of my room on a painful Friday. It was the day I was supposed to say goodbye, although I never imagined I would ever need to take something like that into consideration.

I never had a problem wearing black; as a matter of fact, I loved the elegance of the color. But as I was searching for something to wear, the dark representation of death felt unbearable, tipping my emotions back into chaos.

I had to physically let go of Jenna, even if I would never let her abandon my soul.

"Are you ready?" Brax's voice broke through my silence, steady and patient, as he began helping me lift the zipper to my dress. His hands were much more careful than usual like he understood how fragile I was at that moment.

"How could I ever be ready for this?" I asked, my voice

trembling with words I barely managed to form. In a way, I wished to be like him, colder, more calculated, maybe even impassive to others' feelings. But my friend didn't deserve that.

She deserved my tears.

And she deserved the blood of the one responsible for her death.

Brax never answered my question, just reinforced an arm around my waist and slowly guided me toward the black limo that was waiting for us.

Cole and Ferris were already inside the vehicle, waiting in silence for my arrival. That only seemed to make things harder, pressing down on me like a weight I couldn't lift. Part of me wanted them to bicker over something stupid, like the color of the limo lights. I guess I needed something to pull me out of this haze, but unfortunately, the day forecasted a surreal sadness. Nothing in this world could take me away from that.

I don't even know how I ended up at the graveyard. Everything was a blur. All I knew was I was standing in a large chapel, inches away from the coffin where my friend was lying lifeless.

Strangely, she seemed at peace, more beautiful than ever, and the ombre peach roses that she was bathing in were giving her an angelic look. Ferris must've paid for those too, like everything else at the funeral, since no expense was spared when it came to the location and decorations. But for what? It wasn't like she could see any of the glamour surrounding her, couldn't feel any of it.

I couldn't help but look around me. All the Elite from the university came to see her go. Funny how none of them had wanted her in their lives when she was still breathing. It was like they felt eased that she was leaving and just came to make sure she wouldn't return.

The thought made the room begin to spin in circles. I would have anyone from the Elite present there that day take her place—anyone except for my kings.

Call it a sixth sense, but Cole crept up on me, trying to assure himself I was okay. "It's going to be all right. I promise you."

"How is it ever going to be all right?" I couldn't think of any future for our plan from there on. I couldn't be responsible for another death caused by my actions.

But Cole seemed to see things a lot differently. "Think about all the other families like Jenna's. We're trying to give them a better future, or at least prevent an incoming disaster. You're the one who taught me that. And we're going to be the ones that will change the way this world works. How many residents of the Pit do you think would have died if the riots had continued? Or worse, what if the governor's plan had worked? I know that there's no need to repeat this, but the benefits outweigh the losses."

"My best friend just died, Cole. She's never coming back," I retaliated, as the *losses* he was talking about were affecting me directly.

"And someone else's best friend would have died if the governor's plan would have been put into action. I know that this is hard, and that it affects you, but in one way or another, we've prevented many other *best friends* from meeting the same fate." I understood what Cole was trying to tell me, but even if I knew it was the truth, I was having trouble coming to terms with what had happened.

The minister soon arrived for the last eulogy as I felt I was doing her an injustice again. Everyone who had a special connection to Jenna took the mic to speak—everyone except me. Friends and family spoke about their memories of her, praising the time they spent together. Even Thomas and Darrel gave a short speech while I remained motionless in my seat, aware of all the eyes pointing in my direction, waiting for me to say something.

But what could I have said except, "I did this... I caused this," my lips relentlessly murmuring the words throughout the ceremony while Ferris and Cole pleaded with me to keep quiet.

Brax wasn't there. He was much busier securing the perimeter, ensuring everything developed without any incidents, while I felt that I was the one who could cause an incident. I was like a ticking time bomb in danger of setting off at every moment. I didn't even know what I was doing anymore, constantly oscillating between regret, painful grief, and a strange sense of justice.

I knew I wasn't directly responsible for her death.

I wasn't the one who pulled the trigger.

But I was the one who let her stand in front of my bullet.

I was the one who should be in the coffin, in her place.

I don't even know what really happened during the hour we were there. Just copied speeches, echoing between the cathedral's walls just so that the words would get lost between the bricks.

She was dead, and that was the only thing that mattered. I understood that the instant we abandoned the building and stepped outside.

The clouds were so dark I was beginning to think it was night, as if the sky itself was grieving her death. The whole atmosphere was hazy, like a dark dream that I couldn't escape from was coming to life.

A few guys, including Thomas and Darrel, carried her coffin, walking on what seemed to be a path of thorns, which was painfully carving each one of their steps in the back of my mind.
I remember I was shaking when they finally stopped. The view that spread before me was foretelling the doomed feeling that was about to engulf me. Not that I didn't feel that way every second since she'd been murdered, but the tiny raindrops filling the air reminded me that the time to say the last goodbye was closing in on me.

We finally stopped in front of a pit that seemed to have run down into an endless abyss. I thought I knew pain by then, but the image of her family flooding the ground with their crystal tears tore my soul into shreds. They were reminding me of myself on the day of my mother's funeral. I would have done anything so that she would have stayed... I would even have traded places with her so that she would have stayed.

Jenna seemed so peaceful, still; a stark contrast to the chaos inside me. The pain churned me, threatening to make me sick. I felt I was going to scream until no voice would be left within me.

My responsibility.

My fault!

Despite the thoughts that were driving me to teeter on madness, outwardly, I was numb, unable to speak. Maybe unable to even breathe.

I had no idea what was happening around me, lost in my own torment. I couldn't even tell when they lowered the coffin or when I threw the last handful of dirt over it. All I knew was that I couldn't be there any longer.

The dark sky.

The sea of people that came to say goodbye.

The hypocrisy of the Elite—only present to please my kings.

Too much for me to bear.

"I'm going to take care of her family. They've been through enough." Ferris said softly, sneaking from behind me just when I was about to leave.

I knew he had good intentions, and I also knew what this kind of support would mean for anyone living in the Pit. However, the maddening guilt was preventing me from even thinking straight, let alone take Ferris's own traumas into consideration.

I was a blubbering idiot, and acting exactly like one. "How could that bring a life back? How could that bring Jenna back?" I yelled at him, knowing he would never have the right answer to that.

"Nothing could bring her back, but nothing gives you the right to leave with her. We still need you here." His words were cold and warm at the same time, sharing his pain together with his love.

Maybe we could've gone on with the conversation, and maybe he would have stopped me from my path. But fate never lets you escape the inevitable.

I noticed Brax's men gathering around him for who knows what plan he needed to share with them, while a simple gesture from my mobster's finger made Ferris leave my side to join him. "I'll be right back." The worried look on his face shouldn't have been ignored. Yet, I ignored it completely, being too distracted by my own suffering.

Slithering through the crowd, I managed to walk away without anyone seeing me. The bodyguards, mine included, were distracted by Brax, while the rest of the crowd couldn't care less about where I was heading.

I just drifted away through the maze of imposing tombstones.

The creme of the Elite lay buried beneath this ground.

Such contrast. Jenna lived her life in the Pit, and now she was sleeping for eternity in the Hills. I knew Ferris's reasons for having the funeral in this graveyard. He was trying to compensate for our mistakes, bringing her close to her family since he was probably going to move them to one of his residences in the Hills.

Though what could ever compensate for her death?

I was searching for an answer to that exact question when I stumbled upon a small chapel near the south entrance. A place where people sought solace in moments of despair. It was exactly one of those moments, though nothing had prepared me for the *real* meaning of despair.

The place was so peaceful and calm, I could hear the creak of the old wooden floor as I ventured deeper within to light a few candles. Maybe as a consequence of living with Ferris, but the smell of wax and fire felt like a bridge to the spirit world, hopefully bringing me closer to my friend.

I was just lighting a candle when the same floorboard squeaked, echoing through the chapel.

At first, I suspected it was one of my kings, but something about the sound felt off—almost sinister, like fear curling its way up my spine. I wanted to run away, deflect the danger and surround myself with all the ones dear to me. I felt like a cub that had strayed too far from her nest, too afraid to stay still and wait for an outcome—too afraid to turn and see who was behind me.

Maybe I was exactly a cub since the voice that filled the room hid a parental sound.

A fake parental sound. "Hello, my daughter."

Like an earthquake shattering my world, acknowledging the man's presence seemed an impossible task. My brain was refusing to process *it was him.* Until I finally turned and discerned the face I'd hoped never to see again.

"Father?" I murmured, recognizing the last person I wanted to set eyes on. Everything clicked—his presence, the string of dark events in my life—it all led back to him.

I scanned him from head to toe, noting the strange worker's uniform he wore—a gravedigger. That's how he must've passed Brax's bodyguards and got in unnoticed.

"What are you doing here?" I quivered, although deep down I seemed to know the answer to that question. The glimpse of madness shining from the depths of his mind was making things as clear as day and night.

He wasn't my father.

He was a killer.

"Funny you should ask that," he said, his voice teetering between a simmering rage and an unnerving calm, like hell could break loose at any moment. "You're a smart girl, Bea. You know why I'm here. You took something that belongs to me. You tore apart my business, my life. You destroyed everything I built!"

"What *you built*?" I spat back. "You were exploiting people for your personal interest, including your own family."

"I don't have a family," he sneered. "Your mother was my only family. You were just the burdens she left me with."

I always knew that he felt that way about us, but I never thought his hatred could run deep enough to want us dead.

"You're a psychopath. You killed Jenna, didn't you?" I demanded, my voice cracking with rage.

"I don't even care what her fucking name was. She was wearing your clothes. It should've been you. But I believe things turned out way better for me. Now I get a close-up of your death."

My suspicions were right—he killed Jenna, thinking she was me. The realization didn't linger in my mind for too long before the barrel of the gun pointed straight at me, managing to catch my full attention.

"You're not a parent. You're a monster."

"With children like mine, does it surprise you? You have all betrayed me. And you will all pay the price for that."

"You had us begging strangers for money for years. You were going to sell Natalia to the highest bidder, yet you're the one talking about betrayal?"

"It was about time you ingrates gave me something in return," he spat, venom in his voice. "It was your fault that I needed to get rid of her. You and your stupid ideologies about high schools and colleges. They don't ask you for a fucking degree down on the streets! She didn't need to go to college to gain people's pity."

"No. She needs to go to college to gain self-respect."

"Well, self-respect gets you at the wrong end of a gun," he smiled cruelly, cocking his weapon. The cold detachment of a killer surfaced, ready to send me into oblivion.

My pulse was racing like a wild stallion, and beads of cold sweat were gliding down my temples. The end was closing in on me. I could feel it the same way I felt it on that day back at the governor's house, only this time around, I stood no chance of avoiding my destiny.

A faint squeak, almost imperceptible, caught my attention. A gray shadow slipped between the chapel's pillars, following the path of the darkness until the proximity to my sorry excuse of a father was close enough to create leverage for the man who had just snuck inside. "Drop the fucking gun before I blow your brains out." The click of a second gun cocking filled the air as Cole's cobalt blue eyes gleamed in the dim light of the dying candles.

"Don't test me. I'll kill her before you'll get a chance to pull the trigger." My father was reaching new levels of madness with each second, pushing everything into a frightening carousel of life and death.

"I said, drop it." Cole was going to keep good on his threat as the gun came even closer to my father's skull.

And I prayed that he would pull the trigger, to end it all and avenge all the people he wronged.

"Okay. I'll put it on the ground." my father said, his voice dripping with false calm as he bent to place the metal gun on the ground.

The gesture caught me off guard, too good to be true.

The madness scribbled in his eyes told me he'd never give up on his goal. Though before I came to my senses to warn my king about a possible side plan, my father spun and knocked Cole's revolver away from his hand.

My father's gun never touched the ground, remaining tightly between his fingers.

I couldn't see much beyond Cole trying to wrestle

control, their bodies a blur of frantic motions, but none of it gave away who was winning. And I knew exactly the outcome I desperately needed. As horrible as it sounded, I wanted my father dead.

I tore my eyes off them for a second, lunging for Cole's gun. It had skidded straight under a pew, making it almost impossible to recover without going straight through the two of them fighting.

With unnatural strength, I threw myself on the ground, trying to squeeze between the benches and somehow stretch my arm to get the weapon. Yet nothing could have prepared me for what was to come.

Adrenaline surged, turning the moment into chaos.

My fingers finally closed around the cold metal. I had the gun.

But before I could act, a deafening sound exploded in the room.

Bang!

It was all it took to change my world.

I remembered how I kept looking with horror, struggling to discern what had just happened.

But time doesn't wait for anyone.

My father backed away, blood speckling his clothes, but it was Cole's eyes that haunted me—frozen in a morbid stillness.

A new nightmare was unraveling before my eyes, fueling an unprecedented urge to kill.

Without wasting any more time, I pointed the gun that I'd just recovered from the ground at my so-called parent and shot.

Another deafening *bang* echoed off the chapel's stone walls.

I missed.

A mistake that gave him just enough time to run away.

I emptied the gun barrel in his direction, fury burning through me, the same killer instinct that ran in his blood was vivid in my own veins.

Useless.

I could only watch him seeking shelter within the chapel's dark corners, my last desperate shot, chasing him through the door.

Adrenaline surged through me, amplifying the paralyzing fear of looking down at Cole.

I just wished to delay the inevitable, but the pure desperation running through my veins instantly sent me to hover over him. "Cole, stay with me," I whispered, searching for his powerless hand, silently praying I could give him the strength he needed to hold on.

His lips tried to move, yet no words managed to come out, only fragmented syllables that struggled to form the confession I already knew.

I didn't want him to tell me he loved me. Not like that. I needed the strong, arrogant Cole I used to hate and love so much.

It couldn't be the endgame because it wasn't going to be *The king is dead; Long live the king.* It was going to be the end of the kingdom.

"Someone help him!" I screamed so loud that my voice seemed to reach the depths of the sky, begging God himself to let me keep him for a little longer. "Cole," I pleaded until no sounds were left in my throat. "It's going to be all right. I promise."

Maybe it was a lie. I had no power over that promise. Not like he had over his, *I will always protect you. **Always!***

I never imagined his words would ever prove to be so accurate.

I never imagined it could come to any of my kings losing their lives.

I never left his side. I don't remember even breathing, just praying for a sign that he would beat this.

Our fate was written in the stars. We couldn't escape it, and we couldn't avoid it. All we could do was embrace it. But I would never be ready to embrace his loss.

I begged and cursed the gods, hoping for a miracle. I couldn't be responsible for this too. I couldn't bear being responsible for the death of the man I loved. I convinced myself of that thought, imagining somehow that it would keep him by my side.

Just another way the universe was laughing at me once again.

I tried to crash my lips on his, hoping that I could help him breathe, that I could keep him alive until help would come. But there was so much blood spreading so fast to coat the ground. A devastating image crowned with the last pulses of his heart as I prayed through tears to hear the next beat, and the next.

Until the sounds stopped.

No matter how hard my imagination tried to fool me into believing his heart was still beating, the last flicker of life in his eyes was dying, the blue orbs turning as cold as Jenna's.

My king was gone.

End of Book 3

"Kings of Seduction" is book 3 of The Pleasure Room series, and will be continued!

The Pleasure Room reading order:

1.Kings of Desire

2.Kings of Lust

3.Kings of Seduction

4.The Book of Kings- optional – Kings' POV

5. Kings of Destiny

ABOUT THE AUTHOR

M.O. Absinthe

Ascending author with a sweet tooth for alpha males, and a guilty pleasure of making your darkest fantasies come to life.

Follow me on:

-Instagram :@m.o.absinthe -for sneak peeks and events

-TikTok: @m.o.absinthe

-Facebook Page : M.O. Absinthe
-Facebook Group: M.O. Absinthe's Dark Sinners

-Email : absinthe.is.writing@gmail.com

Sign up on www.moabsinthe.com to my newsletter to get a FREE extra-steamy bonus scene featuring Bea and her kings

BOOKS BY M.O. ABSINTHE

The Sin of You

A vampire dark romance that will make you shiver in unknown temptation

The book is suitable for a mature audience.

I invite you to take a dangerous path where nothing is forbidden. Desire, lust, deceit, and betrayal revolve around an ancient prophecy that can build or break destinies. You're soon to find out if passion and love are enough to stand in the way of antique forces, or it will all be dust with the first ray of light.

"The room darkened with his presence as every step he made towards me took me closer to my downfall. He was death, and life merged in a predator's body. Strength and dominance oozed from his every pore. But it was something else too... Something more that made a cold chill flash through my body. His beautiful absinthe eyes captured the depths of time, making him irresistible, undeniable, but also fatal. All of my instincts were telling me to leave as fast as I could, but there was something stronger that kept me frozen to the spot. An unspoken link from the dawn of time brought me here, in this place, meant to fulfill my destiny. He is the living dead that people whispered about while looking, with fear, out the window... He is a vampire."

Il Capo's Seduction

An enemies-to-lovers passionate mafia romance.

The book is suitable for a mature audience.

One dreadful night changes Angelo's and Elise's lives forever, sharing a dark secret that can never be revealed.

After her mother's tragic death, Elise finds herself trapped in the dangerous Italians' penthouse caught up in a wicked game of smothering lust and wild passion - mind versus feeling.

To escape, she has to win his trust -yet she ends up losing her heart in the process.

"The water drops path while rolling over his inked body was becoming mystical. A sparkling road her famished hands craved to thoroughly follow, to feel his ripped muscle tense beneath them while sliding her fingers towards the wet towel. It felt like a sin, just to be looking at him. "

Blackjack- A game of cards and destiny

Adam Delmont Rocher, Monte Carlo's famous billionaire with a shaky reputation that needs immediate mending offers his teenage crush, Lynette, a deal with a modern devil. A Blackjack game of cards and destiny which finalizes with the fake marriage he desperately needs to keep his company, though sometimes, the word fake can get really blurred when true feelings are involved...

Contrary to what M.O. Absinthe usually writes, this book is NOT a dark romance!

"A feral sound escaped him, bringing down his carved lips on her with an unstilled yearning. The kiss was almost brutal, releasing something chained for too long as his tongue searched hers in crazed swirls, hoping to make the very last drop of her his own."

.

Printed in Great Britain
by Amazon